Christmas Dinner

Cheryl J. McCullough

W9-CJS-874

This is a work of fiction. Names, descriptions, entities, and incidents included in the story are products of the author's imagination. Any resemblance to actual persons, events, and entities is entirely coincidental.

Book cover design by Tracy Jones

www.tracyjonesdesigns.com

Christmas Dinner

Published by Burkwood Media Consulting and Publishing, Inc.

P O Box 29448

Charlotte, NC 28229

Published in the United States

ISBN: 978-0-69256-056-3

ℋCKNOWLEDGEMENTS

Thank God from whom all blessings flow!

This journey started with a dream and a desire to entertain. It began with "The Wedding Party", then "Absent…One From Another" and now the final story in the trilogy; "Christmas Dinner." I am grateful to my readers. You are amazing! Thank you for your feedback and for telling others about my work. I sincerely appreciate all the support.

As I traveled to many cities throughout the country I met many of you, laughed with you and heard you talk about these characters like they are personal friends. I read your emails, the comments on the websites and Facebook posts. The suggestions on how the stories should proceed were particularly interesting!

Very special thanks to the many book clubs and reading groups for including my books in your discussions. Thanks to those who invited me to join the discussion. Your perspectives were interesting.

To my family and friends, thank you for your undying love and support.

Dreams really do come true!

PROLOGUE

"The cancer is back." She kept thinking about what the doctor said. She already had a double mastectomy. The doctor didn't know if the cancer originated in the uterus or cervix. It didn't matter. It had spread. She wasn't sure she could manage the chemo therapy and radiation again. The doctor gave her seven days to make a decision. She gave herself five days.

ONE

Mrs. Rajagopal had not said much to anybody and she had not given Raja any explanation. The reason, she was guilty; she knew her husband's heart attack was due to their argument.

For days she badgered him about Raja and his family. Jill sent the pictures of LaLa like she promised. But that wasn't enough. "Manavendra cannot dictate to his parents how to live," she had said. "He is a disrespectful son." Her mind raced as she thought about all the things they said to each other. They shouted and then he got very quiet and fell to the floor. She thought he was dead. By the time the emergency workers arrived he was barely breathing.

The doctors said they were "cautiously optimistic" about his recovery. Since Raja arrived there seemed to be more doctors involved in her husband's care. But even so, she knew she caused her husband's heart attack. She wasn't a good wife. Good wives were not disrespectful to their husbands. If he ever recovered she would apologize and never question him or raise her voice to him again. If he didn't recover she could not let Raja know she killed his father.

As she sat and thought about all that happened in the past few days, Tara walked in. She was being surprisingly cordial and Mrs. Rajagopal returned the kindness.

"Aunt, may I get you some tea, or a sandwich?" Tara asked. "No, thank you. I have no appetite. I am anxious to talk to the doctor. Where is Manavendra?"

"He will be here shortly." Tara tried to reassure her. They chatted about the décor in the waiting room. Raja came in a few minutes later.

"Mother, based on what the doctor is telling me, Father will not be able to go home with only you there to care for him." Mrs. Rajagopal was sitting there with her hands on her heart. "Oh my dear husband," she said. Tara rolled her eyes. Raja wanted to laugh but he kept his composure, and continued to talk. "We only have two options as I see it. I can hire someone to live with you and care for Father or I can move both of you to Hattiesville so I can supervise his care."

Mrs. Rajagopal stood and walked across the room and back. Tara frowned as she and Raja looked at each other. "Oh son, I just don't know what to do. I know your wife, would not want us there…" "Mother, I will work that out with her. Don't concern yourself with that." Mrs. Rajagopal was clutching her chest as she was listening to Raja talk. Tara was getting tired of the drama and let out a deep sigh. She slowly stood and approached her aunt. "Aunt, my cousin is making you a very generous offer. For him to find care for my uncle here will be very expensive to manage." Tara was trying to choose her words carefully. "It is best that you plan to move home with Raja, at least until my uncle is well and you can care for him at your home." Mrs. Rajagopal looked from Tara to Raja and back to Tara. She nodded her head slowly. "All right son, we shall do as you wish, with your father's approval of course."

"Mother, he is too weak to make any decisions." She started to cry again.

"Aunt, let's go to your home and pack some things, while Raja makes the necessary arrangements here." Tara was stern, she missed Robert and she was ready to go home. But she knew Raja couldn't do all this alone.

When Tara and Mrs. Rajagopal walked away, Raja sat for a few minutes with his head in his hands. Finally he took a deep breath and called Jill. She and her parents had talked and were working out the details for her and Raja to buy their home. They all understood the move may have to happen quickly. Jill braced herself and her mother, who was probably the most organized person Jill knew, had already begun to put things in place. When the phone rang she smiled. She wanted to sound cheerful and put Raja's mind and heart at ease. They talked about LaLa and caught up on things at home. When she asked about his father, they moved to the real reason for the call.

"Sweetie, he is not well. My mother is being so vague about what happened in the days preceding the heart attack; we have to make decisions based on test results and not practical information. It's like she did something to him," Raja said. Jill was thinking, living with her is enough to give him a heart attack. "I am going to bring them back to Hattiesville. That's the only way for me to get back to you and our daughter and my patients. I know I'm asking you for a lot…"

"Honey, it's okay. Really it is. I was expecting you to say that and I'm prepared." Jill went on to tell Raja what she and Ellen worked out and how they planned to accomplish it. As he listened Raja was so grateful to God for his amazing wife and her incredible mother. "How soon are you coming?" Jill asked. "We should leave here in two days; Dad will go directly to the hospital in Charlotte and mom will be able to stay in the visitor's house for a few days."

"Sounds like a plan." Jill said.

$\mathscr{T}$WO

"Where is Natalia?" Blake was asking Chloe. They had been on the road about an hour after Chloe took Nicholas and Blake from Natalia at the playground. "She went home." Chloe glanced in the rearview mirror. Nicholas was asleep but Blake was looking around. It was like he knew something was wrong.

Chloe knew she needed to pull over. She needed to think. She had acted on the spur of the moment. She didn't have a plan. She saw the opportunity to have Nicholas and she took it.

As she approached an exit she decided to stop at a fast food restaurant; the boys probably needed to use the bathroom. And she needed to check her phone. It kept ringing and she knew it was Natalia or by now, her parents or Campbell. She hadn't answered and actually switched the phone to silent.

As the boys ate, they were visibly antsy. They knew Chloe was Natalia's friend who played with them at the park, but they also knew something was odd because Natalia wasn't there. They were asking a lot of questions. Chloe didn't respond to most of them. She had at least a dozen messages and missed calls. Her parents called, Natalia, the Casebier's, Campbell, and the police. The police left a message that she needed to call home as soon as possible. The police. She had not thought this through at all. It never crossed her mind that the police would be involved.

When Chloe pulled away with Nicholas and Blake in her car, Natalia was stunned. For a couple of minutes she just stood there. Fortunately her cell phone was in her pocket and not in the car. She called Chloe twice, but there was no answer. She had to get some help, in a hurry. She called Campbell who was in total disbelief when she told him what happened. "I know it's all my fault." Natalia started to cry. "That's not important now; we need to find Chloe and those kids." Campbell called Chloe; he sent her a text message and then called again. She didn't respond. He got his keys and headed to his car. "I know she won't hurt those boys, but I have to find her," he thought to himself. He called Natalia when he was in the car and told her he would come get her. They needed to go to the Casebier's.

Enoch pulled in the driveway to see a car he didn't recognize. His first thought was he had forgotten something Kirby told him they had to do. As soon as he walked in he knew something wasn't right. "What's up Kirby?" Enoch asked as he looked at Natalia and then at Campbell. Kirby and Natalia were crying. Kirby was trying to answer him but she just put her head on his chest. Enoch's heart was pounding.

Campbell told him why he and Natalia were there. Enoch was listening in disbelief. "I am so sorry Mr. Casebier. I am so sorry," Natalia was saying. Enoch pushed Kirby an arm's length away so he could see her face.

"I told you I didn't trust this babysitting situation you created. I told you Natalia was here under false pretenses."

He had fury in his eyes, looking at all three of them. "I know one thing, somebody better find my kids!" He yelled. "What did the police say?"

"We didn't call yet. We're hoping she will answer and we can convince her to come back." Kirby's voice was trembling. In all the years she had known Enoch, she hadn't ever heard him raise his voice, or seen him angry like this. "Her parents are on their way. I hope they can talk to her."

"Kirby, you're not making good decisions. The police should have been called first."

"Enoch, she's not a criminal, she's a confused young lady."

"She is a kidnapper!" Enoch yelled again, as he reached for the phone.

"Mr. Casebier, I know Chloe won't hurt the boys."

"Shut up Natalia, just shut up!" He called 911. The doorbell rang. Kirby went to the door. Enoch was on the phone with the police.

Roderick and Sandra Matthews walked in, visibly shaken. Roderick was on the phone leaving Chloe another message. There was no exchange of pleasantries; Sandra immediately started asking questions. Natalia answered. While they were talking Campbell was trying to call Chloe again.

"What is the license tag number on the car?" Enoch was asking Natalia. She answered him and he repeated the information into the phone, along with the make and model of the car. "Her name is Chloe Matthews." He listened for a few seconds, hung up and said to the group, "the police are on their way."

$\mathscr{T}$HREE

Clay went back to work but he continued to call Cicely. He went to the employee parking lot at the hospital and finally had his cousin Gretchen call her at work. The person who answered told Gretchen she was on vacation. That told Clay she went home. He knew her brothers wouldn't let him get close to her so there was no point in his going there. He had both her brother's numbers. Eventually he sent a text message to the youngest brother who simply responded "she's fine."

Cicely was online looking at the nurse's schedule. For the first time since she started working at Charlotte Memorial Hospital, she missed six shifts. She was ready to go back to work.

She was alone for a while. Her youngest brother went back to school and the other brother was at work. She sent her supervisor an email to say she would be back and on shift the following Sunday night. She went through her things and packed two suitcases. She would go back to the nurse's residence hall temporarily. Beyond that she hadn't made any plans. At some point she would call Clay. They would have to talk.

Two days later on Friday night, under the cover of darkness, Cicely arrived back in Charlotte. Nobody knew she was coming back. She checked into the residence hall and unpacked. She was hungry so she went back out. There was a deli five minutes away. She went in, ordered food, and flipped through a magazine while she waited. Just as she was leaving a man coming in held the door for her. They slightly spoke. There was a tall teenage boy behind him who looked vaguely familiar.

"Hey Ms. Cicely." She looked back. "Do you remember me? I'm Jeremy. I used to be Clay's little brother." She put on her game face.

"My goodness Jeremy, you have really grown up. How are you doing?"

"I'm good, how you doin'?"

"I am well. Thank you for asking." Just then the man he was with walked back out.

"Ms. Cicely, this is Javier, my stepdad. Jav this is Clay's wife, umm fiancé..." he laughed. Cicely didn't respond. "...Cicely." Javier extended his hand. "Nice to finally meet you Cicely, I've heard a lot about you. Jeremy, go on in and wait for the food." Jeremy walked away. "I think we should talk," Javier said to Cicely.

"Why?" she asked.

"I know what Delia did, and I'm pretty pissed off about it, and I'm sure you need somebody to talk to." Cicely didn't say anything. He gave her his business card. "Call me."

$\mathcal{F}$OUR

Anderson was thrilled to be headed home. Jacksa was meeting him at the airport, and they would go to South Carolina to see his family tomorrow. He fully intended to start the conversation with her about getting married.

But this case had him completely puzzled. It was assigned to Charlotte because one of the key players was a coach at DavisTown College. Anderson was surprised that DavisTown had not done a better job at screening. But these were allegations. It was his job and the job of his partner to make the case or prove there was no validity to it. Who would have thought his first case would have international roots; and something he personally thought was totally insane: athletes using performance enhancing drugs. He spent three weeks in London doing the preliminary work.

The flight attendant announced to the passengers they could engage their electronic devices. Anderson wanted to catch up on his personal email and see how Tiger Woods was playing. He pulled up the golf match, checked the leader board and then went to his email. The first message was from his sister. The subject was "Jacksa's mom". He frowned as he waited for the message to load. The email message started by saying she didn't want him to be caught off guard when he saw Jacksa. She explained in detail what happened to Min, and said Jacksa was a wreck the first few days but better now. He laughed when he read the part about King, but he immediately got angry when he read that Jackson was out of town and didn't call back until the next day. It ended by saying Min was still in the hospital but much better and that their mother and grandmother went to Hattiesville to spend some time with her. The last sentence said "and oh yeah, they stayed at your house!" Anderson groaned at the thought. He was sure they cleaned up so he probably couldn't find anything.

There were a couple of other emails he didn't open and then one from Jacksa. She told him about Min but not in as much detail. The tone of the email was sad. She did mention Jackson being away, just in the context of being by herself to make decisions. She ended the message saying she missed him and loves him. Anderson dozed off watching golf and trying to decide how to deal with Jackson Baye.

IVE

Grammy was getting settled in her new room in her new home. There was so much going on, she didn't have time to think about being in Landridge and away from Hattiesville.

Belinda and the boys were still in the hospital. She was recovering from having a heart attack, and the twin boys, Bryce and Bradley, were still in the pediatric intensive care unit because they were born seven weeks prematurely.

More than anything, she missed her sister Avis. They talked daily but it was different. Auntie had her hands full helping Kirby and Enoch with Blake and Nicholas, but she missed Grammy too. But Thelma was working hard to keep Grammy busy. They were making quilts and baby blankets with other ladies at church to be donated to medical care facilities, and of course they were taking care of Ben, Brittani and Brianna.

Things in the Coffey home were quiet though considering. The girls were trying to keep Ben upbeat, but he was worried about Belinda. She just didn't seem to be bouncing back and so far she refused to see April or Hampton. Ben didn't care one way or the other. All he cared about was his wife getting well, coming home and them being a family. The light in this whole situation was that the boys were making progress every day.

Hampton was better but not good. April threw herself even more into her work. They both asked to see Belinda and she said no, but Hampton decided he was going anyway. He wouldn't tell anybody. Being kicked out was a chance he was willing to take.

He arrived early and went to the nursery window. He could see the boys from a distance. They both had oxygen and other tubes. The nurse noticed him and pushed them closer to the window just for a minute; his grandsons. Then he walked into the intermediate care area without asking anybody if it was okay. Belinda was sitting in a recliner, her legs up. She wore a blue bathrobe and white slippers. She had two blue bands on one arm indicating she had two baby boys. Her hair was in a ponytail and she wasn't wearing any make-up. She looked tired, her eyes looked weak, and she had oxygen in her nose and an IV in her other arm. The television was tuned to the news, but the volume was so low she probably couldn't hear it. Hampton stood there for a minute. When he closed the door she looked up expressionless. She didn't even look surprised to see him. "Hey Belinda."

"Good morning", she replied.

"I came here to talk but now that I'm here, I'm not sure what to say." She didn't respond. "I am very sad about everything that has happened, all the way back to me not finding you when Shona died," Hampton said. Belinda took a deep breath, and exhaled slowly.

"Please have a seat." Belinda said to Hampton. He sat in a chair directly in front of her. He leaned forward resting his forearms on his thighs. He looked at her but neither of them said anything for a few seconds. Just as he started to say something, she interrupted him. "Tell me about Shona, about my mother," she said barely above a whisper.

"She was beautiful. You look just like her, your mannerisms are like hers, she was left handed too and had a mole on her ear like you." Belinda reached up and touched her ear. Hampton leaned back and closed his eyes for a second.

"Did you love her?"

"Sure, but it was young love. We were too young to understand what forever really meant. We talked about me getting drafted, playing in the NFL, having a ton of money, and how we would live. Then reality set in. I was in college, she was in high school. She got angry when she told me she was pregnant and I wouldn't quit school."

"Is that why she told you the baby…I wasn't your child?"

"I didn't realize that at the time, but looking back on it, I think so." Hampton answered Belinda. She looked away from him and didn't say anything for a minute. He broke the silence. "Sweetheart, I don't know how many ways I can say I'm sorry. I sincerely ask for your forgiveness. I love you and I want us to be a family."

"You love me!" Belinda raised her voice, and widened her eyes. Hampton was looking at her thinking how much she looked like her Mom. "You don't know me!"

"Belinda, I know you in my heart." He was determined to keep her calm. "Please don't get upset." She took a deep breath, and then continued talking.

"You want us to be a family. Are you serious? Family is why I'm here." She waved her hand to indicate the hospital room. "And my babies are here way too early, because of my dear sister."

"I know April didn't mean any real harm, absolutely not what ultimately happened."

Belinda interrupted Hampton again. "You mean she didn't intend to shock me into having a heart attack which could have caused me to lose my babies? I pass on the new family." Hampton dropped his head.

Belinda was staring at him. Her emotions were all over the place. She was hurt and angry but she had an inkling of wonder and curiosity about having a father, and her children having a grandfather. She just wasn't sure if she could trust April, and she knew they came as a package.

After a few minutes she finally spoke. "Hampton, I don't know what to do or how to feel. The last couple of weeks have been an emotional roller coaster for me. I have tubes and medicines, my babies have tubes and medicines; that's not how I wanted them to come into the world."

"Sweetheart that's not what I wanted either."

She didn't respond to his comment, she kept talking. "All I can say now is I want to gather my strength, get out of here and be at home with my husband and my children. I don't think you totally understand what I've lost in all this. I may not be able to go back to work. Surgical nursing is stressful. What doctor will want a nurse with a history of a heart attack? Can they trust me in a long, intense surgery? Right now I can't even hold my babies or hug my daughters. Is my heart strong enough to make love to my husband?"

"I promise you all of that is temporary. You are my child and you will land on your feet; stronger than ever. If it takes every dime I have you can and will have the best of everything - private therapy, whatever you need to fully recover." Hampton had tears in his eyes. Belinda did too.

Before either of them said anything else, the door opened and Ben walked in. He looked slightly surprised to see Hampton, but he had fear in his eyes. "Oh, God, what is it?"

21

Belinda said, looking at him and knowing something was wrong. "Is something wrong with the boys?"

"No, darling, not our boys; Kirby's boys."

$\mathscr{S}$IX

Jackson Baye was on a major guilt trip. While he was out of town celebrating his mistress's birthday his wife Min had a major exacerbation of her multiple sclerosis. Thanks to the training of her dog, King, she got some help, but she had a ways to go to full recovery, even back to where she was before this episode. Their daughter Jacksa was angry with her father, and rightly so. She called and left several messages before he finally checked his voice mail and called back the next day. Neither Jacksa nor her brother JJ had a whole lot to say to their dad. In the midst of all that was going on Jacksa called JJ and asked him to come home. She originally told him not to come. But she needed his support. Anderson was away training for his new job and her father was M.I.A.

Jackson knew his affair was the culprit in Min's stress, and he knew stress caused this episode. She was being pretty quiet and Jacksa was really quiet. JJ was very verbal about his mother being in the hospital and his dad taking over twelve hours to call back. Jackson apologized to Min, Jacksa and JJ. None of them were angry that he was out of town, but Jacksa's knowledge of his affair made her furious because he didn't answer when she called. She absolutely intended to address it with him.

Jackson had been frantic when he awakened that morning to three messages and four missed calls. He called Jacksa and JJ before he found out what happened. He started throwing his things into his bag. "Let's go!"

"What's up?" she asked.

"Min is in the hospital. I need to get home as soon as I can."

"Can we get some breakfast before we get on the road?" she asked standing and stretching casually looking out the window.

"Hell no! Did you hear what I said?"

"Don't end my birthday celebration like this!" She screamed. Jackson looked at her in total disbelief. "I'm leaving in fifteen minutes."

The ride from Tampa back to Charlotte was horrible. She cried almost the entire way back. Jackson called Jacksa or JJ every hour. His heart was pounding, and he hadn't said much. When they were about twenty miles from Charlotte he relaxed slightly. "Do you remember what I told you before we left town?" She looked over at him but didn't respond. "This is it for us. For absolute sure, and let me be clear. If I hadn't already decided that, the comment you made about eating breakfast did it!" When they arrived back at her house, he pressed the garage door opener, put the car in park, grabbed his bag from the trunk, jumped in his car and backed out of her garage. All in less than two minutes.

$\mathscr{S}$EVEN

Kathy had not tried to contact Sterling since she got back to New York City. Her feelings were so hurt. She had to admit her part in all this; telling Sterling she wanted her career more than she wanted him, and choosing to go to school in New York. But he had to accept his part to; mentioning marriage to her, and three months later, dating somebody else. There was plenty of fault to go around. She had to move on. Like her dad would tell her and Leah when they were growing up, there are consequences to every decision you make. The fact of the matter was, he had not tried to connect with her either. He knew she wanted to talk to him when she was home that weekend but he had not followed up.

Football practice was over for the day, and Sterling was in his office finishing up some paperwork. He was going straight home and straight to bed. He had not slept well the night before, contemplating his meeting on Friday with the FBI. He was concerned and totally unclear about why they wanted to speak with him; especially because the agent told him not to tell anyone.

$\mathscr{E}$IGHT

Cicely went back to her room, ate her salad and thought about what Javier said to her. He was angry with Delia. Cicely found that very interesting. Maybe she would give him a call tomorrow, and she needed to call Clay. She knew it wouldn't be long before she saw somebody she knew, and she wanted to let him know herself that she was back in town.

The truth was, Cicely loved Clay. She was heartbroken about his still dealing with Delia and especially wanting to have sex with her. She had cried until there were no more tears, but in her heart of hearts she missed him. One of the things her brother said to her was that she had not heard Clay's side of the story. He told Cicely she didn't have to accept anything Clay said but she did need to at least hear him out.

Javier dropped Jeremy off at home and went back to work. He would stay late, until he knew Delia would be asleep. He had been doing that a lot lately. Javier was still ticked off at Delia, and she knew it. She was doing everything she could to make up with him, but he hadn't budged. Their conversations consisted of things about their household or the children.

As he drove back across town, he thought about Cicely, and what he would say to her if she called. He would encourage her to work things out with Clay. In Javier's opinion Clay didn't deserve Cicely and for that matter Delia didn't deserve him, but he knew that it was likely Clay and Cicely would work things out and he and Delia would work things out too. "Maybe we should let them be together and Cicely and I should be together!" he thought to himself and laughed.

Jeremy ate his sandwiches and sat down at the computer. He didn't check his email often; his mom usually checked for information from school or his basketball coach. But he was anxious about a tournament schedule and he was looking to see if it was there. When he looked at the schedule he was surprised the games would be played in the gym at Hattiesville Community Church. "That's Clay's church," he thought. He picked up the phone and called Clay.

When Clay saw Jeremy's name come up on the screen his first thought was to let the call go to voice mail. He thought it may be Delia trying to get him to answer. But he took a chance and answered. "What's up man?" Clay said when he answered. If it was Delia she would know he was not expecting her call.

"Ain't much." Jeremy answered. They exchanged their usual banter and then Jeremy told Clay about the tournament at Hattiesville Community Church.

"Ok, I'll put it on my calendar and try to make it."

"Aight, Clay, don't not show and tell me you forgot!"

"I need to check my travel schedule for work, but other than that I'm there," Clay said laughing.

"I probably shoulda told Ms. Cicely so she could remind you."

"You talked to Cicely?" Clay asked carefully.

"Yeah, I saw her tonight at the deli. She most likely mention it when she get home. She talkin' 'bout how much I changed, all that." Clay laughed because he couldn't think of anything to say that wouldn't let on to Jeremy he didn't know Cicely was back in town.

When he and Jeremy hung up, Clay got up and walked around the house. He didn't know what to do. He wanted to call Cicely but he couldn't bear the thought of her not answering, knowing she was in town. He called Grant.

During the weeks Cicely was gone she had not talked with Sunny. They texted a few times but Cicely didn't tell Sunny where she was and refused to answer any questions about her plans. Eventually Sunny stopped texting every day and stopped asking. But she would always tell Cicely she loved her and she always left the door open for her to call so they could talk. Grant told Clay and Sunny to give Cicely some space and in time she would call. He said that for their benefit, but didn't know if he really believed it. Clay had made some dumb decisions in his life where women were concerned but Grant thought this was the worst one yet. And he told Clay just that.

Clay knew Friday night was Grant and Sunny's date night and he hated to interrupt them but he needed to talk to Grant.

Saturday morning Cicely decided she would leave Clay a message on his work voice mail. He would get it Monday and they would make a plan to meet; maybe for lunch or something like that. She wouldn't go to his house and she didn't want him to know where she was staying. She called his office and was shocked when he answered.

NINE

Brittani, Brianna and Carlotta were at the library. They were there for the last session of the summer book club. There was a special guest today leading the discussion. "Ms. April!" Carlotta noticed her first. "What are you doing here?"

"Hola! Carlotta! I am leading the book discussion today. I'm glad to see you. Have you been participating in the book club all summer?" April asked. Briana and Brittani approached April and Carlotta, and April was obviously surprised. "Ms. April is the discussion leader today!" Carlotta said happily.

"Hi Ms. April," Brittani said as the librarian told them to take their seats.

Seeing the twins shook April. She made it through the book discussion but she wanted, needed, to say something to Brianna and Brittani, her nieces. When the other students were gone, April looked around to see if they were still there. She saw Carlotta and Brittani looking at some DVDs and Briana sitting at a table looking through a magazine. April walked over to the table and sat down across from Brianna, who looked up at her but didn't smile. "You ladies obviously enjoyed the book. Thank you for participating in the discussion." April didn't know the twins well, but she knew Brianna was the more outspoken one. "Ms. April, I know my mom was meeting with you when she got sick. So don't try to make friends with me."

"Bree!" Brittani said as she walked to the table where April and Brianna sat. "Be nice." Brianna looked at Brittani but didn't say anything. She immediately turned her attention back to April.

"I am not going to be nice to her. She made Mommy have a heart attack and she should apologize." April took a deep breath.

"Brianna and Brittani, I am very sorry, terribly sorry about what happened with your mom. I hope all of you can forgive me." There was a thick silence for almost a minute. Finally Carlotta spoke up.

"Bree, it's the right thing to do to forgive people. God forgives us." There was silence again.

"We forgive you Ms. April," Brittani said looking at Brianna, who said nothing.

April walked away, but she didn't feel good about her exchange with the twins. She decided she would go talk to Belinda but she wanted her dad to go with her. She was sure she could talk him into it.

TEN

Ben told Belinda and Hampton all he knew about Blake and Nicholas being kidnapped. Belinda started to cry. She asked Ben for his phone so she could call Kirby.

Hampton took his phone from his pocket. "Don't cry sweetheart, let me help," he said. Ben gave Belinda his phone. They both looked at Hampton.

"Man, I can't play golf with you today." It was the Atlanta Chief of Police answering. "No golf today, I have a serious situation and I need your help."

"What's up Hamp?" Hampton gave the chief the information. "She was in school here and had an apartment here, so it's quite likely she is headed this way."

"I will take care of it."

"Chief, we are more interested in the boys' safe return than having Chloe Matthews arrested. Once they're safe I will let their parents decide if they want to press charges. And, if you have to call in your best to make this happen, I'll cover it," Hampton said, feeling Ben and Belinda's eyes on him. Next he called and quickly explained the situation to Carlos Reyes, the private investigator who gave him the information about Belinda. Hampton told Carlos he talked with the police chief. "If you locate them, let me know and we'll coordinate with the police. I don't want to scare the boys, and I don't want Chloe to panic."

"Take them to our house," Belinda was saying to Hampton. He nodded to her. "Reyes, keep this quiet, but spare no expense."

"Señor, assure your daughter, I will handle this. Put her mind at ease."

"Thanks man, I will." Hampton turned to Belinda. "Don't worry sweetie, we'll find them."

She looked into his eyes. "Thank you", she said with a genuine smile.

&ELEVEN

Sunny and Grant were having breakfast at their neighborhood bistro and talking about their wedding plans. They were worlds apart on what they wanted. Sunny had taken Cicely's advice about not getting married in Eleuthera, but she wanted to get married in a hotel in downtown Charlotte. Grant wanted a small wedding with family and close friends in the chapel at Hattiesville Community Church. He didn't want what he had planned with Leah - hundreds of guests in the main sanctuary of the church. Sunny wanted "grand" and he didn't. "Grant, we will be no more married having the ceremony in the church than we will having it in a hotel."

"Sunny you're right, except we should get married in church; in the eyes of God, it's the right thing to do."

"Right by whose standard?" she asked, putting her fork down, and folding her arms.

"Right by my standards. That's the way I was raised, that's what my family expects," Grant said calmly. Sunny threw her napkin on the table.

"Grant, is this about your family and their expectations or about us, about what we want? This is my wedding, not Leah's," Sunny said angrily. She wanted to take it back as soon as she said it. Grant set his glass down and just looked at Sunny. There she was again. That Sunny he didn't understand. For that matter, the Sunny he didn't like. The

Sunny he first saw in her office that day Janis showed up, and Sunny had slapped her. "Sunny, I love you, I don't want to fight about this."

"I love you too. Please forgive me for what I said about Leah. I just feel like I can't have what I want because of what happened with your last wedding."

"Sunny that's not true at all. Nobody thinks about what happened with that wedding but you. Leah is on your mind, not mine." Grant said to her. She dropped her eyes. "I don't think about Leah or compare our plans to mine and yours until you mention it. You need to let that go." Grant took the last gulp of his juice, wiped his mouth, threw the napkin on the table and walked out.

$\mathcal{T}$WELVE

Min was released to rehab six days after she was admitted to the hospital. The good thing about rehab was, they would allow King to visit. She hadn't seen him since the night she got sick and he saved her life. Jacksa told her King was pretty subdued since she was away.

The hospital was moving Min by ambulance. Jacksa was going to her parent's home after work to pick up a few things, get King and then go to the rehab center. Jacksa was getting some clothes for Min when she heard the alarm beep. She knew it was her dad. This would be their first time alone since all this happened.

"Hello Jacksa." Jackson said very seriously.

"Hi Dad. How are you?"

"I'm good. I guess we need to talk."

"No you need to talk, I'll listen."

Jacksa folded her arms and stood there looking directly into her dad's eyes. He was very uncomfortable. He wanted her to scream at him, to curse at him, to ask a lot of questions....but she didn't. She shifted her weight from one foot to the other, still waiting on Jackson to say something.

"Jacksa, I'm sorry."

"You said that already. I want to know where you were, and why you couldn't or didn't answer my call, and don't lie, 'cause I already know the truth." Jackson wasn't sure what that meant. He didn't know what she knew and didn't know. He had no idea what Thorn told her. She may have been bluffing—or not. "If you have drawn your own conclusions nothing I say is of any benefit."

"That's a stall tactic." Jacksa sighed. She stood perfectly still and didn't take her eyes off him.

"I was in Tampa with a friend. I had a few drinks and fell asleep. I didn't hear the phone."

"You may have been in bed but I doubt you were sleeping." Jackson felt a pang in the pit of his stomach. Then he remembered the comment Anderson made. Going "a round" with Jacksa would be worse than a round with Min. He was right.

"The truth is I made a bad decision and I'm paying for it." He was still side-stepping the issue. She was going to give him about three seconds to confess. "There's nothing I can say to fix it Jacksa. I can't change the past." His time was up.

"Dad, you are having an affair and you and your whore were in Tampa screwing around. Just like you do every Thursday night! Do you think my mother is a fool?" Jacksa was screaming. "I know she thinks because of her condition you have a right to do this but I don't think so and it's not right!" She was going to continue but Jackson cut her off.

"There's no way I can make you understand all this."

"That's for sure," she said sarcastically.

"My decision to get into that situation has less to do with your mom and more to do with my weaknesses."

"Frankly Dad, I don't care what prompted you to get in that 'situation' as you call it. What I care about is your blatant disregard for my mother, your wife, the woman you exchanged vows with. Remember in sickness and health and forsaking all others?" Jacksa was being very animated.

"I love Min." Jackson said quietly.

"I can't tell."

"I didn't ignore your calls Jacksa. I really didn't hear the phone." That was a lie. He did hear the phone, the first two times it rang. He chose not to answer it.

Jacksa went to Min's side of the bed, got her IPad, and opened the night stand drawer to get the charger. Jackson was still standing there. She picked up the bag she packed. As she was walking out of the room, she said to her dad, "When Mom leaves rehab she's going home with me. So you can spend every night with your friend. You won't be limited to Thursdays." She called King and walked out of the house.

$\mathscr{T}$HIRTEEN

"Hello…hello." Clay didn't look at the caller id before he answered the phone. He assumed it was a co-worker. Although it was Saturday morning there were several people in the office. He looked at the screen just as he heard her voice.

"Hi Clay." He swallowed hard.

"Hey baby. How are you?" He clutched the phone tightly, and pressed the receiver hard against his ear. "I'm fine, I just didn't expect you to answer. I was going to leave you a message," Cicely said.

"To tell me what?" he asked. Clay was choosing his words carefully. He didn't want to overreact. He was glad Jeremy inadvertently told him she was back in town. But he would do whatever she asked. "I was going to ask you to call me so we can set a time to talk."

"I'll come to you right now," he told her and meant it. She took a deep breath.

"No, not today, on Monday." He didn't want to wait until Monday but he would.

"Can I cook you dinner?" he asked her.

"Thank you but not this time. Can we meet about 11:00 for brunch, or lunch a little later if that time doesn't work for you?" He didn't care what time she said he would be available. "I can make 11:00. I will pick you up." Clay said hoping she would agree.

"I will meet you at Grizzlies." she said. Clay laughed.

"Okay but I can't believe you are letting me eat at Grizzlies!" She laughed too, because she told him they should call it Greases because the only thing on the menu that wasn't brown was cole slaw. Meeting at Grizzles was strategic. It was five minutes from his office so he wouldn't know where she was coming from or going. Clay wanted to keep her on the telephone but she said she had to go and would see him on Monday. As they were hanging up he said, "I love you." She didn't respond.

After the phone call Clay sat for a few minutes thinking about what he should do. He would have flowers delivered to her while they were at the restaurant, and give her the ring back. No, too much; he would take the flowers to her and not mention the ring. He just wanted to see her, to put his arms around her. He reminded himself not to overdo it, to let her take the lead. He wanted her back so he knew it had to be on her terms.

Cicely sat and thought about Clay. She definitely didn't expect him to answer but she maintained her composure. She wasn't sure what she would say to him. But before she met him she decided she would do one thing; call Javier.

ℱOURTEEN

Tara and Mrs. Rajagopal flew directly to Charlotte. Raja and his father flew to New York before going to Charlotte. Raja decided to have his father checked out at a hospital before continuing on to Charlotte. Mr. Rajagopal stayed in a New York hospital for two days before being cleared to travel to the hospital in Charlotte. He was still in guarded condition. Tara made arrangements for Mrs. Rajagopal to move into her room at the visitor's residence. She explained there was a shuttle to take her to the hospital and bring her back. Tara was going to see LaLa and Jill, then she was going home the next day. Robert wanted her home and she was ready to go.

Ellen Strauss hired a moving company and a cleaning company to handle the work to move both households. Then she made arrangements for Mrs. Rajagopal to stay in a suite at the hospital visitor's residence as long as Mr. Rajagopal was a patient. She raised a lot of money for the hospital and never asked for a favor, so she knew they would accommodate her request. She wanted to buy Jill some time before her mother-in-law moved in. Ellen also decided she would go over and introduce herself to Mrs. Rajagopal. Ellen wanted her to know Raja may be her son but Jill is her daughter and when Jill is unhappy Ellen is unhappy too.

Mrs. Rajagopal was alone for one full day after Tara left and before Raja and Mr. Rajagopal arrived in Charlotte. She didn't realize how tired she was until she woke up hours later than she usually did. Other than going out for a short while for brunch, she stayed in the suite all day. She thought about her husband being sick, and how it would be if he never came home. She thought about living with Jill. She wanted to be close to Raja and LaLa but she was really afraid to live with Jill. Her greatest fear was Mr. Rajagopal would die and she couldn't go back to London, and be at Jill's mercy.

She thought about Tara telling Jill things to turn Jill against her. "But I guess asking her to let the baby live with us didn't help," she thought, as she paced around the room. All she could do was hope her husband got well, so they could go home.

The knock at the door startled her as she stood looking out the window. She expected it was housekeeping. As she walked to the door, she remembered she didn't put the "Do Not Disturb" sign on the door. To her surprise there was a lady standing there with flowers and a friendly smile. "Hello."

"Hello Mrs. Rajagopal. I am Ellen Strauss, Jillian's mother." Mrs. Rajagopal hesitated but invited Ellen in. Ellen gave her the flowers.

"Thank you, please have a seat." After the pleasantries, Ellen told Mrs. Rajagopal the reason for her visit.

"I know you and Jill had a tough start but your decision to ask for LaLa was totally unreasonable".

Mrs. Rajagopal interrupted Ellen. "Mrs. Strauss, neither you nor Jillian understand how things are done in our culture."

"Mrs. Rajagopal, you don't understand. This is America, and here, even people of other cultures do things the American way. Now, I want you to leave Jill and Raja alone. Let them make decisions for their family. My daughter is a wonderful person and when she's happy so am I. But when she's unhappy I take action to insure her happiness." Their eyes met and held for a couple of seconds before Mrs. Rajagopal looked away.

ℱIFTEEN

Cicely took a deep breath and called Javier. "Cicely, I'm really glad you called."

"I'm not sure why I did," Cicely said to Javier.

They talked a few minutes and set a date for a late lunch. As Cicely dressed to meet Javier she started to call him back and cancel. She wanted to make peace with Clay, whether they could work their relationship out or not. She didn't know how meeting Javier would help that, but she concluded it wouldn't hurt.

Delia was worried. She didn't know what Javier had on his mind. He wasn't talking to her and he was sleeping on the sofa. If he was trying to make a point, he made it. She wanted her life back. She was scared things were going to change. She wanted to marry Javier, have a father for her children, live in the house they were building and make a home - maybe even have a baby.

He was in the shower. She didn't know if he was going to work or somewhere else. But she was determined to talk to him before he left. Interestingly Javier started the conversation. "Delia, do a couple of things please."

"Sure, what's up?"

"Change the house appointment to tomorrow after church."

"Okay," she said.

"And I'll meet you at Crystal's game; I won't have time to come back over here," he said.

"That works, but can we talk a minute before you leave?"

"No, we'll talk later," he said walking out of the bedroom. She heard him saying something to the kids and they laughed, so she walked into the living room. He fist bumped Crystal and followed Jeremy out the door.

"Where is Jeremy going?" Delia asked Crystal.

"Jav is dropping him at weight lifting." Delia stood for a moment and thought. Everything in their household was normal except her relationship with Javier.

Cicely wanted to see Javier before he saw her, but he beat her to the punch. He was standing in front of the restaurant when she pulled into the parking lot. She took a deep breath, put a smile on her face and walked toward him. They were seated right away and started talking immediately. The small talk consisted of things about his family in Texas and her family and his job and her job. She finally asked "How did you meet Delia?"
"We met in church," Javier said.

"Really!" Cicely said rolling her eyes. Javier laughed.

"Cicely, I know it's hard to believe, but Delia is a good person. She's a great mother and I asked her to marry me because I believe she will be a good wife." Cicely was looking at him with a puzzled look on her face. He continued. "I know that's not the Delia you met. I can't explain it either, but like you said on the phone, there's something about Clay that brings out the worst in Delia, or in your words, makes her crazy."

"If everything Delia said is true, Clay was wrong. He disrespected me and our relationship."

"You're right but Delia was too. She disrespected me and our relationship. But you know Cicely, I am forgiving Delia and I think you should forgive Clay."

"I'm not sure I want us back together," she said shrugging.

"I didn't say anything about you reconciling with him, I'm talking about forgiveness. That's for you more than him," Javier said to her very seriously. She didn't say anything so Javier kept talking. "You need to talk to Clay…"

"We're having lunch on Monday so we can talk," she said, interrupting him.

"That's good. Be completely honest about how you feel."
"That's what my brothers told me," Cicely said smiling and thinking about them.
Javier laughed. "What else did they tell you?"

"Interestingly, after the first couple of days when they got some perspective and got over their initial anger, they had a lot to say!"

Cicely told Javier her brothers said to be completely honest with Clay. If she doesn't trust him tell him so. They told her the ball was in her court and she was calling all the shots. If they got back together it would have to be on her terms. "They said let him work to get me back, make him court me again, make him earn me," she said.

"If you were my sister, I would tell you the same things. Cicely, I love Delia. I don't for a minute agree with how she handled you and I don't like how Clay handled you either.

But I believe in forgiveness and I believe in love. I made a bad decision that cost me my relationship with my son's mother. I was too dumb to ask for forgiveness and for a while my son was out of my life." As Cicely listened to Javier talk she thought he was a good guy and she could see why Delia wanted him but she still didn't know why he wanted Delia.

"Javier, you are encouraging me to forgive Clay; have you forgiven Clay?" Javier laughed, and he thought for a moment before he answered her.

"As for Clay, I was never really mad at him. He was wrong but it was Delia's responsibility to protect us, to protect our relationship. Sure he was disrespectful but she made the bad decision. Now as for Delia—I am still in the process of forgiving her. I'm not angry anymore but she knows she won't get another chance. What about you? Can you forgive Delia and will you forgive Clay?"

"I don't know, Javier. At this point I haven't forgiven either one of them. I guess when Clay and I talk on Monday and I hear what he has to say, I will start the process of forgiveness."

$\mathscr{S}$IXTEEN

The police arrived at Enoch and Kirby's home to absolute chaos. Natalia and Kirby were crying, Campbell and Sandra were trying to come up with a plan and trying to assure everybody that Chloe would not hurt the boys. Enoch and Roderick were arguing. Roderick was trying to convince him that arresting Chloe was not the answer; she needed help, not jail.

The two officers who arrived first knew the Matthews and the Casebier's. The female officer immediately took charge of the situation. She made everybody sit and had Natalia start at the beginning. When Enoch tried to jump in she wouldn't let him speak. She was able to get a full understanding of the situation, including who each of them was and what their connection was to the situation. The male officer also took notes and when the other officer had a grasp on the information, he made a call to get the ball rolling.

About the same time, Kirby's phone rang. It was Ben telling them they put some things in place on that end in case she was headed that way. "Why Atlanta?" the officer asked.

"Chloe is in college there and had an apartment there, her mother explained. Ben told them Hampton had also hired a private investigator.

"Kirby, let me speak to Ben," Enoch said. She gave Enoch the telephone. He walked into the next room away from the group. Ben could tell how upset Enoch was, but he was firm with him.

"You can't blame Natalia for this, and you can't blame Kirby either. This situation was volatile from day one. Unfortunately our worst nightmare came true." Enoch calmed down some, and Ben told him to remember when this was over he would have to deal with his sons' and his wife's trauma. Enoch hadn't thought of that.

The police officers were preparing to leave so Enoch and Ben ended their call. The officers lay a copy of the police report on the coffee table with their business cards. While Enoch was on the phone, the female officer explained to the group that the FBI would be called in. "I know you want to protect your daughter Mr. and Mrs. Matthews but this is standard procedure in these situations."

Carlos Reyes found out quickly that Chloe used her debit card to get food and gas in Spartanburg, South Carolina. He picked up her trail there. Obviously she was headed to Atlanta, so he went to the apartment. On his way there he called Hampton Josephs.

Hampton left the hospital but assured Belinda he was "on top" of the situation. Belinda told Ben about her visit with Hampton. "How do you feel about what he said?" Ben asked her.

"I'm still processing it, and I can't say I've forgiven him but truthfully I'm not as angry as I was. I think he's genuinely sorry but we're a long way from the family reunion he wants," Belinda said. Ben looked at her and wanted to laugh. For whatever reason she had a new energy, she had her feisty back. As if she was reading his mind she told him she wanted to go to the nursery to see Bradley and Bryce. "I am so worried about Nicholas and Blake. I really need to see my boys." She was sad again. Ben went to the hall to get a wheelchair. "I want to walk," she said taking Ben by the arm, her other hand on the IV pole.

Chloe called a friend of hers in Atlanta. "I'm doing good girl, how are you?" The friend was surprised to hear from Chloe. "I'm good, but I need a gigantic favor."

"Sure Chloe. What's going on?"

"Are you at home, can I come by?" Chloe's friend lived about two blocks from the apartment Chloe lived in previously. Carlos Reyes was sitting outside Chloe's old apartment.

Hampton didn't know much about where Chloe's old apartment was but he decided he would ride around and survey the area. When he stopped at the traffic light and looked at the GPS, he was a half mile from the address Carlos gave him. As he was waiting for the light to change, a red Nissan Sentra went through the intersection. He looked up just in time to see the North Carolina license tag. He turned left behind the Sentra. It was Chloe. It had to be her; there were two little heads in the back seat. Hampton followed her at a safe distance trying to decide what to do. He had to move quickly.

Chloe's plan was to leave the boys with her friend and then call Natalia to tell her where they were. She didn't think, she just acted and now she was in trouble. Chloe knew she couldn't go back to Hattiesville. She would go to D.C. to her aunt. She would understand and help Chloe figure out what to do.

"I want my Mama. I want to go home," Nicholas was saying.

"Me too," Blake said.

"I know boys. I know. I'm going to take care of that soon," Chloe answered them with tears in her eyes.

Hampton decided he should call Ben. They boys would recognize him and that would put them at ease. He had to move fast, he would call the chief first in case Chloe tried to leave. He hoped arresting her wouldn't be necessary.

"Ben, Hampton, I have an eye on Chloe Matthews."

"What? Where?"

Hampton told Ben where he was and that the police chief was sending an officer in plain clothes and an unmarked car.

"Okay, I'll head that way. The girls are with me." "That is probably a good thing. Seeing them should put Blake and Nicholas at ease," Hampton said.

"Let's not call Charlotte until we have our hands on them," Ben told Hampton.

"How close are you, Ben?"

"At least twenty minutes away."

"Get on the interstate and I will have a car pick you up."

"Okay that works." Ben said, impressed that Hampton could make that happen. They hung up and he called the police chief, and told him what he needed.

"Consider it handled Hampton," the chief said.

All of this was a little surreal. Ben and Belinda didn't tell Brianna and Brittani their cousins had been kidnapped, and now the three of them were on their way to hopefully recover the boys, police escort and all. When the police cruiser spotted Ben on Interstate 85 he hit the siren for a quick blast and moved in front of Ben, who put on his flashers and followed the cruiser down the interstate. Brianna and Brittani were startled by the siren and then really frightened when Ben started speeding behind the officer. "Daddy what's the matter?" one of them asked. "It's okay, I'll explain everything in a few minutes."

It finally occurred to Hampton that he had not notified Carlos Reyes of what was happening. Hampton called; quickly updated him and Carlos drove the couple of blocks. Hampton, the plain clothes officer and Carlos met in a parking lot across the street. The officer had a plan but wanted to talk it over with Ben.

When Ben and the police escort reached the intersection where Hampton first saw Chloe, the officer turned off the siren and blue lights. He got out of the cruiser and approached Ben's car. "Sir, because I am in a marked vehicle I won't go any further." The officer gave Ben precise directions to the rendezvous point. Ben drove to the parking lot where the others were waiting.

Chloe parked right in front of the apartment. She sat there for a few minutes before finally taking a deep breath and getting out of the car. She opened the back door and took Nicholas out first. She put both arms around him and hugged him tightly. She held him for a long time. Holding Nicholas' hand she walked around the car and took Blake out. Holding both boys hands she walked to the door and rang the bell.

One of the officers and Carlos Reyes had binoculars and were watching Chloe. The other officer told Ben her plan. "You and I and your daughters will go to the door to get the boys. As quickly as you can get your hands on them, leave the premises with all four children. Once you're gone, I will talk with Chloe." Ben nodded in agreement. The officer turned her attention to Hampton and Carlos. "Mr. Josephs, you and Mr. Reyes should wait here." "That's fine," Hampton responded. She simply looked at the other officer who only nodded. While the officer was talking to Hampton and Carlos, Ben was talking to Brittani and Brianna. "Girls, Blake and Nicolas are in an apartment across the street. It's a really long story that I will tell you later, but we need to go get them." The twins looked at each other but didn't say anything. They simply said okay to their dad.

Chloe hugged her friend, and asked to take the boys to the bathroom. When they finished she sat them in front of the television and walked into the kitchen. Her friend followed her. "I am in a lot of trouble." Chloe told her.

"Why Chloe?" The friend was puzzled.

"I took those boys from their sitter and now I don't know what to do." Chloe said.

"Why would you do that?" Her friend's heart was pounding. Chloe started to cry but she explained to her friend who Nicholas was.

"Chloe you have to take them back."

"I can't go back. I want to leave them here with you. I will let their parents know where they are, and I'm sure they will come get them." As Chloe was talking the doorbell rang.

"It's my neighbor; I'll get rid of him."

$\mathscr{S}$EVENTEEN

Raja and Mr. Rajagopal went from the airport to the hospital in an ambulance. Jill met them there and after Mr. Rajagopal was settled Raja called his mother to tell her they were there. He purposely didn't tell her in advance; he simply couldn't deal with the drama. He was glad to see Jill, and all he wanted was to be home with her and LaLa. Mr. Rajagopal was admitted to Critical Care, which meant Mrs. Rajagopal could not spend the night.

It was a very awkward moment when Jill and her mother-in-law saw each other. "Good afternoon Mrs. Rajagopal." Jill said as pleasantly as she could.

"Hello Jillian. Your mother visited me today, she's a lovey woman, and she brought me beautiful flowers."

"Oh! She didn't tell me." Jill was very surprised.

"It was very nice meeting her." Mrs. Rajagopal wanted to make peace with Jill and her mother. She knew that was the only chance she had to spend any time with LaLa. Raja updated his mother on his Dad's condition. "He's still very ill, Mother. He's weak and definitely not out of the woods." As Raja was talking, Dr. Strauss and Trey, Jill's dad and brother, walked in. Jill made the introductions, but Trey remembered Mrs. Rajagopal from the day she and Mr. Rajagopal came to Jill's house unannounced.

Later, when Jill and Raja were home and LaLa was in bed, he confided in her that if his dad survived he would be on oxygen and basically disabled. "The cardiologist told me my dad's heart has been diseased for years based on the look of it."

"Oh, my." Jill said.

"I am trying to wrap my head around this, but I really don't know how to tell my mother. She will probably die first." Raja said sarcastically. Jill looked at him very seriously. It was hard to determine how he really felt. He teetered from serious to sarcastic.

"Does your dad know he's here?" Jill asked.

"Yes, he was pretty alert in New York and I told him what we were going to do. This morning he asked about you and LaLa, and he told mother he was glad to see her." As Raja talked Jill felt so bad for him. He and his parents had been estranged for three years and now all of a sudden they are thirty minutes away and in his care. Jill hated to think Mr. Rajagopal was terminally ill but listening to Raja she couldn't help thinking that. And then Mrs. Rajagopal would be living with them. What an even more awful thought. In the midst of the awful thought, Jill had an amusing thought. She was looking forward to hearing her mother's explanation of her visit to Mrs. Rajagopal.

ℰIGHTEEN

Kathy took a deep breath and sent the text message. She had deleted and re-typed it several times. She wanted to talk to Sterling. He stayed on her mind. Her mom told her she saw him at church once or twice. She didn't get an immediate response to her text, so she went back to cleaning her apartment. As she was changing the linen on her bed, Kathy heard the alert on her phone. It was Sterling responding to her text. It simply said he was in a team meeting and would call her later. Two hours later she hadn't heard from him. She went to bed sad. Just as she dozed off the phone rang. "Hey Kat, sorry to wake you."

"Hi Sterling, it's okay. I thought you decided not to call."

"Naw, have some pretty heavy stuff going on with the team, meeting went long." After a few minutes of small talk, Kathy decided she wanted to get to the real conversation. "Sterling I want to talk to you about something important."

"What's up?"

Kathy pretended to cough so she could have a second to get up her nerve. "I made a mistake when I left and told you I didn't want to be in a relationship with you." Sterling didn't comment so Kathy kept talking. "I miss you, I want to see you, so can we talk and work this out?" Kathy had practiced over and over what she wanted to say to Sterling but now that she was talking, it wasn't coming out like she planned.

"Sterling laughed. "Woman, you are a piece of work." He laughed again. Kathy was silent. She didn't know how to respond. "I tried to tell you not to go all the way to New York. I tried to tell you our relationship needed to be nurtured and I tried to tell you, you were making a mistake. Now three months in, you want to talk," he said, laughing again.
Kathy was angry that he was laughing. "Is 'I told you so' the best you can do?" Kathy finally said.

"No, but I can't believe you. Do you expect me to just agree with you, accept this now because you miss me, because you're homesick? You totally disrespect my life and in your selfishness you expect me to just adjust?"

"I am not being disrespectful to you. I know you're dating and that's why I need to tell you how I feel. You said we were headed to marriage, now it's puzzling me how you can start a new relationship so fast."

"How did you come up with that?"

"I know about the volleyball coach," she said. "What do you think you know, Kat?"

She sighed loudly. "I know you've been going out with the coach."

"She and I are co-workers and friends. That's it. But even if I was seeing her why does that concern you? You made it clear to me you don't want me," Sterling said matter-of-factly.

"I never said I didn't want you. I said I wanted my degrees more," she said.

"Play with words all you want, Kat. The bottom line is, I moved on. I am not dating the coach, but I am seeing somebody."

NINETEEN

Clay didn't sleep much Sunday night. He was anxious to see Cicely but a bit apprehensive at the same time. The Monday morning staff meeting did distract him so the time went by quickly. He left the office at 10:30 for the five minute drive to the restaurant. He wanted to choose the table and be there when she arrived, flowers in hand.

Cicely worked Sunday night, went to the residence hall, rested for an hour, showered and changed. She planned to arrive at the restaurant at exactly 11:00. She expected Clay to get there early.

She wouldn't let herself think about meeting Clay - what they would say to each other. She couldn't think about his smile or the way she felt in his arms. She couldn't think about the home she was creating for them or the ring that had been his mother's. She just mindlessly prepared herself. She didn't want her heart to get involved. She needed to have this conversation from her head with as little emotion as possible.

Not even thinking, Cicely put on a dress. Clay preferred her in a dress or skirt. The necklace, earrings and bracelet she wore he bought. He bought most of her jewelry. A quick spray of the Coco Chanel perfume he bought her and she was out the door.

She saw Clay before he saw her. He was wearing a shirt she bought him and one of his many watches, the one she bought. Cicely took a deep breath and started toward the table; Clay looked up, stood up and took the few steps to meet her. He opened his arms to embrace her. She pulled away after about two seconds. He watched her slide into the booth and then he slid in on the other side. "Hey baby," he said, staring at her. He was looking for something in her eyes.

"Hi Clay."
"I am so glad to see you," Clay said. He had not taken his eyes off her. They both seemed a little uneasy. The server interrupted them to take their orders. It was a welcome interruption. Cicely wanted to be on offense. She needed to control the conversation. But Clay spoke first. "You look great."

"Thank you." She said with a slight smile. "Clay, we need to clear the air."

"I agree," he said.

"I haven't ever been so hurt, so angry, so humiliated in my life. Even with all I've been through; my mom abandoning us, my dad passing, nothing hurt me as deeply as all the stuff Delia said; telling me you asked her to have sex with you. And in my apartment!" Tears were stinging her eyes, but she willed herself not to cry.

"CeCe…" That was his pet name for her and she didn't want him to say that. Not now, not in this conversation. "…all I can say is, I'm sorry. Can you please, please forgive me?"

"Why should I forgive you?"

"Because I made a mistake. I made a bad decision. I went to Jeremy's game and saw Delia with Javier. I guess I was jealous and I started playing this obviously very dangerous game with her."

"Why were you jealous? If you wanted me, and didn't want her, you could see her with ten men and not care." Before Clay could respond the server brought the food. Cicely did allow Clay to hold her hand while he blessed the food. "You are absolutely right. I have no excuse, no real explanation. But let me say this, in all honesty. I had no intention of having sex with her. None."

"Well why...?"

"To see where her head was. Delia is using Javier. He's paying her bills, taking care of her kids..."

"But why is that your problem?" Cicely asked, widening her eyes. It was an expression Clay knew well.

"In reality it's not, I shouldn't have tried to show her I was right about her all along."

"You and Delia are playing some sick kind of game and I don't want to be a part of it!"

"I don't want you to be a part of any foolishness between Delia and me. I have not seen her since the day she told you all that stuff. She called me and left a message apologizing but I did not respond. I don't want to see her or hear from her again. CeCe, I love you. I love you. I want you and only you. I want to marry you," Clay said sincerely. She just looked at him.

They ate in silence for a few minutes. "I don't trust you Clay." She said matter-of-factly. He sighed and put his fork down. He looked directly into her eyes. "Please give me another chance. Please give me a chance to regain your trust."

They talked for another hour. She did tell him she was back at work but she wouldn't tell him where she was living.

She wouldn't tell him what her plans were. The truth was she didn't have a plan. He told her she could move into the new house. She said no. She told him she had not forgiven him or Delia, and until she did she couldn't consider reconciling with him. "Do you love me Cicely?" He reached for both her hands. She didn't pull away but she didn't answer.

Clay previously told the server to bring the flowers with the check, so he asked for the check. She quickly came back and set the flowers on Cicely's side of the table and the check on Clay's side. Cicely blushed a little. "Thank you," she said.

"Sure."

As they left the restaurant, Clay asked her when he could see her again.

"I don't know. I'll call you."

$\mathscr{T}$WENTY

Grant looked at the clock. He was expecting Clay to call and tell him about meeting Cicely. At the moment he was more interested in their relationship than his and Sunny's. They hadn't exchanged but a few words since Saturday morning when he walked out of the bistro at breakfast. He sat at his desk and thought about being in the pre-martial classes he and Leah took before they got engaged. He and Sunny hadn't taken the classes but maybe they should have. Fighting about what type of wedding to have was totally ludicrous. It was obvious to Grant that he didn't know Sunny as well as he thought. She continued to surprise him and she continued to compare their relationship to his and Leah's relationship. He worked really hard to put Leah in the proper place in his past, but Sunny was stuck trying not to be in Leah's shadow. Grant loved Sunny and wanted to marry her, but they needed counseling and he intended to tell her so.

"Hello Ma, are you busy?" Sunny rarely called her mother this time of day but she needed some advice. She quickly explained what was going on with her and Grant. Her mother listened carefully. "Sunny, what is more important to you; the wedding or the marriage?

"Ma, it's all important."
"But one has to be the priority. Your father and I have been married thirty-five years because our marriage was the

63

priority." Sunny listened to her mother, but the fact still remained she wanted a big wedding. That had always been her dream. "Can you and Grant compromise?" Sunny's mother asked.

"I guess so, but he doesn't want to compromise; he wants his way." Sunny said.

"And you want yours!" her mother said.

"But Ma, I am the bride."

"Yes, Sunny, but you will still be the bride in the church chapel."

She couldn't believe her mother was siding with Grant. Compromise! She was already compromising by not going home to Eleuthera because Grant's father was not well enough to travel that far. Now they wanted her to give up her grand ballroom wedding and trade it for a small chapel. That would mean less attendants and less guests which meant less people would know about her wedding and consequently less money and gifts. Her mother's next statement stung Sunny. "Grant is a good man; don't lose him over the wedding. It looks to me like you care more for appearance than the sanctity of the marriage."

"Ma!"

"Listen to me girl, adjust your attitude and your high and mighty ways before you find yourself single again."

It had not occurred to Sunny that she and Grant's difference of opinion over the wedding would be cause for them to break up. She just figured she would get her way and they would move on.

"I better give this more thought," she said to herself.

$\mathscr{T}$WENTY-ONE

When Chloe saw Ben and the girls walk into her friend's apartment, she was actually relieved, in spite of not knowing what else was coming. "Nicky, Blake!" Brittani got their attention. They both jumped up and saw their uncle and cousins. The boys ran to Brittani and Brianna's open arms. Remembering what the officer said, Ben moved quickly to get the children out of the apartment. The police officer was standing to the side but walked into the living room once Ben and the children were outside. As they walked across the grass to the street he looked back, slightly nervous; the door was closed so he kept walking. The officers waiting across the street met them halfway. Nicholas and Blake were questioning Brittani and Brianna about why they came to pick them up. One of the officers interrupted them. "Hey guys, you okay?"

"Yes," Blake said, holding Brianna's hand. Nicholas was holding Brittani's hand but didn't say anything.

"Are you hungry?" the officer asked.

"No," Blake answered again. Ben was waiting for further instructions from the police, but he texted Enoch. "The boys are safe with me, will call shortly." Hampton was on the phone with the police chief. "I would prefer we take them to Pastor Coffey's home." He gave the chief Ben's address and then nodded yes to Ben. Carlos Reyes walked across the street to get the boys' booster seats from Natalia's car just as the apartment door opened. The officer walked out with

Chloe. She was not in handcuffs but the officer was holding her arm. When the officer realized the children were still there she stopped where they were. Another officer went over, they talked briefly and the second officer told Ben he could leave and the sergeant would come to his home shortly. Ben loaded all the children in the car and drove away.

"It's a text from Ben! He has the boys!" Enoch was yelling. He and Kirby hugged, so did Sandra and Roderick and Campbell and Natalia. "He said he will call shortly." Sandra wanted to know about Chloe, "He didn't mention her," Enoch said. Sandra called Chloe but there was still no answer.

"Pack a bag so we can go to Landridge." Enoch said to Kirby. He was ignoring the other four people in the room. Kirby walked away from them and ran up the stairs. Just as Enoch turned his attention to the group to ask them to leave, Sandra's phone rang.

"Chloe! Oh my God, are you alright? Where are you?"

"Mama, I am in Atlanta at the Fulton County Detention Center. I am not formally under arrest. The officer said it's up to the Casebiers if they want to press charges."

"Chloe, don't say anything to anybody, we'll be there as soon as we can."

"Ma, I am so sorry."

"Not a word Chloe." Sandra gave the phone to Roderick who reinforced what his wife had already said. As Roderick and Chloe were talking, Sandra turned to Enoch. "My daughter is not a criminal; she's a confused young lady who made an impulsive decision. Please don't press charges and I will make sure she gets some help." Campbell and Natalia had pleading looks in their eyes.

"All I care about right now is going to Landridge to get my sons. I will deal with that later. Now please leave, all of you."

The thirty minute drive to Landridge seemed quick. Ben had called Grammy and she and Thelma were at the house waiting. Blake and Nicholas were glad to be with their cousins and glad to see Grammy but they clearly wanted their parents. Once at the house, Brittani called Enoch and each of the boys spoke to each parent. "Mommy I want to come home," Nicholas said to Kirby.

"We are on our way to get you. Why don't you go to sleep in Brittani's bed and when you wake up I'll be there." Kirby was trying her best not to cry. Nicholas gave the phone to Brianna, and relayed his mother's message to Blake. After a sandwich and a bath, both boys went to sleep.

Knowing Grammy would handle everything with the boys, Ben went to his office and called Enoch. He told them everything that happened. "Hampton Josephs handled everything. But we have a question; what do you want me to tell the police officer?"

"Tell them to talk to me in the morning after I've seen my boys," Enoch said.

Hampton left the apartment complex and went to the hospital to tell Belinda everything was fine. He knew Ben would call her but he wanted to tell her in person. Maybe that was an excuse to see her, but he was glad to give her good news. She was genuinely happy to see him and pleased with his report. "Thank you so much for everything." She said to him smiling. "I know Kirby will want to see you when they get here.

"It's a blessing things turned out well. We could be having a very different conversation," Hampton said. "I have another idea Belinda if you want to hear it," he said smiling at her.

She hesitated but then said, "Okay, tell me."

"Ask your doctor if you can be discharged if I hire a nurse to go home with you."

"You just don't learn do you?" Belinda said. Hamp looked at her, puzzled. "You spending money on me is why I'm here. That will just make April angry again. Thank you but no thanks!"

"I can handle April. I just think it's time for you to go home. I think you will be better there, with people who love you."

"But my boys will still be here," Belinda said sadly.

"I know, I'll make sure you get to see them every day. I will hire a private nurse for them too, if that makes you feel better." She was quiet for a minute.

"I don't know; let me talk to Ben about it."

"That's fine, one more thing…" Hamp said taking her hands. "You and your sister need to talk."

TWENTY-TWO

Min's rehabilitation was going well. She was feeling good and ready to go home. There was still tension between her and Jackson but she would deal with that when they were home. She fully intended to tell Jackson she knew what he's up to, and demand that he make a decision to correct his behavior. She knew he would. For all the time Min knew about Jackson's affair it hadn't interfered with their marriage. Now it was affecting her health. Min wanted to be well; she had a lot to live for. The future was bright. Jacksa and Anderson were talking about getting married so she knew they would eventually have children. Min wanted grandbabies!

Jacksa and King walked into Min's room. This was King's third visit to the rehab center. There were a few other patients who had dogs, but King was the star. The staff and other patients knew the story of his rescuing Min.

"Mom, I was talking to the nurse on my way in here and she told me you should be discharged in a day or two."

"Yes, they told me that earlier today." Min was smiling and playing with King. "Ok, I will have everything set up for you to come home. You can have my room and I will move in the guest room."

"Jacksa, what are you talking about?"

"When you get discharged I am taking you to my house."

"Why? For what?" Min asked and shrugged her shoulders.

"I know you don't want to go home to your whorish husband!" Jacksa said.

"Jacksa Lynn Baye, that is your father you're talking about, don't be disrespectful, and yes I am going home, home to my own bed, and my own things." Jacksa was astonished at her mother's attitude about this situation. Min appeared nonchalant, just like she did when she first told Jacksa about Jackson's affair.

"You are going to continue to live with him? Mom, what are you thinking? Why would you do that?" Jacksa was furious that her Mother would even consider being with her father again. "Jacksa, I know you don't understand, I don't expect you to. Marriage is about forgiveness and second chances."

"Mom I get that, but he didn't spend the mortgage money that you can forgive, he had an affair, and didn't come home to see about you!" Jacksa was screaming.

Min didn't raise her voice. "Sweetie, I will deal with this. I appreciate your concern for me but I am capable of handling your father and our marriage."

Neither of them knew Jackson and Anderson were standing outside the door. Anderson was there first. He had started in to stop Jacksa's rant just as Jackson walked up. Jackson stopped him. They stood in the hall and listened. Anderson was furious with Jackson. He definitely sided with Jacksa. Jackson was relieved that Min was coming home. He didn't know what would happen once she was there but at least he would have a chance. Jackson didn't know that Anderson knew who the paramour was, where she lived and that he intended to keep an eye on the situation.

King noticed the two of them outside the door which got Min and Jacksa's attention. Anderson walked in first. He took Jacksa's hand, kissed Min on the cheek and then kissed Jacksa. Jackson spoke to Min and hugged her. Jacksa turned her back to him. Anderson knew she and JJ had a long way to go to re-establish the relationship with their dad.

Anderson wanted some alone time with Jacksa. The case he was working on was tough. She was dealing with her mom's situation and her boss's daughter had kidnapped a couple of kids, and they were dealing with that, so the associates were depending on her to keep things going. She was stressed and so was he. His sister suggested they go to a bed & breakfast. Anderson wasn't sure that was a good idea. That was probably too intimate for them at this point in the relationship. He decided to take her to Catawba to his grandmother's house. She would love on both of them, he could see his mother, sisters and aunt, but they could have some quite time there. He called Jacksa. "Ride to Catawba with me, we can spend the night at Honey's and chill for the weekend." Jacksa thought it was cute that Anderson and his sisters called their grandmother "Honey." He explained to her they did it because their grandfather called her Honey.

"Anderson, what makes you think she will be okay with that?"

He laughed, "She's okay with anything I do!"

"You are such a brat."

"Will you spend the weekend with the brat?"

"I would love to, but...."

"No buts, your mom will be at home with King and your dad. There's no work that can't wait." She sighed, but she knew he was right. They had fun at the river each time they went. Usually they only spent the day; spending the weekend was different.

"If you're sure Honey will be fine with it, then I'll go." They made plans to leave Friday early evening.

Anderson called his grandmother, who was delighted they were coming. "Honey, don't tell my mama or the girls, we'll go see them Saturday. Jacksa and I need some quite time."

"Okay, what do you want to eat?"

"Don't you usually fry fish on Friday?"

"Yeah, but that skinny little girl probably don't eat fried fish." They both laughed.

"The fish is fine Honey! And can I have some cornbread too?"

"Yes, sugar you can and remind me, I have something for you when you get here."

Jacksa called Min to tell her she was going to South Carolina with Anderson for the weekend.

"That sounds like fun." Min smiled at the thought.

"Are you sure you want to go home with Daddy? I can tell Anderson I need to stay....."

"No, absolutely not! You go ahead. Your father and I will be fine." After a few more minutes they hung up and Jacksa called JJ. She told him about the talk she and Min had about Jackson. "Don't worry sis, enjoy your weekend. I'll take care of Mom and I'll handle our dad," he said.

$\mathcal{T}$WENTY-THREE

Kathy had not missed a class since she started. She had cramps today but rather than push through like times before, she decided to stay in and rest. Plus she was heartbroken. Sterling telling her he was dating someone else was hard enough, but knowing it wasn't Coach Foust made it worse. She didn't know what to do. She didn't know how to feel. She was so sure when she left Hattiesville that coming to New York was the right decision. Now she was second guessing herself. When she got up to get something to eat, she looked out the window. It was pouring rain, and dreary outside. It looked just like she felt.

Sterling felt guilty for not telling Kathy the truth. He was not dating Jordana Foust; that was true. But he wasn't really dating anyone else either. He met someone; they had been out once but had not established a relationship. His motive was to hurt Kathy because she hurt him. He shook his head. He was playing games with Kathy like his students played with each other. This was crazy and he knew it. But what was he going to do about it?

Late that afternoon Kathy checked her school email account. There were a couple of assignments and notes from two of her study partners. One message was particularly interesting. The professor asked Kathy to call him, but he didn't say why. Kathy thought that was odd. She was doing well in his class, so he couldn't be calling about her work. Kathy looked at the clock, and expected him to be already gone for the day but she would leave him a message. She wouldn't see him in class for a few days, so she thought she shouldn't wait. Kathy was surprised when he answered. She was even more surprised when he invited her to dinner.

$\mathcal{T}$WENTY-FOUR

Sandra and Roderick arrived in Atlanta late that night and went straight to the police department. They talked to Chloe briefly on the way there and told her not to talk to anybody or answer any questions until they got there.

The officer showed them to a room where Chloe was sitting with her head on the table. She was asleep. "Chloe, sweetheart, wake up." Her mother was rubbing her back. Chloe looked up, looked around the room and remembered where she was. She looked up at her mother and started to cry.

Roderick was in the hall talking to the officer, who was explaining what happened. The officer who brought Chloe in was gone for the night. She had not formally charged Chloe but made it clear to her they could charge her whether the Casebiers decided to press charges or not. She also advised Chloe to get an attorney.

"Chloe, start at the beginning and tell me what happened," Sandra said to her very quietly. Chloe took a deep breath, but didn't say anything for a full minute. Finally she started to talk.

"The day I ran into Enoch Casebier at the post office, Natalia was with me. I told her about Nicholas, and I told her I wanted to take him from the Casebiers.

"Chloe, no wonder…" Chloe interrupted her mother and kept talking as her dad walked in. "She decided to help me see Nicholas. She made friends with the Casebiers so she could let me see him and she sent me pictures when she would babysit for the boys. When I met them at the park Saturday I saw a chance to have him to myself and I took it. I didn't think, I didn't have a plan. I just did it. Then I kinda woke up when we were on the highway and I realized what I did." Chloe started crying again. Roderick sat down beside her.

"Did you tell Natalia what you were going to do?" he asked.

"No daddy, she didn't have anything to do with this. She was putting Blake in the back on the passenger side and when she closed the door I got in the driver's side and pulled away."

"Do you know how much trouble you're in?" Sandra asked.

"I do now. I didn't realize it until I got the message from the police." Chloe's voice was just above a whisper.

"Rod, we need to get her a lawyer," Sandra said, her voice shaky.

As promised, when Nicholas and Blake awakened the next morning, their mother was lying across the foot of Brittani's bed. Nicholas saw her first and when he crawled over Blake's feet to get to his mother, Blake woke up. Kirby held them both tightly in her arms. She cried and whispered "thank you God" over and over. After a few minutes they wanted out of her arms so she started tickling them. Enoch was lying on the sofa. When he heard them laugh he went in to join the fun. A few minutes later the girls ran in and the chaos was in full effect. It was as if nothing had happened. There was nothing abnormal about the scene except that twenty four hours before these two little boys had been kidnapped.

After breakfast Kirby dressed the boys. The police were coming to talk to them. Then Kirby and Enoch were going to the hospital to see Belinda and see Hampton Josephs. The officers arrived promptly. Neither of them was in uniform. Ben had explained to Brittani and Brianna the night before what happened to the boys. They were in the kitchen with Grammy when the police officers came.

"Who's Blake and who's Nicholas?" the officer asked. Nick raised his hand. "So you're Nicholas?"

"Yes."

Blake didn't say anything; he was sizing her up.

"Guys can we have a seat?" Neither boy said anything. They both sat down on the floor. Enoch sat on the ottoman, in front of Kirby who was sitting in the recliner. Grammy, Brianna, Brittani and Ben were standing in the doorway between the family room and the kitchen. "Can somebody tell me what happened at the park yesterday?" the officer asked. The boys looked at each other, and then Blake looked at his dad. Enoch nodded yes, but they still didn't say anything. Brianna tapped Brittani on her shoulder, and they walked into the family room and sat on the floor with the boys.

"Blake, will you tell me what happened at the park yesterday when you finished playing?" Both boys turned their attention to Brianna.

"We asked Natalia if we could get some pancakes. She said yes and we got in the car. Then her friend drove Natalia's car and left," Blake said.

"But we didn't get any pancakes so we told her we wanted to go home," Nicholas said.

"What's her friend's name?" Brittani asked.

"I think its Nikki. She said she had the same name as me," Nicholas answered.

The detective wrote Nikki on her pad with a question mark beside it.

"Did you get anything to eat?" Kirby asked.

"Yeah Ma!" Blake said. They all laughed at the expression on his face.

"What did Natalia's friend tell you?" the detective asked.

"Nothing. It was a surprise and we came to see Brittani and Brianna!" Blake said.

"Did she tell you that?"

"No, it was a surprise!" Nicholas said.

"Did anything bad happen?" the officer asked.

"No, but it took a long time to get here." Blake said.

"Yeah," Nicholas said. "What were you doing before me and Bree & Daddy came to get you?" Brittani asked.

"Watching TV," they both said.

"Can we go outside?" Nicholas asked Enoch.

"Last question, did you guys tell Natalia's friend you wanted to go home?"

"Yeah," they both answered. All four children left the room and Grammy behind them.

"We are going home tomorrow, so I hope you have all the information you need," Enoch said to the detective. "One question for you Mr. and Mrs. Casebier. Do you want to press charges against Chloe Matthews?" Enoch said yes, Kirby said no, at the same time - they were looking at each other. Ben could feel the tension between them.

"Detective, obviously my family has experienced a traumatic event. May we please have some time to discuss this and call you before they leave tomorrow?" Ben said.

"Fair enough," she said, giving Ben her business card. Ben walked the officers to the door to give himself a minute. One of the hardest things in ministry was to counsel your own family but he needed to right now.

$\mathcal{T}$WENTY-FIVE

Mr. Rajagopal was still listed in critical condition five days after arriving in Charlotte. Raja actually thought he was better. Dr. Strauss was cautiously optimistic. Mrs. Rajagopal was spending the day at the hospital but had not made a fuss about being home alone in the evenings. She had actually made a friend. There was another older lady staying in the guest house whose son was very ill. They met in the dining room and started having dinner together each evening.

Ellen didn't tell Jill the full conversation between her and Mrs. Rajagopal. She only admitted to visiting her and taking the flowers. "I'm sure we understand each other," Ellen told Jill with a big smile.

The moving day for Ellen and Dr. Strauss was one day away. After their things were out, the cleaning people would come in and then Jill, LaLa and Raja would move in. Because Ellen and Dr. Strauss were downsizing, they left the furniture in one guest bedroom and the family room furniture that was being moved to the den on the main level so Mrs. Rajagopal could choose her own furniture for downstairs. The only thing Jill didn't like about the new house was that the master suite was on the main level and LaLa's bedroom was upstairs. But Raja insisted it was okay and of course they had monitors. Ellen was helping Jill to be as accommodating as possible. If it didn't work with Mrs. Rajagopal it wouldn't be Jill's fault and Ellen would handle it.

Ellen didn't want to share LaLa anyway and since Raja and Jill were planning to have another baby she was perfectly fine with being the only grandmother of two grandchildren. She was doing what was right, not necessarily what she wanted to do. She really wished Mrs. Rajagopal was back in London.

$\mathcal{T}$WENTY-SIX

Grant knew Sunny was up to something as soon as he walked in the house. She had a full-fledged seduction plan in place; the ambiance, the champagne and especially the thong and bra she was wearing when she greeted him. He stood and looked at her briefly, took the glass of champagne out of her hand. "Go put some clothes on Sunny, we need to talk."

"Can we talk later?"

"No, we need to talk now." She stormed into the other room put on a t-shirt came back, and flopped down on the sofa. Grant used the remote control to turn off the music.

"I want to postpone getting married until we have counseling."

"Counseling! What are you talking about?" Sunny asked casually.

"We need to talk to somebody about all this."

"All this what, Grant?"

"Why I'm seeing a side of you I don't know or understand. Why the wedding is more important to you than the marriage and why you are so concerned about Leah." Grant was very serious. Sunny looked at him, intending to say something harsh. The expression on his face told her that was not a good idea.

"Grant, I love you."

"Sunny, I love you too, but this is not about love."

"Are you saying you won't marry me without counseling?" Sunny had tears in her eyes.

"I'm saying I want our marriage to be forever and the only way to ensure that is to get off to a good start, the right start." Grant said. They were both quite for a moment.

"Are you giving me an ultimatum?" Sunny asked. She raised one eyebrow and folded her arms in front of her. When she realized Grant wasn't smiling she backed down.

"Label it whatever you want to Sunny, I don't want to talk about the wedding until we deal with the marriage and the only way to deal with the marriage is through counseling."

"Do you have a counselor in mind?" she asked. She was furious but was not showing it. How was she going to tell her family and friends the wedding was postponed? She had negotiated with the hotel to get what she wanted. How was she going to back out now? Grant was messing up her plans.

"I called Bishop Robinson and asked if he knows anyone in the area," Grant answered.

"You called Leah's dad to ask for a marriage counselor for us? Why would you do that?"

Grant sighed deeply, loudly. "Before Bishop Robinson was going to be my father-in-law, he was my parent's good friend and my pastor. If we were living in Hattiesville, he would be our counselor."

"And you would just make that decision without us talking about it?"

"Why is dealing with Bishop Robinson a problem?"

"Because I don't want him in our business!" Sunny said.

"Leah is dead, Sunny!" Grant raised his voice. "She is not coming back, and I was over her until I decided to marry you! Leah doesn't cross my mind until you bring her up. Let her rest in peace please!" Grant yelled and walked out of the room.

Sunny took the remote and turned the music back on. She sat for a few minutes deciding what to do. Things did not go the way she planned. If she was going to marry Grant she needed to fix this quickly. She took the t-shirt off and headed to the bedroom. Grant was coming down the hall; he had packed a bag and was leaving. "G, where are going?"

"I'm leaving, Sunny."

"Leaving - what does that mean?"

"I'll call you in a couple of days when I sort things out." Grant said as he walked out.

TWENTY-SEVEN

When the phone rang Cicely answered it half asleep. She didn't open her eyes; she knew it was Clay waking her for work. "Hey you," he said.

"Hi Clay." She sat up in bed and realized where she was and her current life situation came back to her. Her defenses went up.

"Time to go to work," he said. The sound of his voice was comforting to her.

"Thanks for calling, I'm up." Cicely said wanting to get off the phone.

"Will you have breakfast with me when you get off in the morning?"

"Clay, I don't know." She wanted to say yes, but she wasn't sure she should.

"Please CeCe."

"I'll text you on my break," she said.

"That won't work; I need to know what time to get up". He was pouting, she knew it. She knew him well. She couldn't help but laugh.

"Clay, stop acting like a baby."

"I am your baby." he said quietly. She felt a pang in her heart.

"Yes, I will have breakfast with you." Clay pumped his fist in the air. They made plans to meet and hung up so Cicely could get ready for work.

Clay slept off and on. Each time he awakened he thought about Cicely. There were so many things he wanted to say to her but it was all about timing. If they could work it out, he would marry her immediately. He wasn't going to take the time to plan a wedding and all that. He decided in that moment he would call his cousin Gretchen the next day and have her go to the new house and put up the window treatments and put the comforters on the beds. He knew if he could get Cicely to the new house - their house - he could give her the ring back and get back on the right track.

Clay had not been back to the house since the night he found Cicely's ring in the glass of water on the deck. He asked Gretchen to check the house once and he asked Enoch to keep an eye on it since he and his family were in the area now that they lived in Victoria Coffey's house.

As Clay drifted back to sleep, the phone rang. It was late; he hoped Cicely wasn't calling to cancel their date. It was Grant. Over the next half hour Grant told Clay what led to the fight he and Sunny had. Clay was stunned.

"Where are you?" Clay asked.

"In the officers' quarters."

"You goin' back?"

"Not for a couple days," Grant said.

"Does Sunny know where you are?"

"No, and even if she figured it out she can't get in here. I need to clear my head."

After talking a few minutes Clay convinced Grant to come home to Hattiesville for a few days. He said he would.

He got up early the following morning. He sent his manager and his assistant an email saying he would be away for a few days on family business. His next thought was to send Sunny an email or leave a message on her work phone. He thought better of it; he didn't want to have a debate with her. He decided to text her after he got to Hattiesville. But before the thought was out of his head Sunny called. He answered. "Yeah."

"Why didn't you come home last night?"

"I told you I wasn't. I need some air, there needed to be some distance between us," he said. "Why don't we take the day off and get this situation worked out?" she said.

"I have something else to do. I will see you Monday or Tuesday."

"Monday or Tuesday? You're talking about four or five days from now. What are you trying to prove, Grant?"

"I am not trying to prove anything. I'm going home to see my parents. I want to check on my dad."

"Is your dad okay?" Sunny asked softly.

"He's fine. I want to see him; he can't come to me, so I'm going home."

There wasn't a whole lot more to say. He didn't ask her to go with him; his mind was made up. Maybe some distance, as he phrased it, would benefit them. There was no need to argue with him. So she decided to relent. "Are you driving?"

"Yeah."

"Call me when you get there." She said evenly.

"Will do." He hung up.

TWENTY-EIGHT

Min was packed and ready to go home when Jackson arrived. The nurse gave them her discharge orders.

"She really needs to gain a little weight, and the doctor wants her to be on a high protein diet." They talked about the four weeks of in-home physical therapy and occupational therapy. Jackson asked if she should return to work. "Sure, if she wants to and feels up to it."

The ride home was quite, except for some small talk. When they were almost home Jackson asked Min what she had for lunch. "A chicken sandwich. Why do you ask?"

"I am going to cook dinner for you. I was just thinking what I need to get from the store."

"I would really like to have a steak on the grill," Min said.

"Steak it is! "Jackson said smiling at her. "Do you think Jacksa and the detective want to join us? Min laughed at her husband's tone of voice.

"No, they are visiting his family for the weekend."

"Oh I see."

King was excited to see Min, and she was excited to see him. They played while Jackson brought Min's things in. A few minutes later the next door neighbor was at the door. Jackson decided to go to the store while the neighbor was there. For a split second Min wondered where he was going or if he would make a call while he was out. She quickly dismissed the thought. Those thoughts are what landed her in the hospital. While Min was in the hospital she admitted to the psychiatrist that she was completely stressed about Jackson's affair. She felt it was her fault. She said her MS sent him to that woman's bed. The doctor was clear with her that it wasn't her fault; the illness or Jackson's infidelity.

Regardless of the front she put up for Jacksa, Min was sick about Jackson's actions. She had sleepless nights, and tearful days. As much as she knew he loved her, as attentive as he was to her, there was another woman in his life. At least there had been. Min decided not to hire a private detective; she didn't want to know who she was. She had made a conscious decision not to confront Jackson and keep quite. Keeping quiet made her sick; she wasn't going to keep quiet anymore.

On the ride to S.C., Jacksa and Anderson played "What If". They each took turns asking the other questions that started with the phrase "What If." "The only rule; you have to be willing to answer any question you ask," Anderson told Jacksa.

Jacksa went first. Laughing, she asked "what if there was no more crime in the world?"

"I guess I would be out of a job." His turn.

"What if there no coffee in the world?"

"This would be a cranky world!" They laughed.

They went back and forth until he asked "What if we get married next year?" Jacksa swallowed hard. She really didn't know how to respond. She didn't know if he was playing the game or asking her to marry him. She decided to play the game.

"Then I need to find something to wear!"

Jackson was back from the store in about a half hour. He had steak, baking potatoes, asparagus and cheesecake. The neighbor was gone and Min was unpacking her things. She was obviously stronger; moving around without her walker. Jackson took a deep breath and walked into the bedroom.

"Can I help you with any of that?" Jackson asked Min.

"No, I'm about done. Thank you. I'll do the laundry tomorrow," she said casually. He walked over to her, put his arm around her and hugged her tightly. They held each other and neither said anything for a moment.

Honey was sitting in her favorite spot; on the screened porch on the side of the house when Anderson and Jacksa pulled into the driveway. After hugs all around, and chatting for a few minutes, Anderson put Jacksa's things in the pink room; the girl's room they called it when they were growing up. He put his things in the boy's room, the blue room. Honey was in the back yard, frying fish in the black pot. Jacksa was making tea and watching the food in the oven. Anderson walked past her, patted her on the butt and went out the back door. As Honey took the last two pieces of croaker out of the hot grease, Anderson doused the fire. She covered the fish with aluminum foil. As he reached to pick up the pan she put her hand on his shoulder and gave him a dark blue velvet box. He opened the box and saw a set of wedding rings. It was obviously an old set but very nice. "And you....are...giving...me...this...why?" He asked pausing between each word.

"Clean it up, have it reset, whatever you want to do and ask that girl to marry you." Anderson put the box in his pocket and carried the fish into the house.

Honey, Anderson and Jacksa ate a lot and laughed a lot. They cleaned the kitchen together. Anderson watched the interaction between Jacksa and his grandmother. He liked that they got along so well. He left the kitchen and went to his grandmother's room. She had a king sized bed decorated with lots of pillows. He took his shoes off and climbed in bed like he did when he was a little boy. He leaned back on the pillows and closed his eyes.

"Where did Anderson go?" Jacksa asked.

"I bet I know where he is," Honey said. When the ladies walked into the room Anderson had dozed off. His grandmother motioned for Jacksa to get on the bed beside him. She got in on the other side. He looked at Honey and then at Jacksa and lay back on the pillows. For a couple of hours they talked and laughed. No stress, no pressure, just the love of his grandmother. That was what he wanted, and what he wanted for Jacksa.

After a while Jacksa went to her room to call and check on her mother. "Thanks for the rings," Anderson said to his grandmother. Why would you give them to me now?"

"Anderson Thorn, don't ask me a bunch of questions. Just handle your business," Honey told him.

He laughed. "Yes ma'am."

Min and King played around in the backyard, while Jackson cooked. They decided to eat on the deck. Dinner was delicious. Min took one small bite of her cheesecake.

"Jackson, I need to know if you intend to continue your affair."

Jackson was caught off guard by Min's question. He cleared his throat to give himself a second to think. "Min, please forgive me. Please forgive me for everything." Min didn't immediately respond. She looked directly into his eyes, and then took another bite of her dessert.

"Why should I forgive you, Jackson? Why would I forgive you?"

"I made a mistake, a bad decision. I got caught up"

Min interrupted him. "Which decision are you talking about? Having an affair or not coming home to see about your wife?"

"I'm sorry for all of it, I sincerely apologize. I came as soon as I got the message."

"I knew months ago you were having an affair. I just didn't know what to do about it."

Jackson's body language was tense. He didn't know what to do with his hands, and he couldn't look her in the eye.

"You know JJ and Jacksa want me to kick you out, and in my head, somewhere in my intellect, I agree with them. But my heart is telling me 'no.' My head says take everything you have, sue her for alienation of affection, bankrupt you both and move on with my life. But my heart says don't give up on thirty years."

"I can't fix the past, but I can make the future better," Jackson said.

Min ignored his comment and kept talking. She was looking away as if he wasn't sitting there. "There was a point in my thinking about this when I was in rehab, that I thought I was too sick, too weak, and too dependent on you to live on my own. I thought I needed you because no one else would ever want a 55-year-old woman whose body is deteriorating." As Min was talking Jackson was watching her. She was strong and confident, and he really didn't know what she was going to say. He had no idea how this conversation was going to end. And he hated that she even had a thought of someone else wanting her. "But you know what Jack; if I decide to dismiss you, and be with someone else, that's my option." He was stunned. He did not know this woman sitting across the table from him.

"You are my wife. I love you. I don't want to lose you." His voice and his eyes were pleading with her. As he talked, he felt his phone vibrate in his shirt pocket. He knew it wasn't Jacksa or JJ but that was the third time. It shouldn't be her, but he was afraid to take that chance and pull the phone out. They hadn't communicated but she had attempted several times to reach him. Min was looking right through him, and again she didn't respond to what he said.

"What would our parents think if they knew the state of our relationship?" she asked. "What would your father say?" She didn't wait for his answer she kept talking. "My father would say, I told you the black American was not good for you! My mother would cry because she loved you so much." Tears were forming in Jackson's eyes. She repeated her question and waited for his answer. "What would your father say?"

"He would be very disappointed," Jackson said as the tear spilled over and ran down his cheek. "And my mother would be very angry," he added. Neither of them said anything for a few seconds, and then Min got up from her seat. Jackson stood to help her.

"I'm okay," she said, "just going to the bathroom."

Jackson took a deep breath. He had to fix this. He did not want his marriage to end, but the ball was in her court. He leaned back in the chair and closed his eyes, and then thought about the phone. He looked at the screen. There were two calls; one actually was from Jacksa and the other from a co-worker. He listened to the messages. As Min was headed back to the deck she saw him on the phone. "How dare him, "she thought. When she walked back out he looked up at her.

"Jacksa left a message. She was trying to call you." He also told her about the message from his co-worker who wanted to know if she had gotten settled and if they needed anything. Her countenance softened. "That was very nice of her."

"May I use your phone?" He gave it to her. She called Jacksa back and assured her everything was fine. "Please tell Anderson and his grandmother I said hello." They talked a few more minutes and Min got up from the table. "Let's go King," she said. "Thank you for a great meal Jack." Min said with a smile. It was a lovely evening.

"You're welcome, sweetheart." King came up the stairs to the deck and followed Min into the house. After Jackson cleaned up he came to the bedroom. Min was sitting on the side of the bed putting lotion on her arms when he walked in. "Can I get you something? "He asked while taking a t-shirt out of a drawer.

"No, thank you," she said. "And when you finish your shower you need to sleep in the guest room."

$\mathscr{T}$WENTY-NINE

Carlotta was having a pool party and sleepover for her birthday. Brittani and Brianna were spending the day with her, now that everything was okay at home. Ben, Enoch and Kirby were meeting Hampton at the hospital. Ben and Enoch went to the nursery to see Bryce and Bradley. Kirby went straight to Belinda's room. She told her sister how painful it was for her boys to be gone and how she knew Enoch blamed her for what happened. While they were talking, there was a knock at the door.

"Yes, come in."

Hampton walked in and was surprised that Belinda was not alone.

"Hello ladies," he said looking from Belinda to Kirby. They both spoke, and then Belinda made the introductions.

"Hampton, this is my sister, Kirby Casebier. K, this is Hampton Josephs." Hampton had hoped she would introduce him as her father.

"Hampton, thank you for all you did to help us find our boys," Kirby said to him. Belinda was watching Kirby. She was still holding his hand.

"You're welcome. I'm glad I could help, and glad it turned out as uneventfully as it did."

"I am too. I don't want to think about how else it could have turned out," Kirby said.

Ben and Enoch came in. Ben introduced Enoch and Hampton, and Enoch thanked Hampton too. They all talked for a while and then Enoch and Kirby left. They were going back to the house to get Blake and Nicholas so they could head back to Hattiesville. After Kirby and Enoch left, Hampton told Ben about his offer to get Belinda a nurse so she could be discharged from the hospital. Belinda wanted to tell Ben herself and she didn't appreciate Hampton bringing it up first. She shot a look at him that let him know she did not appreciate him mentioning it. Hampton and Ben saw the expression on her face.

"I told him no," Belinda said to Ben. She rolled her eyes at Hampton. He thought how much she looked like Shona.

"My daughter is concerned that her sister will be opposed to the idea. I asked her to let me handle it."

"I am in the hospital. I had a heart attack because your daughter…"

"She's your sister Belinda." Hampton said, cutting her off.

Belinda ignored his comment and continued talking. "I had a heart attack because April told me my mother …" she paused and then whispered… "killed Ben's mother." She cleared her throat. Ben could feel the tension between Belinda and Hampton. He knew he needed to jump in. "Hampton, why don't you let me and Belinda talk, and I will call you."

Before Hampton could respond, Belinda added, looking at Hampton, "And stop calling me your daughter. You don't know that for sure. You just think I'm your daughter." Hampton sighed loudly. He leaned back in the chair, looked at the ceiling and stretched his arms above his head for a few seconds.

"Belinda… he sighed again…I had DNA done."

"How did you get my DNA?" Ben looked at Belinda.

The squint of her eyes told him she wanted to claw Hampton's eyes out.

"I had my DNA tested against Bradley and Bryce. The result is I am related to them…

"How dare you!" Belinda screamed.

"Calm down babe. Hampton, why would you do that without talking to us about it?" Ben asked him, trying to keep his cool.

"What gives you the right…?" Belinda was screaming at Hampton again, before he could answer Ben's question.

"Belinda, please don't get upset. Let me explain." She folded her arms and looked directly at Hampton. "I bought life insurance and made you the beneficiary and set up college trust funds for all four children and made some changes to my will. My attorney thought having proof of paternity would nullify any contest of my Will."

"Why would you do that?" Belinda asked, her attitude having softened.

"That's what grandfathers do for their grandchildren. It was supposed to be a surprise," Hampton said. Everyone was quiet for a moment.

Finally Belinda asked, "How did you get access to my boys' DNA?"

Hampton smiled before he answered. "I have a friend who works in the lab. I asked her to swab their cheeks for me and she did and I sent the samples to a private lab."

"Hampton, how do you know somebody won't use that information, or tell our private affairs before we're ready to talk about it?"

"Ben, I assure you and Belinda that won't happen. That's why I went to the private lab."

"Do you think people who work in private labs don't talk?" Belinda said.

"Honey, I wield a lot of power in this town. Nobody in that lab will cross me. Trust me on that." Belinda wasn't sure how she felt about that comment, but she didn't respond. She just looked at Ben.

$\mathscr{T}$HIRTY

Publically, Sandra Matthews became a "mama bear" protecting her cub. Privately she was a mess. She was worried sick that her daughter was going to prison. Sandra felt very responsible for the situation. She and Roderick had given Chloe anything and everything she wanted except allowing her to keep her baby. Sandra knew she convinced Roderick that a baby would ruin Chloe's life and she was the one who insisted on putting the baby up for adoption. Now four years later Chloe snapped and snatched her baby back.

Sandra called a friend from law school that referred her to a lawyer in Atlanta. The lawyer was able to get Chloe released and get permission for her to go home to North Carolina. She was formally charged with kidnapping and child endangerment. The Casebiers did not press charges, but the Atlanta Police Department charged her anyway. The lawyer Sandra and Roderick hired was described to them as "a bull". They were told he would run over anybody in his way. That's what Sandra wanted. She fully intended to get Chloe help and prison was not the answer. Chloe was very quiet. Her attorney advised Sandra to get a medical and psychological evaluation as soon as they got back home.

Roderick contacted the dean at Spelman, explained the situation and told her Chloe would be back in January. He prayed that to be so. He also took over a lot of Sandra's responsibilities in the office. By the time Sandra and Roderick were back in the office, Jacksa had called a full staff meeting, briefed everybody on what happened, made some reassignments and told them to "hunker down." She didn't know the total impact the situation would have on the office but she knew the work had to get done. The entire staff stepped up. Nobody really understood what Sandra and Roderick were going through but they all wanted to help.

Jacksa asked Natalia not to come to the office for a couple of days. She needed to talk to Roderick about how to handle that and she didn't know if Natalia was in any legal trouble. Natalia tried several times to call Chloe but hadn't talked to her. She and Campbell talked and he assured her Chloe was okay, but needed some time, "a few days," to process what happened. Natalia said she understood but she felt totally responsible for the whole situation. If she had not tried to help Chloe see Nicholas none of this would have happened. She knew everybody was angry with her.

Campbell put up a good front for Natalia but he was terrified. He knew he was ultimately responsible for the whole situation. He got Chloe pregnant. He agreed to put Nicholas up for adoption, he agreed to the open adoption, and most of all he didn't get her the help she needed. Campbell knew Chloe was clearly in trouble before she took the boys but he thought she would be okay. He had apologized to her parents and to Natalia.

He talked to Kathy Robinson and told her the story. Kathy felt bad because it was her idea for Enoch and Kirby to adopt Chloe and Campbell's baby. She tried to reassure Campbell that there was no way he could have seen this coming. Kathy also thought – "How will her parents get her out of this?"

Enoch and Kirby hired an attorney too. They didn't know if they really needed one, but the law enforcement officials in Georgia were asking them questions and Enoch decided they needed some counsel on the situation. Kirby wanted to keep Blake and Nicholas home for a few days but after one day they wanted to go back to school to see their friends. The boys were fine, but Kirby and Enoch were afraid to let them out of their sight. They hadn't said very much about the incident. Kirby talked to the director of their school and she assured Kirby she would keep a close eye on them.

The first day Chloe was home she slept most of the day. The second day she spent some time with Campbell. They talked and she told him the same thing she told her parents; "I didn't think, I just did it." Campbell wanted to know how he could help and he assured her he would support her totally. He meant what he said, but he didn't know what he was getting himself into. What he did know was the life he and Chloe planned had changed drastically.

The third day Chloe was home she called Natalia and asked her to come over. When Natalia got there, Chloe was home alone. Natalia expected her to be down and depressed. Chloe greeted Natalia dressed in jeans, a DavisTown College t-shirt, and flip flops. She looked just like she would on a regular day. They hugged for a long moment and then sat down on the sofa in the den like always. Chloe was not one to beat around the bush, so she didn't.

"Sis, I am really sorry for taking Nicholas and Blake from you. I realize I made a spur of the moment decision without thinking about the consequences." Natalia started to say something but Chloe stopped her. "Natalia, I told everybody, my parents, the attorney and the police that you didn't have anything to do with what happened."

"But I am guilty too, Chloe, because I started letting you see Nicholas."

"You did me a favor and I took advantage of it."

"He is your son and you love him. I can't say I wouldn't have done the same thing," Natalia said.

"Please don't ever say that again! What I did may be sending me to jail for a long time."

"I heard your dad say the Casebiers didn't press charges."

"True, but the police did." Chloe said.

Natalia got up from the sofa and walked around the room. She looked back at Chloe over her shoulder.

"I've been giving this some thought. I think you have PTSD". Chloe actually laughed.

"Post-Traumatic Stress Disorder; are you serious?"

Natalia walked back to the sofa and sat down beside Chloe. "Hear me out, Chloe. You have been through a lot. Being pregnant at sixteen, putting the baby up for adoption, then realizing you want him back. All of that is traumatic and stressful. I think that should be your defense, and I am going to tell your mom what I think."

"Nat, have you talked to Mr. and Mrs. Casebier?"

"No, I called but they didn't answer. I left a message, but nobody called me back. But, I'll see them at church on Sunday. Are you coming?"

"I doubt it; don't want to see a bunch of people."

"I think you should come. Sit with your parents and Campbell, look gorgeous as usual and keep your head up." Natalia was pretending her hand was a mirror, and patting her hair. Chloe was laughing. "You are fine. You had a temporary lapse in judgment."

"Maybe I should hire you as my defense attorney."

"Maybe you should," Natalia said confidently.

Later that day, Jacksa called Natalia and told her to come back to work the following day. Natalia was glad, she needed to work but she knew if she was allowed to go back no charges were being leveled against her. There were two truths nobody was discussing and Natalia never intended to bring it up. First, she took Blake and Nicholas to the park under false pretenses, so their parents could accuse her of helping Chloe. Secondly, Chloe asked her to bring the boys to the park. She told Natalia she wanted to see Nicholas before she left for school. If anybody knew, it could be said that the act was pre-meditated. Natalia thought about the commercial on television that said, "Life comes at you fast." That was so true right now.

In the office the next day things were really busy, and there was a lot of tension. Finally, at the end of the day, Natalia knocked on Sandra's office door. "Mrs. M, may we talk for a few minutes?" Sandra took a deep breath and exhaled slowly. She motioned for Natalia to come in and be seated. Sandra was a little afraid of what Natalia was going to tell her. Her gut told her there was more to this story than Chloe was sharing.

THIRTY-ONE

The Rajagopal family were in their new home. Raja, Jill and LaLa were upstairs and Mrs. Rajagopal's things were downstairs. She had not unpacked. Since she moved out of the visitors' residence at the hospital, she had barely done anything. She heard the knock at the door but she didn't respond. "Mother, may I come in?" Raja slightly opened the door to the bedroom. She still did not respond. "Mother, we should get ready. The people from the funeral home will be here any minute."

Mr. Rajagopal had passed away two days before. He seemed to be better early that day but passed in his sleep. Mrs. Rajagopal was devastated. Nothing anyone said could console her, and her self-imposed guilt, the feeling that she was responsible for his heart attack, made it worse. They were having a small memorial service for him in Hattiesville and then flying his body back to London for a funeral and burial there. Tara and Raja were going with Mrs. Rajagopal. The dilemma now was whether to leave her in London or bring her back to Hattiesville permanently. She was too distraught to even discuss it with Raja. The only time she smiled in the past two days was when LaLa hugged her. That exchange made Raja feel as though she needed to come back. He loved his mother, and would love for her to have a good relationship with Jill and LaLa. There were other Indian people in Hattiesville and DavisTown. She could find some peers and make some friends. "Mother, are you ready?"

"Oh, Manavendra, my dear son, I will never be ready for this, I cannot believe that my dear husband is gone. I cannot believe it."

"I know. It's hard for me too. But find peace in knowing he loved you very much." Mrs. Rajagopal started to cry. She sat on the sofa with her hands in her head.

"Son, it is my fault that you no longer have a father. It's all my fault."

"It's not your fault. A heart attack is not anybody's fault. The doctor said his heart was diseased."

"But I fought with him and he became ill and now he is gone," Mrs. Rajagopal said.

"Mother, what are you talking about?" Raja asked.

Mrs. Rajagopal told Raja about the argument she and Mr. Rajagopal had, about how he collapsed and that the doctor in London told her he would not live. "So you see, I am responsible for my own husband's death." Raja wanted to tell his mother if their disagreements were the real reason for his father's heart attack and his death, he would have died a long time ago. She had harassed him and his father as long as Raja could remember.

"Mother, I assure you that is not the case." But now Raja knew why his mother had not said much to the doctors when his father was first admitted to the hospital. Her reluctance had definitely cost them time, but probably not cost him his life. "Father was obviously very sick for a long time before it showed up." As Raja was about to say something else, he heard LaLa laugh. She and Jill were coming down the stairs. She hugged her dad around his legs and then held her arms up to her grandmother. Mrs. Rajagopal picked her up. LaLa hugged her grandmother tightly around the neck.

"Who is that LaLa?" Jill asked.

"It's Dadi!" LaLa said very clearly. She had learned to call her grandmother by her Indian name. It was the first word she learned in Punjabi. Mrs. Rajagopal hugged LaLa with tears in her eyes. LaLa wiggled from her grandmothers arms just as the doorbell rang.

The memorial service was well attended - mostly Raja's colleagues and friends. A DavisTown College professor from India made remarks and offered a prayer. Raja and Tara talked a little about Mr. Rajagopal and Tara told funny stories about her uncle. The whole thing was over in less than an hour. The repast was held at the Country Club. Mrs. Rajagopal was quiet and barely made eye contact with anyone.

Ellen came over early the next morning to stay with LaLa so Jill could drive Raja, Mrs. Rajagopal and Tara to the airport. She and Mrs. Rajagopal had not seen each other except at the funeral, since their encounter at the hospital visitors' residence. When Ellen and Jill talked, Jill told her mother that it was more than likely her mother-in-law was here to stay. Ellen's advice was for Jill to stand her ground. "You are the lady of the house. It is your home. She will be there through your kindness, and if she forgets, I will remind her."

$\mathscr{T}$HIRTY-TWO

Grant woke up in his twin sister Gretchen's guest room. She let him sleep late. They had stayed up late the night before talking like they used to when they were growing up. Gretchen told him he should talk to their dad. Grant shared the whole story about Sunny and how she had changed. "It sounds to me like she cares more about the wedding than she does about marrying you, GP." Gretchen rolled her eyes when she said it. But, they both knew Paul would give Grant good advice. Their father was a very reasonable man.

"Hey Ma."

"Hi darling. How are you?"

"I'm good. Can I speak to Daddy?" Grace smiled and gave Paul the phone.

"Hey son, what's up?"

"Can you go out to lunch? I need to talk to you privately."

Paul frowned as he listened to Grant talk. "Why don't you pick up some food and come over here. Your mother is leaving for a while, so we'll be able to talk here." Grace looked at Paul and shrugged her shoulders, questioning what her husband was talking about.

Paul explained to Grace that he and Grant needed some privacy. "GG told me he is having second thoughts about marrying Sunny."

"Of course she told you that." Grace shook her head. "I'm sure Grant didn't share that with her for her to tell you."

"I think he did." Paul said. "He wanted me to have time to think about it before we talk."

"Well, what do you think?" Grace asked.

"I am going to hear him out. If it sounds like cold feet, I'll encourage him to move forward. If it's something else I will be absolutely honest with him including telling him not to marry her if he's not sure." Grace knew he meant what he said.

THIRTY-THREE

Breakfast was just okay. Cicely was tired, she had a hectic night at work, and she was pretty upset about one of her patients. Clay didn't talk about anything personal; he just wanted to be in her company.

Driving to work from the restaurant Clay listened to the Steve Harvey morning radio show. Steve was having a conversation with a listener. "A man can change, a man will change. But there's only one woman he changes for. The question is, are you that woman?" Clay didn't hear her response but throughout the day he kept thinking about what Steve Harvey had said. Cicely was that woman, she was the right woman, the one he would change for; the one he had changed for. He needed to tell Cicely she was that woman. Interestingly, Cicely was listening to the same radio show. When she heard what Steve said she thought about Clay. "I thought I was the woman Clay had changed for," she thought. Suddenly Cicely was sad.

Clay went to the break room and two female co-workers were their getting coffee. "Morning, ladies." They both spoke but didn't really stop their conversation. He got a bottle of water and walked out of the break room, then backed back inside the door. He asked the one he was friendly with to come by his office. They had worked together for years, had a brief relationship early on and actually maintained their friendship. She was the one who helped him call Delia's bluff when she said she was pregnant.

Five minutes later she came into Clay's office and sat in the chair in front of his desk. "What crisis can I help you avert today?" She set her coffee down and reached on his desk for a note pad and a pen.

"You don't need to take any notes, I just need a woman's opinion on something." She chuckled, took a sip of coffee and leaned back in the chair. He told her about the comment he heard Steve Harvey make. "Do you think that's true?"

"It's absolutely true." She gave him a couple of examples and then Clay told his friend what happened between him and Cicely, and he wanted to fix it.

"I want her to know she is the one I changed for." After a few minutes they came up with a plan.

"Pop, I think Sunny is more interested in a wedding than she is in being married." Grant was telling his dad about the events that led to him leaving Sunny in D.C.

"I told her we need to go to counseling and she got pissed off because I called Bishop Robinson for a recommendation."

"Son, she is fearful that you are still connected to Leah. She doesn't want you to compare her or your relationship with her to Leah." Paul was saying that to Grant more to see where his head was.

"Dad, she's the one who's obsessed with Leah. I don't think about Leah until Sunny brings her up," Grant said.

"I thought you had cold feet, but sounds to me you have real cause for concern. I agree counseling is the way to go. But, maybe you should seek another source for referral. That should lessen Sunny's apprehension."

"That's fair." Grant said nodding his head.

"What if …."

Paul interrupted Grant before he finished his question.

"If she says no, you need to move on. I know that's not what you want to hear but it's the truth." Grant leaned back in his chair and looked at the ceiling. He didn't say anything. His head was spinning.

THIRTY-FOUR

Sunny and Cicely hadn't talked much since Clay and Cicely broke up. But Sunny did know that Cicely was back in Hattiesville, and she wanted to know what Grant was up to. She called Cicely.

Cicely had just gotten in when the phone rang. She really didn't want to talk to Sunny but she answered to keep from having to call her back. They exchanged pleasantries although Cicely thought Sunny was being nosey. Sunny wanted to know where she was living and if she talked to Clay. Cicely did tell her she and Clay talked but did not tell her where she was staying. Cicely couldn't be sure she wouldn't tell Grant, who would absolutely tell Clay. Cicely still wasn't sure she wanted Clay to know where she was. She wasn't sure about anything where Clayton Sturdivant was concerned. "Cicely, have you seen Grant?"

"Grant's in town?"

"Yes, he's been there a couple of days."

"No, I haven't seen him. I didn't know he was here."

"He said he was coming to see his dad, but we had a big fight and I know that's why he really left." Cicely sat in the chair and put her feet up on the coffee table. She looked around the room. It was comfortable, but she knew she couldn't stay much longer without giving the supervisor some kind of explanation. When Cicely tuned back in to what Sunny was saying, she was talking about her fight with Grant.

"Why are you so obsessed with the wedding?"

"What do you mean?"

"Sunny, you planned a wedding with no consideration for Grant's dad! That was selfish and showed you weren't thinking about anybody but yourself!"

"I changed my plans, Cicely."

"Yeah, after I brought it to your attention. And I don't think counseling is a bad idea. If Clay and I had had counseling we wouldn't be where we are now. We may not have gotten married but things wouldn't have ended up like they did." The volume of Cicely's voice got lower as she talked. Sunny was stating her case for not believing she and Grant needed counseling. Cicely heard her phone beep. She looked at the screen. It was Javier. "Hold on Sunny." She clicked over. "Hi, how are you? Can you hold on Javier?"

"Yep."

Cicely told Sunny she had to go. "I will see what I can find out about Grant and call you back." "Javier, your timing is incredible! She laughed. "I was listening to a friend of mine talking about her troubles with her fiancé. Ugh!"

Javier laughed. "I wanted to check on you, see how things are with you and Clay." Cicely let out a long, deep sigh.

"Things are good, really. He is trying hard. I just don't know what to do."

"What are you apprehensive about?"

"Javi, he lied to me, and I'm afraid. He hasn't regained my trust."

"Does he know that?"

"I haven't said it in so many words, but I think he knows. I haven't even told him were I'm living."

"Cicely, I've told you before; Clay was wrong, but Delia created this situation. She told you all that stuff to hurt you and get back at Clay. If you hadn't seen her that day you two would be married by now."

"But I would be married to a lie." Cicely said.

"No, you would be married to a man you love."

"Why do you continue to defend Clay?"

Javier laughed. "I know it sounds like that but I'm not defending him as much as I am pulling for you. As men we tend to do stupid stuff. We don't always make good decisions; but he is hanging on by a thread and he knows it. He won't do it again. Forgive him and get your life back." They talked a few more minutes and then Javier told Cicely one last thing.

"Delia and I are getting married this weekend."

"Are you serious?"

He laughed. "Yep."

"Wow, I don't know what to say. You really have forgiven Delia."

"Life is too short to walk around unhappy." Javier said. He told her they were getting married in the chapel at their church, having a family dinner after, and then going on a cruise.

"I'm happy for you Javier. You are a great guy and you deserve to be happy." Cicely said quietly.

"You deserve to be happy too, Cicely."

$\mathcal{T}$HIRTY-FIVE

Kathy agreed to meet her professor, but for coffee, not for dinner. She thought dinner was too much because she didn't really know what he wanted. They met at a dessert spot on the edge of campus. He was there when she walked in.

"Kathy, thank you for joining me. Please have a seat." Dr. Gasquet was one of the younger professors. He came to work at Columbia a few years before. "You're welcome, but I am curious and unsure why I'm here – why you want to meet with me."

"I have observed your leadership and your work is impeccable. I am absolutely impressed." Dr. Gasquet said seriously.

"Thank you sir."

Before he could continue the waiter brought their order. After sweetening his coffee and taking a bite of his cake, Dr. Gasquet continued. "Kathy, I have an opportunity in my department for a graduate assistant. I would like to discuss the opportunity with you." They talked for about fifteen minutes. Kathy only asked a few questions. She wanted to know how accepting the graduate assistant position would affect her scholarship. He assured her it wouldn't, and she would receive an additional stipend.

At the conclusion of the conversation Kathy told the professor she would think about his offer and get back to him in a few days. When Kathy got home, she was ecstatic. The GA position was a dream come true. She would get to facilitate labs, interact with students and oversee projects. She liked Dr. Gasquet and the additional stipend was gravy. She was pumped, and she loved that her leadership and academic success earned her the offer. The only downside to his offer; he didn't recommend she continue to take a full course load with the added responsibility. Translation; she would be in school and in New York longer.

Kathy's cousin, Michelle, was in New York visiting from Virginia for the weekend. Kathy was excited to share her news. Michelle listened and congratulated Kathy on the offer and then asked the question Kathy had not asked herself. "What bout Sterling?" Kathy sighed loudly before she answered.

"I can't worry about Sterling, Michelle. He told me he's dating, he really has moved on."

"But if he was available would you be as excited about this GA position?"

"Yes, I would."

"Kat, you need to make a decision. Do you want Columbia University and the grad assistant position and all your degrees and to be the president of a college or do you want Sterling and love and a family?"

" 'Chelle I…"

Michelle interrupted Kathy before she finished her answer. "Whatever you say this time Kathy, you have to stick to it.

No back and forth, no Sterling today, school tomorrow. So maybe you better think about your answer."

THIRTY-SIX

A few days after Anderson and Jacksa spent the weekend in Catawba with his family, he called Min to see if they could have lunch. She thought that was very sweet of him and agreed immediately. Jackson was back at work and there was a caregiver with Min part of the day.

Twice a week the therapist came and once a week a nurse came to give her an infusion. Min and King were tired of all the company. King had actually growled at the therapist. Min remarked to Jacksa she was going to dismiss them all "very shortly."

Jackson was being a model husband. He was cooking, cleaning, and coming home right after his haircut on Thursday - not out watching games with his friends. Min was amused. At her insistence he was still sleeping in the other room. She wasn't sure he had ended his affair and she wasn't sure she could do anything about it if he hadn't. She was sure she would not stress herself out about it. Min wanted to live and she wanted to have a good life. As far as she was concerned Jackson could do whatever he wanted to do. She wasn't angry with him anymore, she was numb.

Anderson arrived with sub sandwiches, chips, cookies and sweet iced tea. One thing he and Min both loved was sweet tea. Min was delighted to see him and as usual he made her laugh. He doted on her, waiting on her hand and foot. When they finished eating, Anderson told Min he had something to show her. He reached in his pocket and showed Min his grandmother's rings. She was surprised. She could tell from looking at them they were valuable, and a very traditional style. "Oh, Anderson, how pretty. Your grandmother is so sweet!"

"Yeah, she's a doll!" he said, laughing. "I know this set is pretty old fashioned so I want you to help me figure out what Jacksa will like; actually love."

Min smiled. "Anderson, how much time do I have to think about this?" She said it very carefully. She didn't want to imply she was rushing him or trying to spoil his surprise.

He was really serious when he answered her. "I don't really know. I'll know when I know. But I want her to love the ring." He was sincere. They talked about what Jacksa liked, whether he should trade it in and get something more contemporary. Min told him about a ring with an orange plastic stone that she used to wear when she was a little girl. They didn't make a decision.

While Anderson was visiting with Min he received two messages. The last one troubled him. He left the Baye's home headed to DavisTown College.

THIRTY-SEVEN

Chloe's attorney sent Sandra an email with relatively good news. The Casebiers didn't want to pursue the case further so he was trying to convince the assistant district attorney to drop the case. She offered to send Chloe to counseling and community service. The goal was to avoid a conviction so she could still go to law school. The ADA was amenable to those terms but wanted Chloe to be assessed by a psychiatrist. Sandra was a little nervous about the psychiatric evaluation. What if they determine something is wrong with her? Sandra wasn't afraid of anything until now. She went to Roderick's office to tell him what the email said. They were at odds about how to handle this situation. Roderick thought Chloe should take responsibility for what she did. Sandra wanted to protect her. They argued about it. "What are you going to do if the psychiatrist determines she has a problem?" Roderick asked Sandra.

"I don't know, sweetheart. In all the thoughts and plans and dreams I had for Chloe, I could have never imagined anything like this. Even after she got pregnant, I never thought she would snap."

Roderick wasn't saying anything; he was just listening to his wife. He knew Chloe's problems were not mental or emotional. His daughter was spoiled and protected, and reality had set in. For the first time in her life, Chloe Nichole Matthews was having to take responsibility for her actions. As horrible as it was, it was the truth - her truth, their truth.

"Rod, why aren't you saying anything?" "Because I'm tired of fighting with you about this." "Roderick!" Then Sandra started to cry. But this time he didn't take her in his arms and comfort her. He stayed behind his desk and let her cry.

$\mathscr{T}$HIRTY-EIGHT

Brittani and Brianna were ecstatic and totally surprised when they came home from school and their mother was there. Hampton finally convinced her and Ben to let him hire a nurse so she could go home. She cried and cried when she had to leave Bradley and Bryce. But Hampton assured her she would see them every day and he would get them home too as soon as they were strong enough. The doctors told Ben the boys were doing "remarkably well". Things were coming together for the Coffey family.

The girls updated Belinda on everything going on at school. Although she talked to them every day, she felt like an outsider in their world. They grew up in the weeks she was away from them.

The house was spotless and organized. The babies' room was ready for them. The brown and blue with the argyle pattern on one wall was exactly like she wanted it. There were two of everything. Grammy told Belinda that some people came and examined the nursery. They told Grammy and Thelma they were there to delineate what needed to be done to safely bring the boys home. They looked for the electrical outlets; they discussed where they could install a generator and other particulars. They were waiting for the go ahead before they installed anything.

Grammy wasn't sure she liked Hampton Josephs. She was glad he helped save Blake and Nicholas but she told her sister Avis, "He just has too much power in this town."

Avis told her that men with a lot of money wield a lot of power. "I saw it all the time when I lived in Washington."

"This isn't Washington, D.C., this Landridge, Georgia. I know he's Belinda's father - and by the way I'm not sure how I feel about that either - but he's trying too hard to be in her life. And that daughter of his, I don't trust her either. There's a fly in this buttermilk," Grammy said with attitude.

Avis laughed. "Victoria, I hope, I pray, you're wrong. I'm pretty sure you're wrong about Hampton. He may be trying too hard but I think he's sincere."

"Umph" was all Grammy said.

"He missed a lot of her life through no fault of his own. All he's trying to do is take care of his daughter, and you can't hold him responsible for what the other daughter did."

They went back and forth and eventually Grammy conceded that Avis was right. As Grammy was thinking about her conversation with her sister, the phone rang. On the screen the display said "April Josephs."

"Umph, we talked her up," Grammy said aloud as she reached for the telephone. April asked if she could speak with Pastor or Mrs. Coffey. Grammy told her that Ben was not there and Belinda was not available. April was very professional and explained that she was calling about their new house and left a message for either of them to call her. Grammy would tell Ben, she would not bother Belinda.

April needed to talk to Ben and/or Belinda but she didn't really want to. Her dad insisted she talk with them about the incident at the hospital and from a business perspective they had to talk. They were in a delay due to Belinda's hospitalization. April was genuinely glad Belinda was well enough to be at home.

Grammy went down the hall to check on Belinda, and see what she wanted for dinner. Belinda was on her iPad talking to Kirby on FaceTime. Grammy didn't interrupt. Kirby updated her on all that happened with Blake and Nicholas post kidnapping and the legalities. Kirby told Belinda it was amazing how the boys had not missed a beat. "You would think nothing happened." Kirby said.

"K, to them nothing did happen. They didn't know they were in danger. But, have you seen Natalia?" Belinda asked.

"I have not seen her. She left me a couple of messages, and wrote me a letter to apologize."

"Have you responded?"

"No, I'm still very angry with her."

"Sis, please try to forgive her so both of you can move on."

"I am angry, I'm not over her deception."

"I understand, I feel the same way about April." Belinda said.

"April, your sister. I'm not sure how I feel about that....yes I do. I'm sure I don't like it. I don't like her, I don't like her being in your life and I don't like how she treats you. I hate that you have her as a biological sister."

"Kirby, you are my sister. I love you. I don't care if Hampton is my father and April is my half-sister, she could never take your place in my life or my heart," Belinda said sincerely. Neither of them said anything for a long moment. Finally Kirby said "Thank you for saying that."

"Don't thank me, it's the truth."

Belinda took a deep breath and blew it out quickly when Ben told her April called. "She wants to schedule an appointment to see us," Ben said. Belinda looked at him with a blank expression. "Sweetie, I know you don't want to deal with April but she is building our house, and the truth is, not seeing her is only prolonging the inevitable." Belinda still didn't say anything; she just rolled her eyes at him. He laughed. "You are so cute when you're mad!"

"I'm not mad," Belinda said rolling her eyes again. "She just needs to state her business and leave. I'm not ready for the talk!" she said, moving her fingers in the quotation sign. "Whatever you want babe," Ben said reaching for her schedule.

The first week she was home the nurse was there around the clock. The second week she left about 10pm, and this week she was leaving at 8pm. Belinda went to the doctor at the end of the week. If this went according to plan, they would trade some of the nurse's hours for the physical therapist. She hated to admit it but Hampton's plan was working well.

The nurse accompanied her each day to visit Bradley and Bryce. Belinda was able to feed them and hold them and she asked if they could go home with a nurse and the equipment. She told the doctor about the assessment being done. The doctor was aware of it, but he wasn't quite ready to let the boys leave. As much as she wanted them home, she knew better than to rush them.

Ben scheduled the appointment to see April on the afternoon Belinda did not have therapy. He wanted her to be rested. April arrived exactly on time. She brought the revised drawings of the house and the new church. Ben knew he needed to facilitate this meeting and try to be as neutral as he could. He invited April into the dining room. While she was getting set up he went to the back of the house to get Belinda. He pulled out a chair for her and stood her oxygen tank in the corner. April felt a pain in her stomach when she saw oxygen. "Hello April."

"Hi Belinda. How are you?"

"Do you really want to know or are your being polite?" Ben couldn't believe Belinda responded like that. April took a deep breath.

"Belinda, I really want to know. I am very, very sorry about all of this. I never imagined when I told you we are sisters and told you about your mother that you …" April's voice trailed off.

"You never imagined that telling me all that and telling me that mother caused the accident that killed my husband's mother would cause me to have a heart attack." Belinda was looking directly into April's eyes. Ben knew it had to happen so he just stood back. He kept his eyes on Belinda to make sure she wasn't breathing too hard, or wasn't getting too upset.

"Yes, Belinda, yes. I had no intention of making you sick, but I fully intended to make you angry - angry enough to have nothing to do with my dad. I didn't want him to do all the stuff he was doing for you. I didn't want him to spend any of my money – the money I made for the company – on you. I didn't want to share. Perhaps I'm selfish but that's the truth."

"But you're okay with making money off my church and off my family," Ben said to April. "Pastor Coffey, that's business. I am the best architect in this town, so the money you spend on my services is an investment and you won't get better for the money, for any amount of money. Success is important to me and I work hard to be successful. Daddy does his part, and he built the company but it's mine now, and when he retires I want it to be an empire." April was smiling as she talked, and there was light in her eyes. Belinda wasn't saying anything; she was listening to April. Ben was thinking how alike she and Belinda really were. They were both strong-willed and passionate about their work and both very ambitious. "April where is your mother?" Ben asked.

THIRTY-NINE

"Hi Grant."

"CeCe! What's up girl?"

"You tell me what's up. Sunny called me looking for you."

"Did she tell you why she hasn't heard from me?"

"Yes, she told me and I told her how wrong she is."

"I hope she listened 'cause she was having trouble hearing me."

"What are you going to do, Grant?"

"I still don't know, Cicely. I love Sunny, but I don't think I know her."

"Give it one more chance, Grant. Maybe this time away has given her some time to think too."

"What about you, Cicely? Are you going to give Clay a second chance?" Grant asked.

"I'm going to work on the relationship. I need to know I can trust him." Cicely answered.

"Do you still love him?" Grant asked.

"Yes, I love him, but love doesn't mean much without trust," she answered.

"You're right, and I don't trust Sunny not to change on me."

"You and Sunny need to date again. You don't need to live together, and you have to insist on counseling. Grant, you can't take no for an answer."

After Cicely and Grant talked, Grant felt better. He knew what he needed to do. Cicely was so sensible. He knew why Clay loved her and prayed they would work it out. It was time to go back to Washington to face the music with Sunny.

Cicely didn't want to talk to Sunny so she sent her a text message. She simply said "Grant is fine. He will call you soon!" Of course when Sunny read the text she wanted more explanation, but Cicely didn't respond.

ℱORTY

Clay paid extra to have the flowers delivered to the hospital at night. He wrote a note that made Cicely cry.

"Hey babe, my dad used to sing a song to my mom that I thought was so lame. But now I understand. His favorite line to sing was 'there's no me without you' and that is the absolute truth. It is said a man can and will change, but for only one woman; the right woman. You are the right woman, the one I have changed for. God didn't make but one woman for me and that's you. I love you and I want you to trust me again. Let me earn you and show you I am the man you fell in love with. I am thinking about you right now. Call me when the sun comes up, I'll be dreaming about you. I love you with every beat of my heart. Clayton."

For whatever reason, tonight Cicely welcomed Clay's words. She re-read the note and it warmed her heart. The fact that he stated what she heard Steve Harvey say on the radio the day before may have made the difference or maybe it was the way he signed his name. He told her "Clayton" was the serious side of his persona. What he didn't know; she was working a different shift tonight. Her shift ended at 11:00. She would be off when the sun came up.

Grant told Gretchen and his parents he was leaving the next morning. He and his father had another conversation and Grant told him about his talk with Cicely. "I am moving back to my apartment, and giving Sunny one more opportunity to agree to counseling. If she says no, we will go our separate ways.

"Are you sure son?" Paul asked.

"Yes sir. I'm sure."

"Well, you know I support whatever decision you make."

One last thing before he headed home. A rematch of Madden Football on X-box with Clay and Enoch. The competition had been going for years, and this trip was no different.

When Cicely's shift was over she took the flowers and went back to her room. She looked in the zip compartment of the bag she had not unpacked, and took out the keys - a key to his house and one to the new house. They were on a keychain with the "S"... for Sturdivant, the new last name she had been so excited about. She dropped them in her purse and looked at the clock. It was almost midnight and Clay wouldn't want her to drive the thirty miles all the way to Wyndham this late, but it was necessary. She showered and dressed, but before she left she took a few of the flowers from the bouquet and arranged them in a small vase and wrote a note.

"Hey babe, I don't think your dad's song is lame at all, I think it's pretty romantic. The truth is, there's no me without you either, and that is the absolute truth. I believe I am the right woman for you, the one God made for you and the one you will change for. Show me the man I fell in love with. When the sun comes up I will be in your arms. Stop dreaming about me, I'm really here. I love you with every beat of my heart. CeCe"

Cicely was tired and hungry but she had to get to Clay. She grabbed her overnight bag and headed for the car, flowers in hand. Less than halfway there Cicely felt herself getting sleepy. She turned up the music and rolled the window down. A few more miles and she ran off the road.

$\mathscr{F}$ORTY-ONE

Tara and Raja flew back to the states the day after the funeral. Mrs. Rajagopal was going to stay in London for a few weeks. Yash was helping her get things settled and then she was coming back to Hattiesville. All of them were tense about it but they had to make it work. Raja was really sad. He felt guilty that his relationship with his father was strained when he died.

Raja arrived back at home and went right back to work. He had back-to-back critical surgeries, two in two days. Then he went to Chapel Hill a day later for another one. Being busy kept him from thinking or dealing with his feelings. He talked to Yash and his mother daily. He wasn't talking to Jill about how he felt but she knew he was having a hard time. She carefully suggested he go to counseling. He not so carefully declined. Jill let him get away with the attitude for a couple of days, but when he snapped at LaLa he crossed the line. "Raja! I know you are grieving but why are you biting her head off?" Raja didn't respond. He walked out of the room. Jill was stunned. For a few seconds she couldn't think what to do or what to say. She finally went down the hall to address him. She found him upstairs. He was sitting on the floor in LaLa's room, crying. She was standing between his legs with her arms around his neck. Jill backed out of the room quietly, and let them have their moment.

A half hour later Jill went back to LaLa's room. Raja had put her to bed, and he was sitting in the rocker watching her sleep. Jill didn't know what to do or not do, for that matter. She didn't imagine Raja would take his father's death so hard. They hadn't communicated regularly in three years. Besides that their relationship was so formal. There was no emotion or affection between them. "I guess that doesn't mean you don't love somebody," Jill thought to herself. She wanted to suggest to him again that he seek some grief counseling but she wasn't sure how he would feel about it. As Americanized as Raja was, he still had some ideas from his native culture, and seeking outside help was not something they embraced. One thing was for sure, Jill knew she needed to figure out how to deal with all this before Mrs. Rajagopal came back. But for tonight she just let him be.

FORTY-TWO

Campbell talked Chloe and Natalia into going out to eat. Chloe hadn't gone out on purpose and Natalia felt guilty, so she wouldn't go out either. He picked up Chloe and then Natalia, and took them to a Japanese restaurant. He knew Natalia especially liked the chef's antics as he cooked right in front of them. It was one of those American things the girls from Haiti didn't take for granted. Chloe liked to laugh at and with Natalia and all her childish innocence. Campbell knew he made a good decision when they got off the exit and Natalia squealed. Chloe and Campbell laughed loudly.

The hostess showed the threesome to their table. Chloe almost fainted when she sat down and Kirby Casebier was across the table from her. Directly in front of her was the woman who hated her the most in the world. The woman whose children she had kidnapped. The woman who had adopted her son so she could go to college and stay on the planned trajectory of her life. The only thing separating them was a hot table that Chloe was sure Kirby wanted to lay her on and let her fry.

"Natalia! It's you!" Blake said loudly as Nicholas got down from his chair and ran to her.

"Hey guys!" She squatted and opened her arms wide. They both ran to her. She hugged them tightly. Both boys started firing questions at her. She knew she needed to look back; to see what everybody else was doing. She wasn't even sure who as there. The boys were telling her how the man was going to make fire on the table. One of them was holding each of her hands. She looked up to see Enoch, Kirby, and Aunt Avis on one side of the table and Chloe and Campbell on the other side.

"Hello Auntie Avis, Mr. and Mrs. Casebier," Natalia said smiling as she took Blake and Nicholas back to their seats.

"Hello Natalia," Aunt Avis said. Enoch spoke to Natalia, shook hands with Campbell, but just looked at Chloe. Kirby didn't acknowledge any of them. She did have the presence of mind to know they couldn't leave the restaurant. It was Aunt Avis' birthday, but also Nicholas and Blake wouldn't leave without a fight. Kirby was hyperventilating. Enoch put his arm around her, and leaned over to say something in her ear. Before he was close enough for Kirby to hear him, she stood up. "Chloe! Bathroom!" Kirby screamed at her.

FORTY-THREE

The nurse was concerned that Min wasn't progressing as much as she needed to. But Min refused to go back to the hospital. "You just give me some time," Min told her. Min didn't really know what time would do, but she wasn't leaving home. Just to be on the safe side she called the doctor to make an appointment. Her doctor was away for a few days, so she agreed to see the physician's assistant. Her neighbor took her. She didn't want Jacksa or Jackson to go. Either of them would insist on being with her during the exam.

When the PA walked into the room, Min was surprised. She had not seen him before. He was very handsome, but not as handsome as Jackson, she thought. He was immediately very charming. "Mrs. Baye, my name is Dr. Ryan, I am the physician's assistant."

"But you're a doctor." Min was thinking out loud more than asking. He explained he was a retired military doctor. "But retirement didn't agree with me, so I took the job part-time."

"I understand," Min said. As he examined her, she told him about teaching part-time, and they talked about her family. She bragged about JJ playing college basketball at Duke and Jacksa preparing for the law school entrance exam. "She has a great job as a paralegal; I don't know why she wants the stress of being a lawyer," Min said to Dr. Ryan.

"Why don't you want her to be a lawyer?" he asked.

"That's what I always wanted for her until recently."

"What changed?"

Min sighed before she answered him. "I don't want my daughter to be stressed in a career that may cause her to be where I am when she's my age. I want her to enjoy her children and always be able to be a wife to her husband."

He looked at her, puzzled. Min went on to explain her situation with Jackson, and how she knew her disease contributed to it. She surprised herself at how open she was being to a man she didn't even know. "I want better for my daughter."

"I understand," was all he said. He was typing some notes into the computer. When he finished he looked up at Min over his reading glasses. "Mrs. Baye…"

"Please call me Min."

He smiled. "Min, I want to do a little blood work but I think you're okay. The nurse's concern about your strength and energy concern me too, but let's check your levels and see what we need to do. I will call you tomorrow when I get the results and we will come up with an action plan."

The next day Dr. Ryan called Min. Her vitamin D, potassium, iron and blood pressure were low. All the medicine was depleting the vitamins and minerals in her system. He wanted her to come in to see him the next day. They made the appointment and hung up. For the first time Min was looking forward to going to the doctor.

$\mathscr{F}$ORTY-FOUR

Kathy was quiet for a moment. She wasn't sure how to respond to Michelle's comment. "Michelle, why are you so interested in this? Why do you care whether Sterling and I are together or apart? Why can't you be happy for me either way?"

Michelle laughed. "Kathy you invited me into this, and truthfully my investment is minimal. But I am really tired of how wishy-washy you've been about all this."

"Michelle, you're the one always talking about having options. I have options!" Now Kathy was laughing.

"Having options is one thing, manipulating a situation is something else. You want Sterling when things aren't going the way you want in school. But when that changed, then he became second. Make a decision and stick to it. You're out of options."

"'Chelle, are you jealous?" Kathy asked mater-of-factly.

Michelle swallowed hard. "Yes Kathy. Yes I am," she replied quietly. "My career is going well, I make plenty of money, I have a lot of things, and I have a lot of friends. But the thing I want the most, a man in my life - a husband, children - that eludes me. And although I am content, I am not happy. So yes I am jealous that this great guy wants you."

"You don't need a man to make you happy. You're intelligent and beautiful…"

"And lonely." Michelle said not letting Kathy finish her statement. "No, I don't need a man but I want one." She paused for a few seconds. "I think I'll call Sterling."

Anderson Thorn walked into Sterling Chance's office not sure what to expect. All the info he and his partner had been able to obtain pointed to Jordana Foust being involved in doping while she participated in the Olympics. Anderson needed to know what Sterling knew.

He was thinking on the drive to DavisTown that this had the potential to be a big case for him - a rookie agent. He wasn't a rookie investigator but he had only worked for the agency a year. He didn't want to be the one to give DavisTown College the black eye but he had to do his job and doing it well should secure his assignment to the Charlotte bureau.

Anderson and Sterling shook hands and Anderson sat down in front of Sterling's desk. He was leaning back in the chair. The only sound in the room was the chair squeaking.

"What's up, Coach?" Anderson asked. "Man, damn, I don't know where to start." Sterling didn't respond.

"Have you talked with Jordana?"

"Yes, briefly." Anderson answered.

"You two should talk again but here's what I know."

Sterling told Anderson about Jordana's admission that some of the Olympic athletes used performance enhancing drugs. "She stopped short of saying she used them," Sterling said. He continued saying it was not just U.S. athletes but athletes from several other countries, and not just volleyball players, and both men and women.

"Why do you think she confided in you?" Anderson asked Sterling.

"I think she knows you're onto her and she's looking for me to have her back."

"You think she expects you to lie for her?"

"I hope not 'cause I won't. I like Coach Foust. She's a good person; she is a good friend and colleague. She's a great coach and the students like and respect her. But I think doping is whack; all drugs and drug use for that matter, and I will not lie for her. I hate what this can do to her, to the college, but those kids came to her to get a degree and play ball. Many of them can't do one without the other and that's not fair to them." Anderson shifted in his chair as he listened to Sterling talk. He knew Sterling was absolutely right, but if he could prove she was involved, she broke the law and she had to be accountable for that.

"Coach, do you think she will tell me the truth?"

"I don't know," Sterling said, shrugging his shoulders. "I think what she tells you will be the truth; she just may not tell you the whole story."

"Well, in my business that's lying," Anderson said. They talked a few more minutes and Anderson left. As he was headed back to the parking lot, he saw Jordana Foust and her players working out. She was doing wind sprints with them. She was competing with them to make them better.

𝓕ORTY-FIVE

A Volunteer firefighter driving behind Cicely on the interstate saw her weaving. Just as he reached for his phone to call the police to report a drunk driver, he saw her run off the road. He slowed down, put on his blinkers and stopped a few feet behind her.

It took Cicely a few seconds to realize what happened. She started to cry. She had to get to Clay but she was so tired, so sleepy. She would call him and spoil the surprise but he would come get her. She noticed the lights flashing behind her and then the man at the window startled her. "Ma'am are you okay? Can I help you?" Cicely lowered the window just a little. The man showed her his id card. She was crying. "Ma'am have you been drinking?"

"No, no," she said. "I worked twelve hours and I am really tired but I have to drive to Wyndham, to take these flowers because he loves me and I love him and he wanted me to call but I want to go and he doesn't know I'm coming and I need to go and I'm awake now..." She was babbling like she was drunk. They both saw the blue lights at the same time. The police officer approached the firefighter, before he approached Cicely's car. They talked briefly and the officer approached the car window.

"May I see your license please?" She was thinking they were holding her up, she needed to go. She had to get to Clay, take him the flowers and the note. She gave him her license. "Officer, I am awake now. I really need to go." She was crying. "I would rather call somebody for you." He could look at her and tell she was in no condition to drive.

"But I ...."

"No ma'am I won't let you leave," he said as he handed her license back. She looked over to see the firefighter still standing there. He nodded his head "yes."

"Okay," she whispered.

Clay was walking to his car still trash talking with Enoch and Grant. He had successfully beaten them at X-Box. The three of them had a good talk and Grant was going back to Washington the next day with a clear head.

Clay looked at his watch. He would drop Grant off and then head home to get some sleep and hoped Cicely would call early. Just as he cranked up, his phone rang. He didn't recognize the number but this time of night it had to be important. "Sturdivant," he said very businesslike. "Mr. Sturdivant this Charlotte Police Officer....Cicely....off the road...not hurt...." Clay only heard bits and pieces of what the officer said. His heart was pounding. He sped out of the neighborhood and onto the main street.

"Tell her I am on my way." When he was on the interstate Clay called Cicely. She answered quickly, and started apologizing.

"Sorry for what baby? Listen to me. I will be there, everything will be okay in a few minutes." Clay was glad Grant was with him. He didn't know what kind of shape Cicely was in or why, but he would fix it, whatever it was.

When he passed her on the southbound side of the highway he blew the horn and she immediately felt better. In about five minutes he pulled in front of her on the shoulder of the road. He jumped out of his car and she jumped out of her car. He reached her in about two steps. He grabbed her and hugged her tightly. She was shaking. He kissed her forehead and looked deep into her eyes. "Let's go home and sort this all out." She just nodded yes.

Grant got out, talked to the police officer and the fireman and thanked them both. Clay put Cicely in his car, buckled her in and walked back to where Grant and the other men were standing. He shook hands with them, and thanked them and they left. He went to Cicely's car. He saw her purse, and the overnight bag and then the flowers sitting in the cup holder. He smiled. "Take CeCe's car home and I'll get it tomorrow," Clay said to Grant. Clay put the overnight bag in the back seat, but gave Cicely her purse and the flowers. She started to explain but he wouldn't let her.

"Not now, you relax and we'll talk when we get home." She dozed off thinking about the word "home."

FORTY-SIX

April swallowed hard before she answered Ben's question. Nobody ever asked about her mother. She hadn't thought about her mother in a long time. Nobody was saying anything. They were waiting for April to answer. "I don't know where my mother is. I haven't seen her since the day after my sixth birthday. She took me to the airport to meet my dad. He was taking me on vacation. When we got back a week later, all my things were at his house and his housekeeper had set up my room." Belinda was thinking about April saying she and Hampton went on vacation, just the two of them. At that moment Belinda was jealous. Not because it was Hampton, but because April had a dad who could and did take her on vacation; at six years old. "What did Hampton tell you?" Ben asked.

"He told me I was going to live with him. I didn't really understand that meant forever and without my mother at the time, but she never came back and eventually I stopped asking. Why do you care where my mother is?" April asked.

"I am just trying to understand what motivates you. What makes you so successful but at the same time so hateful." When Ben called April "hateful" it stung. Belinda still wasn't saying anything. She was watching the exchange between her husband and her alleged sister.

"Ben, I am not a hateful person." April said.

"You hate me so much you caused me to have a heart attack and I could have lost my babies." Belinda said, making her first comment. April sighed heavily.

"Belinda, since I was six years old I have had my dad, our dad, to myself. I had his love, his attention, and his admiration. All of a sudden he discovers you and I am not the apple of his eye anymore. What I did turned out to be a bad decision, but my only motive was to keep what I worked so hard for. Belinda, I'm sorry. With every fiber of my being, I apologize. I can't turn back the hands of time so all I can do is move forward."

"What if I say no, I won't forgive you," Belinda said.

April shrugged her shoulders. "That is purely up to you. I just hope we can keep our personal lives and business relationship separate. If you don't want to be my sister and Hampton Joseph's daughter, that's up to you. I don't really care one way or the other."

Ben was watching April's body language as she talked. She really didn't care. She cared about being successful and her soft spot was her mother.

"I am having a really hard time forgiving you April. But I have to. I have to for my husband, for my daughters, and for my sons who are not still living inside me where they were safe; thanks to you." Belinda was very calm. She was looking directly into April's eyes. "When Hampton offered to get me a nurse so I could come home I only accepted because I needed to be here for my girls and Ben. This has to be costing him a fortune." Belinda smiled. The smile was directly related to the look on April's face; the horror in her eyes. "Obviously you didn't know," Belinda said to April. She was enjoying the look of surprise on April's face.

"Belinda, you may have our father's money but I have his heart. And my own money."

FORTY-SEVEN

As it turned out, Raja had an emergency surgery so Jill had to get Mrs. Rajagopal from the airport. She took her mother and LaLa with her. Ellen convinced Jill to take LaLa in to greet her grandmother. "Let's get off to a smooth start," Ellen told her.

Jill saw Mrs. Rajagopal before her mother-in-law saw her. She was in traditional dress. She looked like she had aged and she looked tired. She did manage a slight smile. "Dadi! Dadi!" LaLa said as she scrambled from her mother's arms and reached for her grandmother. Mrs. Rajagopal held her tight and LaLa lay her head on her grandmother's shoulder. Jill was able to quickly snap the picture for Raja to see.

"Jillian, I have more luggage," Mrs. Rajagopal said as Jill picked up the bag she had carried off the plane. After getting four big bags from the luggage carrousel, Jill went to get the car while Ellen waited with Mrs. Rajagopal and LaLa. LaLa was fascinated, running between Dadi and Grandma. Jill was glad she drove the SUV. One of the sky caps loaded the car and Jill thanked him with a hefty tip. On the drive back to Hattiesville, Mrs. Rajagopal sat in the back seat with LaLa. A few minutes after they were on the road Ellen looked back and LaLa and Dadi were asleep.

When they were home, Jill put LaLa to bed to finish her nap. Trey met them to help bring in Mrs. Rajagopal's things. Ellen was determined to help her unpack. She was not going to let her daughter's home be cluttered.

Mrs. Rajagopal had her things very organized. She told Ellen two of the big bags could be put away. "Some of them are winter things and there are a few of my husband's things I will look at later." Her voice was just above a whisper. After the three of them unpacked the other two suitcases, Mrs. Rajagopal sat and slowly began to take smaller bags from her carry-on luggage. At the very top was the tea pot Jill had given her when they first met. It looked like a stack of gifts with a lavender bow on top. Jill had given it to her when she and Raja went to London for his cousin's wedding. They were just dating then and Jill took the tea pot as a peace offering. It hadn't worked so Jill was surprised to see her mother-in-law still had it. Next she pulled out a white china tea set. The pot and cups had fourteen karat gold trim. It was a replica of a set from the Taj Mahal. It was exactly like the gift Raja gave Jill on their first Christmas as a couple. She noticed it immediately. Jill was surprised. Mrs. Rajagopal set both on top of the bookshelf in the den. She reached in the bag again and took out a black velvet jewelry roll. In one of the zip compartments she took out a gold ring and a gold watch. She looked at Ellen. "I hope you never have to give your son his father's things. It's painful." Mrs. Rajagopal wiped tears with a handkerchief she had tucked in her sleeve. Ellen simply reached over and patted her hand. In another zipper compartment was a pair of cuff links with an "R" engraved on them. In other compartments were coins, a lapel pin, a tie bar and a ring that belonged to Raja's grandfather. Most of the things in the pouch had more sentimental value than actual value. After she showed Jill and Ellen all the things she brought for her son she replaced them, tied the ribbon back around the roll and gave it to Jill. "Jillian, please give this to Manavendra. I can't bear to do it. I am too sad."

The other things in the bag were gifts for LaLa and a gift for Jill. She gave Jill a long red velvet jewelry box. She opened it and saw a lovely vintage gold bracelet. Jill and Ellen made eye contact. Jill took the bracelet from the box. She looked at it closely. It wasn't her style but it was very lovely. There were several flat white ornaments between the gold links with a pink rose painted on each one. Jill remembered her grandmother having a bracelet very similar to this one. She showed it to her mother. Ellen recognized the style and had the same thought Jill had; that her mother had worn a bracelet very much like it. "That bracelet belonged to Manvendra's paternal grandmother. My husband said his mother wanted me to have it, because I was her first daughter-in-law. But now I want you to have it."

"Why would you give it to me now? Jill asked.

"You mean rather than you getting it when I pass away?" Mrs. Rajagopal asked.

"Well…yes," Jill said wondering if there was a catch to the gift.

"Now is the right time. My husband would want you to have it now," she said, wiping tears again before she continued. "I will give Leah her gifts when she's up from her nap. Will you please excuse me? I need to rest for a while." Ellen stood and started to leave the room. She looked back and Jill was still sitting there with a blank expression on her face. Ellen cleared her throat to get Jill's attention. Jill looked up and then stood.

"Thank you for the bracelet. Please let me know if you need anything."

"I will be fine. I'm just very tired," Mrs. Rajagopal said.

"I don't know what time to expect Raja but we can have dinner whenever you're ready," Jill said.

"I will wait and have tea with my son when he gets here. Thank you."

FORTY-EIGHT

Kathy was getting a handle on her schedule. The additional responsibilities of being a graduate assistant added hours to her day. One thing was bothering her. Dr. Gasquet was asking for more and more of her time but some of it was more personal than professional. He wanted to have dinner and wanted her to stay after class to talk. Kathy couldn't determine if he was just lonely or if he was a "dirty old man" like Michelle called him. He wasn't really old but Kathy determined he was too old to be interested in her, for any personal reason.

She talked to her mother about him. "Do you feel harassed, Kathy?" her mother asked.

"No, but I am uncomfortable."

"Are you uncomfortable to the point of needing to report the situation to someone?"

"I don't want to overreact. I'll let it go for a bit."

"Kathy, don't be passive about this. Keep your guard up."

"I will Mama."

Kathy knew her mother would tell her dad. There was no point in asking her not to. She just hoped her dad wouldn't overreact.

A few days after Kathy talked to her mother about Dr. Gasquet, he called her into his office. He explained plans for his classes over several days.

"Please be sure the other GA has the password for the new online course." Kathy was puzzled why he made that comment.

"I will handle the online course myself," she responded.

"No Kathy, I need you to accompany me to the conference," Dr. Gasquet said casually. "Accompany you to the conference. Why?" Kathy asked, shrugging her shoulders.

"You are my assistant," he said without making eye contact with her.

"Dr. Gasquet, I can't miss my other classes. I also have a project I am working on with some other people." Kathy gave him a good argument why she couldn't leave town. He listened and then there was silence between them.

Finally he said "I will email you the travel arrangements," and left the room. Kathy sat there briefly, totally astonished at his disregard for what she said. She wasn't going. He could do or say whatever he wanted to. Kathy was incensed. She couldn't believe he was being so arrogant. But at the moment she decided she needed to cover herself. She would be sure to keep the email he sent her and keep notes about the conversations.

ℱORTY-NINE

April left the meeting with Ben and Belinda, glad they could now move forward with the construction projects, but not happy he mentioned her mother. As a matter of fact, she was ticked off. "Who does Ben Coffey think he is?" she thought to herself. But as the days passed her mother was in the forefront of her thoughts. The only person she could talk to about it was her father. After all these years he owed her some sort of explanation.

Hampton met with Bryce and Bradley's neonatologist and the pediatrician. The boys needed at least two more weeks in the hospital before they would consider letting them go home. The doctor made it clear to Hampton he was calling the shots. It didn't matter how many nurses Hampton hired, the doctor had the final word. Hampton didn't like to be told no but he decided to back off. All he wanted was to make Belinda happy.

His thoughts were interrupted by his phone. "Hey darling,"

"Hi Daddy. Are you coming home for dinner?"

"Yep, headed that way now. What's up?"

"I'm cooking so I'll add you to the list of dinner guests."

"List? Who else is coming?" Hampton asked frowning.

"Nobody, I'm teasing. See you in a bit."

Hampton and April had dinner and talked about work. He mentioned the church project and the Coffey's new house before she did. She was glad. That gave her a good segue into what she really wanted to talk about. "When I met with the Coffey's last week, we talked about more than the projects."

"Good, I hoped you and your sister talked," Hampton interrupted her.

"Yes, but it didn't go well. Belinda hates me, and I don't care for her either."

"Your sister does not hate you....."

"Stop calling her my sister!" April raised her voice at her dad.

"She is your sister. Both of you are my daughters." Hampton did not raise his voice and he did not take his eyes off April. She met his eyes only briefly.

"Well, Pastor Coffey asked about my mother." Now April wasn't taking her eyes off Hampton. He squirmed in his seat. "What did he want to know?"

"He asked where she is and I told him I don't know. I haven't seen her since I was six years old." Hampton didn't comment. There was an uneasy silence between them. Finally April spoke. "Daddy, where is my mama?"

Hampton moved his plate from in front of him, but didn't say anything. He took a long drink from his glass, but still didn't say anything. He was trying to decide how to answer April's question. He cleared his throat, folded his hands on the table in front of him and looked at April. "I don't know where your mother is. I heard from her a few years ago. She was in California leaving for Milan the next day. I haven't heard from her since then.

"If it was a few years ago, why didn't she call me?" April asked.

"Same reason she left you at my house twenty-two years ago and never looked back. She's selfish."

He had a look of disgust on his face.

"So why did she call?" April was pressing Hampton. He sighed loudly and heavily. He took another drink of his tea. It was time, so he might as well deal with it.

"She called to tell me her mother passed and there was an insurance policy that you were the beneficiary for. I told her to send the documents to my attorney. When the check came I had him add it to your trust fund."

"So let me get this straight. My grandmother who I don't remember, left me some money, and my mother, whom I haven't seen in over twenty years, called you and not me to see how to handle it, and you make the decision as to what to do with the money. Am I eight or twenty-eight?" She paused. "Why do you - or my mother for that matter - think you can make these kinds of decisions for me?" April raised her voice again.

"You were in college, I was taking care of your expenses, and you didn't need the money." Hampton replied.

"Daddy, it's not really about the money. My issue is you making decisions for me and my mother ignoring me."

"April, I will always make the decisions I think are best for you given the circumstances. Now, as for your mother…"

"Yes, let's talk about my mother. Who is she, where is she, why did she leave?"

"Melissa left because she didn't have a maternal bone in her body. Melissa cared about Melissa." Before Hampton could continue, April asked another question.

"So was I a mistake, a surprise?"

"No, just the opposite. We planned the pregnancy. I wanted a child. We talked about it for over a year. When she told me she was pregnant I was ecstatic!" April smiled at her dad. "Then she went to California for three months and I was pissed."

"Why were you pissed?"

"Because she didn't have to go. Even pregnant she was more career-minded than she was concerned with being a mother." Hampton went on to explain to April that he and her mother didn't get married because Melissa told him she didn't want to be wife. "She didn't want to be accountable," he said. He told April that Melissa said once that she did him a favor, having a baby for him. When April asked why she lived with her mother for the first few years of her life, Hampton explained that things eventually changed. "After you were born she started to come around. She treated you like a baby doll, changing your clothes all day, but she did feed you and keep you clean." As Hampton talked it occurred to him how much had happened and how much time had passed. And how he and April had gone on without Melissa. Neither of his girls had their mother. What did that say about him? As far as he was concerned it said he was a great father to April and he raised her well. She was the apple of his eye. It also said he now had a second chance with Belinda and they would have a great relationship, and he would take care of her children the way he would have taken care of her. He was absolutely intrigued with Brianna and Brittani. He wanted his granddaughters to have every opportunity available to them.

Hampton and April talked for a couple of hours. He told her honestly that he didn't know where her mother was and he didn't care. The last he heard she was still working for the fashion magazine and was probably still living in Europe somewhere. "Sweetie, I am more interested in you maintaining your status as the top architect in this part of the country, creating an empire and the fortune that accompanies that, than I am in you wasting time being concerned about your mother. She didn't want to be a mother to you when you needed her, and you don't need her now. You are who you are, no thanks to her."

Later, when April was alone, she replayed in her mind the conversation she had with her dad. He was right. She was successful - very successful - and her own hard work and her dad's guidance had gotten her there. For whatever reason she thought about Belinda. Belinda had done well for herself too. She didn't hate Belinda; she just didn't want to share her dad, and deep down inside she was envious of her sister; actually. Belinda had it all; career and family. She thought to herself, "Maybe it's time for me to work a little less on career and more on family."

$\mathscr{F}$IFTY

There was a power outage at Jackson's office so he came home early. To his surprise, Min was not there. There was no note, but of course she wasn't expecting him. She had not sent a text message or called. The truth was they were not communicating much anyway. Maybe she and Jacksa were out together.

Min was looking forward to seeing Dr. Ryan. She didn't expect him to tell her anything was wrong. She just wanted to see him, to talk to him.

Dr. Ryan didn't disappoint her. He was charming and engaging. He made her laugh. They talked about her care plan but mostly they just talked. She didn't want him to go but he had other patients to see.

"I don't need to see you again for three months unless there's a problem." Dr. Ryan told her. "What if I just have a question, may I call you?" Min asked.

"Sure, as a matter of fact, you can reach me through our Doctor Hours program on the computer." Dr. Ryan went on to explain how it worked and gave her the card with the sign-on information. He only participated one day per week. He was being very professional. Min knew she needed to say okay and let him go but she didn't want to. She liked his attention. "Thank you, Dr. Ryan. I will let you know if I need you," Min said to him, and swallowed hard.

When the cab pulled into the driveway, Min saw King in the backyard. That meant Jackson was there. She paid the driver and went in the house through the front door. She could smell something cooking. It smelled good.

"Hey honey, I was worried about you."

"I'm fine."

"You shouldn't be out alone."

"I'm a big girl, I can manage."

Jackson didn't immediately respond to her remark. She went down the hall for a few minutes and when she came back she went to the patio door to see why King was barking. It was only squirrels in the tree.

"Where were you?" Jackson asked. His back was to her, he was cooking.

"I went to the doctor." Her response was rather dry.

"Who drove you? What did the doctor say? Why didn't you tell me you had an appointment?" "Jackson please! What's with the twenty questions?" He turned to face her but didn't say anything. "It was a routine visit and I took a cab," she finally answered.

"A cab, why? Min, I know you are angry with me but you are my wife and still my responsibility."

She rolled her eyes at him. "Jack, I'm your responsibility when it's convenient for you. I never know when you may be away on another tryst with your whore!" There was fury in her eyes. At that moment he knew how angry she still was and he knew that she still had not forgiven him. Before he could say anything she opened the door and walked out on the patio.

Jackson stood there for a few minutes. He had to say something; to do something. It didn't matter how many good meals he cooked, the way to her heart was not through her stomach. As he was thinking he felt his phone vibrate. He looked at the screen, it was a message from her; the woman he had allowed to create this mess.

$\mathscr{F}$IFTY-ONE

Kirby was shaking. She was so furious at seeing Chloe. She walked into the bathroom. Chloe was a few steps behind her. Chloe was ready for the confrontation. "What! What do you want Kirby?"

"You want to know why I stole my son and took him away from you." Chloe was screaming at Kirby. "He is my child. I wanted him with me and away from you. Was it wrong? Yes! Would I do it again?" Chloe's voice cracked and tears rolled down her face. Then it was Kirby's turn. She was surprised at how Chloe acted. "No, you will not take my children again because you will never get that close to them again!" Now Kirby was screaming. "What gave you the right to …?"

"I wanted him back, I miss him so much. You know how you felt when he was away from you for a day, I feel that way every day!" Chloe was crying.

"Chloe, you couldn't take care of Nicholas; that's why you wanted us to adopt him. And you took Blake too. I could prosecute you on that alone." It never occurred to Chloe that the Casebiers could still make a case against her. They went back and forth and at times they were screaming at each other at the same time. Chloe wasn't ready for Kirby to back her against the wall. When she realized what was happening Kirby had her forearm across Chloe's neck. The bathroom door opened, which got Kirby's attention. It was Aunt Avis and she could see Enoch standing on the other side of the door.

"Kirby, Kirby. Let Chloe go," Aunt Avis said calmly. She put her hand on Kirby's back. Kirby took one step back and Chloe relaxed a little and started toward the door. "Chloe, clean your face," Aunt Avis said, still speaking very calmly. Chloe wiped her face, took a deep breath and walked out of the bathroom, looking back at Kirby over her shoulder.

Kirby turned around and looked directly into Avis's eyes. "She stole my children. She better be glad I didn't kick her ass."

"Get yourself together. Enoch is out there. When you both come back to the table, have a smile on your face and we'll talk about this when we get home. Blake and Nicholas are fine and they want to celebrate my birthday." Aunt Avis went out and told Enoch that Kirby would be out in a minute.

Chloe walked back to the table and faked a smile. Natalia was sitting between Nicholas and Blake and they were eating salad and laughing. Campbell met Chloe a few steps before she reached the table. "I'm fine. Really I am."

"Do you want to leave?" Campbell asked.

"No, I don't want to go," she answered.

"We can go if you want to." Enoch said to Kirby putting his arm around her. She didn't answer immediately. As they turned the corner and she saw her boys having such a good time Kirby told Enoch she want to stay.

Dinner went well all things considered. There was tension only because the adults at the table knew the situation. People at other tables cheered when the family sang Happy Birthday to Aunt Avis. Kirby was quiet on the ride home, and Enoch didn't push. He knew they would talk later when they were alone.

Chloe started to cry as soon as she was in the car. Between her sobs she told Campbell and Natalia what Kirby said to her and how she acted. "I probably made everything worse," Chloe said. "Instead of saying I'm sorry I argued with her. Oh my God, she said she could prosecute me for taking Blake, without even considering Nicholas. Oh, God, what am I going to do?"

"Chloe please stop crying. Please. She didn't make you leave the restaurant. It's really going to be okay," Natalia said to Chloe.

"She's right babe, I think she just needed to get it off her chest and now it's over," Campbell said, hoping to calm Chloe. But he wasn't sure if he really believed what he was saying.

Kirby and Aunt Avis were in the kitchen talking while Enoch got the boys ready for bed. Kirby told her how Chloe reacted, the things she said. "Honey you know a good offense is the best defense," Aunt Avis said to Kirby.

"I know, but she thinks she's off the hook because we didn't press charges. She needs to learn a lesson. Chloe has always landed on her feet. She needs to bump her butt so she'll know life has real consequences."

"So what are you saying?" Auntie asked seriously. "I am going to tell Enoch I want to prosecute Chloe. That girl needs to learn a lesson."

FIFTY-TWO

Cicely slept lightly on the thirty minute ride to Clay's house in Wyndham. The light in the garage awakened her. They had not talked at all. Clay had held her hand most of the way there. It dawned on her as she came fully awake, that she didn't know where her car was. "Where is my car?" she asked Clay. He smiled at her.

"Grant took it home, to Gretchen's house. We can get it later." She just nodded. He carried her things in the house, and she followed right behind him. She looked around; the house looked the same and she felt comfortable but it seemed like she hadn't been there in a long time. When they reached the bedroom Clay turned on the light so he could get a good look at Cicely. Her hair was in a ponytail and she wasn't wearing any make-up. She looked so innocent and pure and vulnerable. She stood there like she didn't know what to do. He moved some clothes out of the chair, took her hand and led her to it. She sat, not taking her eyes off him. He sat on the bed facing her. "Baby, what happened?" he asked softly. She reached in her purse to get the note she wrote him. She handed it to him with the flowers. As he read she explained. They were both quiet for a moment. Finally Clay spoke. "At this moment, I love you more than I ever have, and I promise you I will never ever hurt you again. Thank you for forgiving me, thank you for believing in me, in us, thank you for coming back." Tears were streaming down her face. He reached in a drawer and gave her a handkerchief. "CeCe, baby, I don't know what I would have done if you had gotten hurt tonight."

"I'm sorry; I thought I could make it." Just then the phone rang.

"What's up GP?"

"Making sure everything's okay with Cicely."

"She's good, thanks for checking man." While Grant and Clay talked, Cicely took a couple of things from her bag and went to the bathroom. When she came back she had changed into a silk night shirt. He was off the phone and watched her as she came across the room. She stood between his legs and put her arms around his neck. She kissed his forehead and then pulled his shirt and undershirt over his head. He looked up at her but didn't say anything.

"Clay, I love you. I missed you so much while I was gone. I want us to get back on track."

"I want that too babe," was all he said. He pulled her into his arms and they lay side by side. He held her tightly for a few minutes. Neither of them was saying anything. They were both lost in their thoughts and glad to be together. They held each other like their very lives depended on it. Finally Clay whispered "be right back."

He turned on the lamp and turned off the overhead light. When he came out of the bathroom Cicely was under the cover, and had his side of the bed turned back too. Unlike their usual process of her being under the sheet and comforter and him just under the comforter, she had all the covers back so that when he got in they would be side by side; nothing protecting them from each other. He got in, turned off the light and pulled her close. His only thought at that moment was to ask her to marry him. The ring was in the safe, in the closet in the other room. While he was deciding to go get it, she spoke. "I want us to be fully back together, fully committed to each other again. I want to be completely yours." She looked up at him and they shared a long passionate kiss. "I know I said we have to wait until we get married..." Cicely was saying when he interrupted her.

"And we will wait. I want you so bad. But there can only be one first time, and I don't want us to be all caught up in the emotion of tonight." His body was aching for her. "I want to wait until our wedding night," Clay said.

FIFTY-THREE

About an hour into the drive back to Washington, Grant called Sunny. They had not spoken in days, they only exchanged a few text messages. She was generally glad to hear from him, and the sound of her voice soothed him. He told her he was headed back and they needed to talk when he got there. She agreed.

He originally left for four or five days; he was gone seven days, and Sunny was a wreck. She was truly worried. She had no idea what was on his mind. The house was clean, she even changed the comforter and curtains in the bedroom to a set she made a year ago but hadn't used. She didn't really buy any groceries while he was away, so she decided to go to the store and buy all Grant's favorites and prepare dinner for him.

Sunny was almost finished cooking when Grant called. "Do you want to meet me somewhere, get something to eat?"

"Grant, I cooked dinner."

"Oh, okay, I will see you shortly."

Sunny was puzzled, and all of a sudden panicked. She was afraid Grant wasn't coming back there to stay. She took a deep breath. "Maintain your cool," she said out loud to herself.

When Grant walked in he wasn't surprised with what Sunny had cooked. He smiled. She had one of his favorite meals;

baked tilapia with mango salsa, garlic mashed potatoes, asparagus and a bottle of white wine. He was glad she hadn't pulled out the lingerie. While they ate she asked about his trip, his parents and Gretchen. He told her about Cicely and the incident on the interstate.

"Thanks for dinner, it was delicious," Grant said as he poured another glass of wine.

"You're welcome," she said. There was a huge silence between them. He took a sip of wine, set the glass down and leaned forward on the table.

"I thought about us and our situation most of the time I was gone." She started to say something – he stopped her. "The bottom line is we need to rewind. I am moving back to my quarters, and we can set a wedding date after we have counseling." Sunny's body language showed relief. She had been afraid he was going to call off the engagement. "I hear you not wanting a counselor recommended by Bishop Robinson, so I will leave it to you to find somebody. I recommend you start with the Employee Assistance Program," Grant said.

"Okay, I will. Thanks for understanding," Sunny said just above a whisper.

"But hear what I'm telling you. If this doesn't happen, the engagement is off." Sunny was quiet. "Say something, Sunny." Grant said sternly.

"I love you, Grant."

"That's beside the point Sunny." She sighed loudly and sat back in her chair. They didn't take their eyes off each other.

"I will call tomorrow," she replied.

173

"Ok, let me know so I can arrange my schedule." Sunny was thinking Grant sounded like he was discussing business, not their future. As she completed her thought, he got up from the table, and took both their plates to the kitchen. Sunny walked in behind him.

"Do you want another glass of wine?" she asked him.

"No, I'm beat. Need a shower and the remote." Grant said. Sunny laughed.

"Okay, I'll unpack your bag, and the remote is all yours!"

"I'm not stayin'. I'm going back to my spot. We're not spending the night together again unless we get married."

"Grant! Please! What are you talking about?"

"I'll see you; we'll spend some time together. But while we're in counseling, no overnights. I love you Sunny. I really do, but marriage is forever and it's going to take more than love to make it last." Sunny couldn't believe he was sticking to this but he was.

"What are you angry about?" she asked.

"I'm not angry about anything, but I need to know we are on the same page. You flip when things don't go your way."

"No, I don't!" She raised her voice and then caught herself. He looked at her and shrugged, but didn't say anything. He yawned.

"We aren't going to hash this out now. I'm going. I'll talk to you tomorrow." He kissed her lightly on the lips and left her standing in the kitchen.

FIFTY-FOUR

She called Jackson several times but he did not answer or respond to her messages for him to call her. Finally, early Saturday morning, she sent a text message; 'Mom passed Wednesday. Funeral today 1:00 please come.' Jackson looked at the clock. For a split second he considered driving the hour to her hometown to attend the funeral. Just as quickly he thought better of it. He sent her a message back 'my condolences to you and your family.' He deleted her message.

Jackson was worried. Jacksa wasn't talking to him at all, JJ was only talking to him if he initiated the conversation and Min had changed. She seemed happy but was very short with him. He had apologized profusely and he just didn't know what else to do.

His thoughts were interrupted by Min's laughter. She was on the phone. He quickly realized she was talking to Anderson. When he knew she was off the phone he approached her. "Min, ride to Home Depot with me to get the new ceiling fan." He said it very casually.

"I will later," she said. "I'm expecting Anderson."

"For what?" Jackson asked, frowning. She didn't answer him. She just laughed.

When the bell rang Jackson went to the door, with King at his side. As usual King growled at Anderson as soon as he came in. That was Jackson's intention. "What's up Mr. Baye?" Anderson said as he extended his hand to Jackson. "I'm glad you're here. I want to talk to you and Mrs. Baye."

Min came down the hall. "Hello sweetheart," she said, greeting Anderson with a hug. Min asked about his mother, sisters and grandmother. "How is Honey?" Min asked.

"She's good. I talked to her on the way over here. She wants you to call her later," Anderson replied.

"Sure will."

"Speaking of Honey, here's what I did with her rings." Anderson took a velvet ring box from his pocket. He opened the box and handed it to Min.

"Anderson, it's beautiful. Jacksa will love it." Jackson was just sitting there, feeling left out. He finally spoke up.

"Is that an engagement ring?" Min smiled and gave the box back to Anderson, who gave it to Jackson.

"Yes Sir," Anderson said. "I am going to ask Jacksa to marry me and I would appreciate yours and Mrs. Baye's blessing." Tears formed in Min's eyes. Before she could say anything Jackson spoke.

"Thorn, I never made any secret of how I feel about you and my daughter. You're a cop. You carry a gun - that is not what I want for her. I don't want to worry about my daughter being a young widow."

"Jackson!" Min said looking at him frowning. He kept talking.

"But if you make her happy and you are good to her then there's not much I can say. But don't let me have to use that gun on you." Jackson was serious, and it was taking every

176

ounce of restraint Anderson had not to tell Jackson he was in no position to talk.

"Sir, my career may increase the chance of something happening to me, but I could work in an office tower and some fool crash an airplane into it." He shrugged his shoulders. He made his point. Jackson didn't say anything.

"Anderson, I am proud to have you as a son-in-law. I know you will make Jacksa very happy. You are a good man. But I want you to consider one thing before you marry Jacksa." Min was speaking. Jackson had a slight smile on his face. His wife was going to support him. Maybe they could get rid of Anderson Thorn. "When I was her age, I was beautiful and active just like Jacksa; I had big plans for my life with my husband and children. And then this happened to me. My body betrayed me, I have a debilitating illness and because of it, my husband betrayed me. My condition sent my husband into the arms of another woman."

"Oh Min!" Jackson said. He couldn't believe she said that. She didn't meet his eyes.

"Mama Min, I won't address that, but I can answer you that there isn't anything that could or will make me cut out on Jacksa. Please don't worry about that." Anderson looked at Jackson. "I love Jacksa. She is the only woman for me. When I say in sickness and in health, I will mean it." Jackson felt like he had been punched in the gut.

FIFTY-FIVE

April got online and Googled her mother's name. As she typed she wondered why she hadn't ever done it before. There were three people with the same name. The one she determined was her mother was connected to the magazine she worked for. There was no personal information but it appeared she still lived in Europe.

She sat and thought for a while; trying to decide what to do. Should she call? Should she write? If I send an email it will probably go to an assistant, and she'll never see it, April thought. It occurred to April that she didn't have anyone to talk to. She had a few friends but she wasn't close to anyone; not close enough to discuss something like this. Then she thought about Belinda. "I never wanted a sister but I guess now that I have one I could talk to her, if she didn't hate me," she said to herself.

April didn't have an active social life. She hadn't had a real boyfriend since she was an undergrad. She laughed aloud. "Wonder where he is?" she thought. "I bet I can find him on Facebook." With that thought it occurred to her she may find her mother on Facebook too. "I guess I better have a few kids if I don't want my daddy to spend all the money on Belinda's kids," she said aloud, and laughed.

Ben and Belinda were surprised when they got to the hospital to see Bradley and Bryce. Neither of them were on oxygen and the nurse said Bryce had four ounces of milk and Bradley had four and a half. "Good that I brought this then," she said as she gave her the cooler with the breast milk she had pumped. The nurse took the cooler and walked away. When Belinda turned around to see the boys, Ben was standing over them, obviously praying. She quickly pulled out her phone and took the picture. They would know one day that their dad continuously had them covered.

After a few minutes visiting, the doctor approached Ben and Belinda. "I am going to start the process of sending Bryce and Bradley home," the doctor said.

"What does that mean exactly?" Belinda asked. Ben put his arm around her.

"Tomorrow they will be moved to a regular room, we will run a few tests, and also wean them off all the meds in twenty-four to forty-eight hours."

"If everything goes according to plan..." Ben said.

The doctor finished the statement "we will send them home by the end of the week."

"If it doesn't go according to plan then what?" Belinda asked.

"Then we will decide what needs to be adjusted," the doctor answered. Belinda's eyes lit up. "So you're saying they may be home by the end of the week. Will they need a nurse or anything, any equipment?"

"I don't expect that, but I'll know in a few days," the doctor said, handing Bryce's chart to the nurse. They talked a few more minutes, he gave the nurse some instructions, and he

179

left. Ben and Belinda stood there for a moment very quiet. They had come so far and this part of the journey was almost over.

Quickly they started to talk about what needed to happen to make this all work. They knew the first call needed to be Grammy. The conversation was interrupted by Bradley crying and Belinda's phone ringing. Ben went to see about Bradley. Belinda took a deep breath and answered. It was April.

"Hi Belinda, are you busy?"

"Yes, we're at the hospital with the boys."

"How are they?" April asked.

"Doing very well. Thank you for asking. May I call you back?" Belinda said very businesslike. "Sure, please do," April answered.

"That was April," Belinda told Ben. "I wonder what she wanted."

"Why didn't you talk to her?" Ben asked.

" 'Cause I don't really care," Belinda said, rolling her eyes. Ben looked up and his facial expression changed before he responded.

"Ben, Belinda" – Hampton was walking toward them. Belinda let out a big sigh.

"Glad to run into you two." Hampton said, hugging Belinda slightly. "How are my grandsons?" "They're fine," Belinda said.

"Really good. May be going home by the end of the week," Ben told Hampton.

"I'm glad to hear that. Is there anything I can do to make it go smoothly?" Hampton asked.

"If we need to keep the nurse, may we?" Belinda asked.

"Sure, but why don't we get a pediatric nurse?" Hampton answered, glad Belinda was letting him in even if just for the boys.

They stayed a few more minutes and they all left together. Ben and Hampton talked a little about the church and the three of them talked about the house. The church was ahead of schedule and the house was on schedule. The thought of all the moving made Belinda tired. As if he was reading her mind, "I am going to hire someone to pack your things and move you, sweetie," Hampton said to Belinda. Her response was simply a smile.

When they were in the car Ben asked Belinda if she was going to return April's call. "No Ben, I'm not. Why should I? I don't want to hear anything she has to say."

"Belinda, she could be calling about the house," Ben said.

"Well her dad just updated us on that".

"Her dad, Belinda?"

She reached in her purse to get her phone. She saw him from the corner of her eye looking at her.

"Hey Grammy! We're on our way home. Do you need us to bring anything?" She looked at Ben and rolled her eyes.

ℱIFTY-SIX

Dr. Gasquet was very cool toward Kathy after she didn't show up at the conference. He called her and texted her when it was clear to him she wasn't coming. When he returned he told her she missed important information at the conference, and that he was disappointed that she defied his request. Kathy decided she needed to address this once and for all. "Excuse me Dr. Gasquet, but I think you are confused about the nature of our relationship. I am your graduate assistant. The position does not call for me to have dinner with you or accompany you to conferences. And if that is your expectation you need to get another assistant." In response he just waved her away. She walked out of his office, with no intention to return.

Kathy went straight home and called her mother. "You made the right decision honey." Katherine told her. "I hope you're right Ma, because I don't know what the repercussions will be."

After Kathy talked with her mother and Michelle, she settled down to study. She was startled when she saw an email from Dr. Gasquet. He copied her on a message he sent to the Graduate Assistants Administrator. The email stated she was insubordinate and as a result he dismissed her. "What in the world? " Kathy yelled aloud. "Is he crazy? That is not what happened!" She picked up the phone. "Daddy, I need a lawyer."

FIFTY-SEVEN

"Mom, I know she's going through our things when we're not here!"

"Jillian, how do you know that?" Ellen asked, laughing.

"I see things moved around."

"Are you sure you aren't imaging that?" Ellen was still laughing.

"Mom! I'm glad you see the humor in this."

Things had settled down at the Rajagopal residence. Mrs. Rajagopal stayed downstairs most of the time, but she spent as much time with LaLa as she could. She was even teaching her some words in Punjabi. LaLa enjoyed having "Dadi" around and she was much more relaxed around her grandmother than Jill. Raja missed his dad terribly but he was glad his mother was there with them. Tara's advice to Jill was not to let her guard down.

Jill mentioned to Raja her concerns about his mother. "She probably is, sweetie," Raja said. "But unless we can prove it, I can't confront her. I think you should set a trap for her and see if she takes the bait."

Jill looked at the clock when she heard LaLa cry. It was 12:47am. She had gone to sleep hours before. As soon as Jill touched her she knew LaLa had a fever.

Jill was up with LaLa for hours before she finally went back to sleep. It seemed to take the medicine a long time to work. While she rocked her, Jill was thinking through how she would work her schedule the next day. When she went back to bed at 5:00, Raja was getting up. He had an early surgery. "Were you up all night? How is she?" Raja asked.

"Okay for now."

"What does your day look like?" he asked.

"I have a couple of meetings I don't need to cancel, but I will. She can't go to pre-school with a fever and I don't know if she's teething or if it's a virus. I guess I can get my mom to go to the meetings for me or get her to come over here while I go. I'll call her in a little while," Jill said. "Doll, you know we have another option," Raja said from the bathroom.

"What?" She asked.

"My mother ... my mom is downstairs," Raja said casually. He didn't expect immediate agreement.

"Are you kidding me?" Jill said, with a smirk on her face. "I am still adjusting to her being here and you want me to leave my baby with her?"

"That's her granddaughter ..."

"Yeah, the granddaughter she was going to kidnap and take back to London with her. I pass!" "Why don't we give it a chance Jillie?" She ignored him.

After Raja showered and got dressed he went down the hall to check on LaLa. She was coughing. "Sounds like a respiratory situation to me," Raja said.

184

"How do you know?" she said, slapping his bottom. "You're not a real doctor. You only cut people!"

Raja got his stethoscope, listened to LaLa's chest and took her temperature. "We need to get her an antibiotic, I'll call her doctor. And, Jill, we need to let my Mom care for her today." Jill sighed deeply, and nodded okay.

Between appointments Jill picked up LaLa's medicine and took it home. It could have been delivered but she really wanted to check on LaLa and Mrs. Rajagopal. When she walked in LaLa was asleep and her grandmother was sitting in the rocking chair watching her sleep and reading. She looked up at Jill over her reading glasses, and put her index finger to her lips to indicate Jill should be quiet. They walked down the hall before they said anything.

"How has she been?" Jill asked.

"Very fussy, but I held her and rocked her to sleep. I gave her a little tea and the fever broke," Mrs. Rajagopal answered.

"You didn't give her the ibuprofen?"

"No, that wasn't necessary. I brewed her some tea with basil, cardamom, pepper, and licorice mint. It's called tisanes. I added some honey - no sugar. She had two ounces and then four more later. The fever went away." Jill didn't know what to say. But she finally asked her mother-in-law where she got the herbs. "I brought the ingredients with me when I moved here." Jill glanced at the clock. She needed to go. Without commenting on the tea, Jill explained to Dadi how to give LaLa the medicine. She went back to LaLa's room and kissed her. Her head was not warm. She felt her arms and legs. Mrs. Rajagopal was right; the fever was gone.

FIFTY-EIGHT

Kathy told her father the story about Dr. Gasquet, "Why are you just telling me about this?" Lee asked.

"Because I never thought it would escalate to this level. The man is a brilliant professor. I had no reason to expect he was a fool!"

"This wouldn't happen if you were at a local university."

"Daddy! What does that have to do with anything? I have a situation here and I need your help!" Kathy was yelling. This was the first time she had raised her voice at her father. Neither of them said anything for a few seconds.

"I apologize baby. You asked for my help, not an editorial. I will make a call in the morning and get this handled," Lee said very calmly.

Kathy didn't sleep much that night. She was furious; she was nervous, and a little afraid. When she heard her phone around 8:00am she expected it to be her dad. It was Sterling. She was glad to hear from him but surprised and puzzled that he called.

"To what do I owe the pleasure of this call?" Kathy said sarcastically. It was a defense mechanism. She wanted to be on offense.

Sterling chuckled. "I dreamed about you."

"Is that so," Kathy said and laughed.

Sterling continued without commenting. "You were in some kind of trouble and you were running. I could see you but I couldn't get to you." He said it very matter-of-factly. Her demeanor softened a bit. He continued to tell her about the dream. She listened without interrupting. "Your dream was partially correct," she said. "I am in a bit of trouble but I'm not running." Kathy went on to tell Sterling about the situation with Dr. Gasquet.

"Do you want me to come up there and kick his ass?"

"Sterling, there you go with the locker room mouth."

"That's beside the point. I will knock him out! He is not going to disrespect you!"

"It's okay, my dad is going to handle it."

"Your dad is going to handle it diplomatically; with words. I'll bring a couple of my boys up there and rough him up." He went on a couple more minutes. Kathy was listening but puzzled why he was so emotional about the situation.

"Sterling why do you care?"

" 'Cause you my girl and I don't appreciate his sh..."

"Sterling!" Kathy interrupted him. She would often get on him about his choice of words. They both laughed.

"Why do you care what's going on in my life?" Kathy asked him softly.

"I care about you," he replied.

"The last time we talked you said you were seeing someone."

187

Sterling inhaled and then exhaled slowly. "I lied, Kathy."

Before he could continue she interrupted him. "Why would you, did you, lie about something like that?"

He was quiet for a couple of seconds. "I was hurt that you left and I wanted to hurt you."

Now she was quiet. He continued. "I love you, and you know that, but you made all these decisions to move and be gone for four years like I didn't matter and we didn't matter."

Kathy swallowed hard. Before she could respond, her phone beeped. It was her dad. "I'll call you back. That's my dad."

"Make sure you do," Sterling said.

When they hung up, Sterling dialed Katherine's number. He intended to leave a message but she answered.

"Good look Mrs. Robinson." She laughed.

"Thanks for the info. We talked, I told her the truth, that I lied about being with somebody, told her I love her." Katherine's eyes lit up. She wasn't sure calling Sterling to tell him about Kathy's problem was the right thing to do.

"I embellished it a little, but she got the message. Her dad called so we hung up. She's supposed to call me back."

"Yes, I can hear him talking to her now. Thanks for letting me know. Let's talk later!" Katherine hung up with a smile on her face.

Sterling leaned back on the pillows propped against his head board. He laughed out loud.

Mrs. Robinson calling to tell him about Kathy's situation with the professor was gold. He was a good actor. Telling

Kathy he dreamed about her was a good move. He meant everything he said. He did love her and he would kick the professor's ass. Sterling didn't know if he could get Kathy to come back to Hattiesville, but at least she would be back in his life.

$\mathscr{F}$IFTY-NINE

Sunny was incensed. Grant was holding fast to his plan. He was staying in the officers' quarters at the hospital. They had lunch once and she invited him. She waited for a couple of days before looking for a counselor, but Grant wasn't budging. She lied and told him she left a message for someone to call her back. Sunny's mother called too but she didn't answer. She knew she would eventually have to face that music too. Her mother told her to handle things differently with Grant, but she hadn't and here they were.

The Employee Assistance Program directory listed several pre-marital counselors. Sunny looked at the profiles and pictures of a few of them. She decided to call an African-American female. As she called she thought to herself a female will understand her position and help her convince Grant they should go ahead with their plans. She figured an African-American female would feel her pain. Sunny was the only one in her circle of friends who was in a committed relationship, and she liked being the center of attention. Since she and Grant got engaged it was all about her. There was no possible way she could not get married. Her friends accepted and understood they couldn't get married on the island because of Grant's father's inability to travel. They would never understand her not getting married at all. If that happened, her value in the circle would go down.

The counselor Sunny called wasn't very attractive by Sunny's standards and she was fine with that. She didn't want Grant to pay her any attention. Her assistant gave

Sunny an appointment for the following week. "Wow, I was hoping we could get in a little sooner," Sunny told her.

"I'm sorry Ms. Dorsett, I don't have anything earlier, but I will call you if anybody cancels."

"That will be fine, thank you." The assistant went on to explain to Sunny the procedure; five to six sessions, the first two as a couple, then two to three individually and the last one as a couple. "Five to six weeks! Are you kidding me?" Sunny raised her voice. The assistant didn't respond. "We want to get married right away. Another six to eight weeks is not acceptable! My fiancé is an officer..." "Then I'm sure he understands order and procedure!" The assistant responded. "Now do you want the keep the appointments or not?"

"Yes." Sunny was somewhat taken aback by the assistant's response. "Keep my eye on the prize," she said to herself. One good thing the assistant told her, the preliminary packet of papers could be emailed. She asked her to send Grant's directly to him. That way he would know Sunny did what he asked without her telling him.

A few minutes later the email arrived. The forms were attached and in the body of the email the appointment time was confirmed. "Splendid!" She thought. She would wait for Grant to call her.

$\mathscr{S}$IXTY

Things were basically back on track for Cicely and Clay. He proposed again, she accepted and she accepted the ring. They decided to get married in the church office, have Bishop Robinson perform the ceremony and ask Mrs. Robinson to be the witness. Then they were going to Hawaii. They would have some type of celebration later. Clay said they would have his cousin Gretchen work on that while they were gone.

Cicely moved out of the nurse's residence and into Clay's house. There were both pretty clingy. Other than work, they were together. He wanted her to move to the day shift at the hospital, but there were no openings. Some nights he took her to work and picked her up the next morning before he went to work.

The travel agent worked things out, and they both requested two weeks off and coordinated things with Bishop Robinson's office. Cicely would have to take one week without being paid for it because of the time she took off when she left Clay. When she told him, he shrugged. "You know that's not an issue," Clay told her smiling. "Baby, you aren't on your own anymore. If you never made any more money we'll still be fine." Cicely felt a sense of security that was foreign to her.

Bishop Robinson insisted that they have some counseling. He allowed them to forgo the formal classes but Clay met with the bishop, Cicely met with the first lady and they had two sessions with both of them. They accomplished all of that in two weeks.

During the counseling everything was revealed. Clay admitted the situation with Delia. Bishop Robinson asked tough questions but in the end he was satisfied with Clay's answers, and satisfied that repentance and forgiveness had taken place.

In the midst of counseling, she was unpacking, repacking and planning for them to move to their new house. She hired someone to help her. It was amazing to Clay how much she could get done in a day.

On Tuesday, prior to their getting married on Friday, they were checking off the list and going over the loose ends. "How are we going to tell our family?" Cicely asked Clay. He laughed.

"I think we should leave a note or send them a text message!" He kept laughing. Cicely laughed too. "Clay!"

"Well, I'm just sayin'." He was still laughing.

"You know Gretchen will want to plan a wedding and Aunt Gracie will want her to. I don't want to do all that." He lowered his voice. "I want to marry you Friday, go to Hawaii on Saturday and be in paradise for ten days. I don't know how much longer I can sleep in that bed beside you and not reach over there and grab you," he said looking directly into her eyes. She smiled and bit her bottom lip. They were both quiet for a moment.

"Why don't we write a letter and mail them Friday. By the time they get the letter on Saturday we'll be on our way to Honolulu."

"A letter that says what?" Clay asked.

Cicely got a sheet of paper and Clay gave her a pen. They went back and forth and finally came up with more of a note than a letter; short and sweet.

Dear Family,

By the time you read this we will be headed to Honolulu for our honeymoon! We were married Friday afternoon! There's no point in you calling, we're not answering. We will be back in two weeks. We need this time together… alone. Thank you for loving us.

We love you,

Cicely and Clay

Mr. and Mrs. Clayton Paul Sturdivant

They printed copies of the letter to go to Cicely's brothers, Clay's Uncle Paul and Aunt Grace, Grant and Sunny and Gretchen. Also in Gretchen's envelope was a copy of their itinerary and a note to start planning a reception and a check to get the ball rolling.

$\mathscr{S}$IXTY-ONE

When Roderick's phone rang at 8:00 am and he saw the Georgia attorney's phone number, he was surprised. He walked into the other room away from Sandra.

"Roderick, the Casebiers have changed their minds. They are prosecuting Chloe." Roderick was stunned. He went on to tell Roderick the details. "To keep from fighting the parental rights, adoption thing in this setting…"

"They are going to prosecute on the other child," Roderick said, completing the attorney's sentence.

"Right," the attorney said.

"Damn, "Roderick said.

The attorney told Roderick, "Chloe needs to turn herself in by 5:00 pm tomorrow. She'll make bail and then we'll try to work something out with the Casebiers' attorney."

Roderick thanked him and ended the call. He sat thinking for a few minutes. They had to face the music.

"Chloe, Sandra - come in here for a few minutes." Sandra came out of the bedroom. Chloe didn't respond. "Chloe".

"Yes, Daddy, down here."

He motioned for Sandra to follow him down the stairs. Roderick didn't beat around the bush. He told them what the attorney said. Sandra started to protest, but there was no point. Chloe had to face the consequences of the decisions she made. Chloe dropped her head. "I messed it up Ma."

"What are you talking about Chloe?" Sandra asked.

"I had a big argument with Kirby Casebier the other day. Campbell, Natalia and I ran into them when we went out to eat." Chloe went on to tell her parents about the incident. Roderick slammed his fist on the counter.

"Damn it Chloe! Why didn't you just keep your mouth shut?" Sandra was saying something but Roderick talked right over her. "Do you realize you can go to prison? Do you realize if you go to prison you cannot take the bar and probably won't get any type of meaningful job?" Chloe was crying, but he continued. "Everything we worked for will go down the drain if you can't take over the business. Do you know how much money we are spending on your education?"
"Yes Daddy I do realize all of that!" Chloe said in tears.

"Stop crying Chloe, just shut up! I am not moved by your tears! You made some serious decisions, and now you have to suffer some serious consequences." Roderick picked up his phone and keys and walked outside.

Sandra was stunned. Chloe was almost twenty-one years old and her dad had never raised his voice at her. Everything he said was right but she wished he had said it differently. Chloe walked into the den and sat on the sofa with her head in her hands. Sandra walked in and sat beside her. "Your dad is angry but you know he loves you," Sandra said rubbing Chloe's back.

"I know Ma, but he's very disappointed in me, and he has every right to be." There was sadness in Chloe's voice.

"Honey, you didn't make good decisions, but I still think we can work this out. You know I believe anything can be negotiated," Sandra said attempting to make Chloe smile.

"My mother, forever the optimist," Chloe said standing and stretching. "Mama, facts can't be negotiated. I'm going back to Atlanta to face the facts."

SIXTY-TWO

Labor Day was the following Monday, school started on Wednesday and basketball season was around the corner. This would be JJ's final college season. He had no real expectation of being drafted into the league so he was pursuing opportunities in sports broadcasting and looked forward to an interview with Duke University's sports information director. He and Jackson talked earlier in the day and JJ shared that news with his dad. Jackson was glad they talked and hoped that meant they were repairing their relationship. Jackson was excited about JJ's news and wanted to tell Min all about it when he got home.

He walked in to hear her laughing. She was in the den sitting at the computer. He could hear a man's voice. He stopped right inside the kitchen door. Jackson couldn't clearly hear him or Min but he heard enough to know the man was the doctor. He walked further into the room. Min knew he was there, she heard him come in, but she didn't acknowledge him. He walked out onto the deck where King was. A few minutes later he noticed Min was no longer in front of the computer so he went back in. "Hey doll, how was your day?" he asked casually.

"It was fine. How was yours?" She responded just as casually.

"It was pretty hectic." She didn't engage him in conversation. "What do you want to do about dinner?" he asked. "Jacksa is coming over and bringing dinner."

"I hope she's not bringing the detective with dinner," Jackson said with a groan. Min still did not respond. He tried again. "What did the doctor say?" She looked at him but didn't answer. He repeated the question.

"Why do you care, Jackson?"

"Min I care because I love you. I care because you are my wife, I care because I'm concerned about you."

"None of those are good reasons," she said starting to walk away. He slammed his fist on the counter. The noise startled Min. "Why are you acting like this?" he asked her.

"Acting like what? Acting like I don't want you in my business? Because I don't," she said, raising her voice. "Jackson, if I was financially able to live on my own, you wouldn't even be here!" Min said. The look in her eyes told him she meant what she said.

"I messed up and I'm sorry. I don't know how many times I can apologize, and I don't know what else I can do to fix this situation between us." Jackson sounded sincere and deep inside she knew he was. But she couldn't let her guard down.

"I don't really care what you do or say, Jackson. I really don't." As Min turned to walk away, Jackson grabbed her. He intended to kiss her but she lost her balance. He caught her before she actually fell but not before Anderson and Jacksa walked in.

"Daddy!" Jacksa screamed. Anderson pushed past Jacksa and grabbed Min out of Jackson's grip.

"Step back Mr. Baye." Anderson said evenly. Jackson didn't move. "Back sir." This time Anderson raised his voice. Jackson took a couple of steps back. Anderson got Min to a chair. "What happened here?" Anderson asked. Jacksa was kneeling in front of her mother but looking at her father. Anderson had shifted to Detective Thorn.

"We were arguing and he grabbed me." Min said.

"Mom, are you hurt? Did Daddy hit you?"

"Jacksa, you know better." Jackson said.

"I know what I saw." She responded not taking her eyes off him.

"We were disagreeing, she started to walk away, and I grabbed her to stop her. I wanted to kiss her, I wanted to try to make her understand how much I love her. I must have caught her off guard 'cause she lost her balance. I was trying to keep her from falling when you two walked in."

"Mrs. Baye, do you want me to arrest Mr. Baye?

"Thorn! Arrest me for what?"

"Sir, I am a law enforcement officer who takes domestic violence seriously."

"Domestic violence! Thorn you are taking this too far," Jackson said in protest.

Jacksa stood beside her mother, not knowing what to do or what to say. Anderson repeated his question. "Mrs. Baye, do you want to press charges against Mr. Baye?" Min knew she had to say something. She felt certain that Jackson was shaken up so she was satisfied.

"No Anderson I don't think that's necessary, but I want him out of my sight."

"Why don't you take a walk, Mr. Baye?"

Jackson stood there for a few seconds; all eyes were on him. Finally he picked up his keys and went out through the garage.

SIXTY-THREE

Jill had to admit the tea Mrs. Rajagopal made worked to get rid of LaLa's fever. She also had to admit coming home a couple days a week with dinner ready was wonderful. Mrs. Rajagopal was getting settled. She made a few friends in the Indian community, which seemed to be good for her. Raja told Jill he knew she was still very sad though; he had caught her crying.

One evening when Jill came in late, Raja, LaLa and Mrs. Rajagopal were in the family room singing. It was a children's song in Punjabi. They explained later it was a song Raja learned as a child too. Jill still didn't trust her mother-in-law, and she couldn't relax. Late that night Raja and Jill were lying in bed talking. "I think we need a vacation." Raja said to Jill, taking her hand and kissing it.

"Do we want to take LaLa out of pre-school this soon and get her off schedule?" Jill asked.

"I said 'we need a vacation'; you and I."

"And what do you suggest we do with our daughter?"

"Leave her with her grandmother," he said.

"That's not an option. Even if I trusted your mother to keep her. She can't get her back and forth to school. Your mother doesn't drive. If an emergency came up, she can't get her to the doctor," Jill responded.

Raja was quiet for a moment. Jill rolled over on her side and leaned up on her elbow. "Babe, you need to forgive my mother." Now Jill was quiet. Finally she said, "That's easier said than done."

"As much as you talk about letting stuff go, and forgiving people, you need to take your own advice."

She sighed heavily. They talked, and went back and forth for a while. The last thing Raja said before he turned over to go to sleep was, "I'm calling the travel agent in the morning, so work it out. Clear your schedule and your head."

$\mathcal{S}$IXTY-FOUR

Brittani and Brianna were surprised when they came home from school and their two little brothers were there. There was a lot of commotion in the house. Belinda didn't know what to expect from them, but she did expect a little more excitement or at least some curiosity. After a few minutes they went upstairs, changed clothes and started on their homework.

When Grammy called them down for dinner, she asked how they felt. "I'm not sure what you mean, Gram," Brianna said.

"The boys being home causes a lot to go on around here, and that includes adjustments for you two."

The girls looked at each other without saying anything. Grammy knew they had talked about it. Neither of them responded, and they were both quiet during dinner. Ben and Belinda noticed it but didn't mention it.

"Grammy, May I please be excused from cleaning the kitchen? I need to study for a test," Brittani asked.

"I got you Britt," Ben said.

"Thanks Daddy."

"Gram, you get a break tonight too. Leave everything to me and my assistant Brianna!"

"No, you can be my assistant!" They all laughed.

Ben and Brianna started cleaning the kitchen and Grammy went to check on Bryce and Bradley while Belinda pumped more milk. When the doorbell rang Ben frowned. They weren't expecting anyone. It was Hampton Josephs.

"Evening Ben, sorry to drop in unannounced. Hope it's okay," Hampton said as they shook hands.

"Well, we weren't expecting company. We have our hands full," Ben chuckled.

"I know, just want to check on everybody, and I have something for the girls. I'm sure they're a little overwhelmed."

Ben was amused that Hampton picked up on that. The other interesting thing was that he and the girls had not been introduced. He wasn't sure how Belinda would feel about him being there.

Ben asked Brianna to go upstairs to get Brittani. He decided he would make the introductions and ask Belinda for forgiveness later. Grammy came in just as Ben and Hampton sat down in the den. Ben didn't know how she was going to react either.

"Hello Hampton. How are you?"

"I'm doing great Mrs. Coffey, how are you?" He stood when she walked into the room.

"Doing fine. Is Belinda expecting you?"

"No, and I won't be here long," Hampton said.

Before Grammy could respond Belinda walked in, and Brittani and Brianna were with her. "Hampton, I'm surprised to see you."

"I know, just wanted to check on you and the boys and bring the girls a gift."

Brianna and Brittani looked at each other a bit puzzled. "Girls, I know you recognize Mr. Josephs from church, but I need to tell you something else." Ben was speaking. He wouldn't look at Belinda or Grammy. "We found out recently that Hampton is your mother's father; he's your grandfather." Neither of the girls said anything. Belinda was looking at Ben. She was wide-eyed. She couldn't believe Ben was telling them this without talking it over with her.

"What do you mean, you found out recently?" Brianna asked.
"Do you remember we talked about your mom and Aunt Kirby growing up in foster care?"

"Yes," they said in unison.

"The reason your mom was in foster care is her mother died and her father didn't know. After we moved here, Mr. Josephs discovered he is her father." Ben said.

The girls were frowning, but Brianna spoke. "So you're our grandfather and Ms. April is your daughter."

"Yes," Hampton said smiling.

"So that means you know your daughter was the cause of my mama getting sick."

None of the adults responded. Grammy folded her arms. Belinda looked at Ben, who did not meet her gaze. She rolled her eyes. Hampton was looking at the girls. "Yes, sweetie, that was an unfortunate situation, but I hope we have worked through all that," he said.

"I haven't worked through it. I'm still mad." Brianna was the one talking and all eyes were on her. She kept talking. "And my little brothers were born early and they could have died and my mama could have died." She had her hands on her hips and she was looking directly at Hampton.

"Brianna Coffey are you being disrespectful?" Grammy asked about the same time they heard one of the babies on the monitor. Belinda started out of the room but Grammy stopped her. "I'll see about him." Grammy said, leaving the room.

The den was completely silent. Finally Brittani broke the silence. "Mr. Josephs, my sister doesn't mean to be disrespectful - this is just a lot."

Hampton couldn't tell the girls apart, but he was totally impressed with them, even considering the circumstances. "It's a lot because they made it a lot!" Brianna said.

"Bree, be nice!" Brittani whispered to her sister.

Hampton looked at his granddaughters closely. He was looking for some little thing to help him tell them apart. "Brianna and Brittani, I agree this is a lot, and I can only hope that when you're a little older some of this will be easier for you to understand. In the meantime I hope we can all get to know each other better and become a real family," Hampton said.

"Sir, I'm not sure we want to get to know each other better and become a real family," Brianna responded.

Before she could continue, Ben finally said something. "Brianna, let's let your mom, April and Hampton work that out." Both girls looked at their mother. She nodded her head yes with a slight smile. She was furious with Ben and he knew it, but she was trying not to show it.

Hampton stayed only a short while longer after his run-in with Brianna. He did not get to see the boys and he left the girls' iPods he bought them with Belinda. Brittani and Brianna were upstairs when he left. They didn't know he was gone.

Upstairs in Brianna's room, the girls discussed "Mr. Josephs". "How do you think Mommy feels about having a dad now?" Brianna was asking Brittani. "She's probably glad because she didn't have any parents." Brianna said.

"And you shouldn't have been so mean to him, Bree. It's not his fault what April did."

"I know, I was just giving him something to think about!" She laughed.

They talked a few more minutes and decided if their mother liked Hampton they would like him too, and if she could forgive April they would too.

As they talked there was a knock at the door. It was Belinda. "Hey Ma!" Brittani said.

"Hi girls," she said, sitting on the foot of the bed. "I guess the information about Mr. Josephs came as a surprise," Belinda said.

"Yes, Mommy, it did and like we told him that's a lot." Brittani said.

"How do you feel about all this? Are you glad to have a daddy?" Brianna asked.

Belinda let out a big sigh. "I'm not sure how I feel. I'm still trying to get my thoughts together." Belinda didn't want to say too much. She needed to process all this before she attempted to influence their thoughts; and she needed to talk with Ben. He told the story without talking to her about it. That was unlike him, but she needed him to make her understand why he thought that was the right thing to do.

"Mommy, what's in the bag?" Brianna asked. Belinda forgot she brought Hampton's package upstairs.

"Mr. Josephs left you two these gifts."

"Mommy, are you going to call him Daddy or Mr. Josephs?" Brittani asked.

Belinda chuckled. "I don't know - what do you think?"

Brittani started to answer but Brianna stopped her. "Let us think about it and we will let you know."

Belinda gave Brittani the bag and she took out one box and gave the bag to Brianna. There were two cards at the bottom of the bag that neither Brittani nor Belinda saw, addressed to each of the girls. Brittani opened the box to see the turquoise IPod. Brianna opened the card. The note said; *"When you have time, let's get together and download some music. Enjoy! G-Pop."* "I'm impressed with this note card." She looked at the back and noticed his monogram at the top of the card. "But he has bad penmanship like Daddy!" Both girls laughed as Brianna made the comment and handed the card to her mother. Brittani read her card which said basically the same and she laughed at 'G-Pop'.

"G-Pop" she said frowning. Is that what he wants us to call him?"

"I guess," Brianna said. "We'll have to think about that too."

$\mathscr{S}$IXTY-FIVE

Grant and Sunny had different approaches to counseling. Grant wanted to make sure they should get married, because marriage was forever. Sunny wanted to be married forever too but she wanted to do it as quickly as possible. She had to save face. The differences showed up quickly and the counselor was not fooled.

Sunny sized up the counselor and decided she better play along. This woman was serious. She had credentials and rank. She was married with children. She was very professional, not the "girlfriend" type Sunny expected. Sunny wished she had vetted her more closely.

The counselor was straight down the middle. She didn't lean either way. At the end of the first session, Grant was satisfied they were off to a good start. Sunny was indifferent but she knew better than to let on. The next session would be for Grant alone, then Sunny alone. Sunny decided she would tell Grant after her session that the counseling was done and they could get married. She would tell the counselor they decided not to continue. The challenge would be to keep Grant away from her and get him to set the date. In the meantime, Sunny's mother had called a couple of times over the weekend so she needed to call back.

"Hi Ma, how are you?"

"I am fine. How are you and how is Grant?"

"All is well Ma. We are doing the counseling and we're going to confirm the date in two weeks."

"That sounds good honey, I will go ahead and make my reservations." Mrs. Dorsett said that more to see if Sunny would change her story. She knew how much her daughter wanted to have a wedding.

"That's good," was Sunny's reply.

"How is the counseling going, sugar?"

"It's good, better than I thought. I guess it was kind of necessary. I have a session and Grant has one, then we're through; actually his is first."

Sunny's mother knew that wasn't the whole truth. She and Grant had not met in person but Sunny introduced them via Skype and they communicated regularly. More regularly than Sunny knew. When she hadn't been able to reach Sunny she called Grant. He told her the whole story and gave her the details of the counseling process. "So you didn't undo any of the plans you made when Grant told you no wedding without counseling?"

Sunny was stunned when her mother said that, but she recovered nicely. "I couldn't get my deposits back so I left everything as it was. But we'll finish counseling in time to make it work anyway." Sunny said easily.

"Does Grant know you changed the counseling schedule?" her mother asked.

"I didn't change it, we're doing so well we only have to do the two individual sessions."

"Don't you have homework?"

"Yes, Ma, we do it at night before we go to bed."

"You little lying heifer! I know Grant moved out and I know you have a total of six sessions. I also know Grant told you not to make any plans until the counseling was done! Girl, if you don't stop lying you are going to lose that man for sure!" Mrs. Dorsett was yelling at Sunny.

"Ma! I am not lying. Not really. You said that sometimes you make decisions and present it to Daddy like it was his decision. That's all I'm doing." Sunny sounded like she believed what she was saying.

"Crazy girl, I do that when we're buying paint or I want him to clear out the gutters. I don't deliberately lie to my husband." Sunny still didn't realize how her mother knew all this. They went back and forth until finally Mrs. Dorsett told Sunny, "You have one day to correct all this or I am going to correct it for you."

When Sunny hung up there were tears in her eyes. Things were not going according to plan. Her mother didn't make idle threats and she knew it. She had to come up with another plan. Sunny gathered her things and walked to the reception area. She told the receptionist she wasn't feeling well and was going home for the remainder of the day. When she got in the car she called Grant. "Come for dinner. I'm fixing crab legs." She had to leave a message. She stopped at the store got the crab legs, some shrimp and vegetables. She had everything else she needed at home. By the time she got home Sunny decided to call her mother's bluff. There was no way her mother would make good on her threat, not in one day.

Grant called to tell Sunny he was on his way. "Will you get the mail on your way in?"

"Yep, see you shortly."

SIXTY-SIX

The sun was shining, and there wasn't a cloud in the sky. It was the type of day Cicely had always pictured for her wedding day. She and Clay were pretty quiet all morning. They dressed separately and when she walked into the room his breath was taken away. She was wearing a white lace dress, strapless with the diamond necklace and earrings he bought her their first Christmas together. Her hair was down and her make-up was flawless. He was wearing a charcoal gray suit, white shirt and a light gray and peach tie with a matching pocket square.

Like clockwork the doorbell rang. It was the photographer they hired. He took pictures for almost twenty minutes before the limousine arrived. The photographer took a few more pictures and then followed the limo to the church. On the ride to the church Clay gave Cicely a small diamond bracelet that matched the other jewelry.

The driver pulled the limo into Bishop Robinson's garage. They didn't want an audience. The security guard met them at the elevator and escorted Cicely to Mrs. Robinson's suite. The Bishop wanted to see Clay. Mrs. Robinson's assistant came in and hugged Cicely. She brought Cicely a glass of cold sparkling water and she lay the bouquet of peach colored roses on the table. In less than a minute Mrs. Robinson came in with a big smile. They prayed and then chatted for about ten minutes, when the assistant came back to tell them Bishop Robinson was ready. Mrs. Robinson held Cicely's hand while they walked down the hall. Cicely noticed Clay was wearing a peach rose bud boutonniere. He winked at her as she approached him.

The ceremony didn't take long. The photographer took a few more pictures then excused himself. They signed the license, chatted a few minutes and left. The limousine took them to a hotel in Charlotte where they would spend their first night as husband and wife. The next morning they would leave for Hawaii.

Clay hadn't missed a detail. He made arrangements with the hotel to use the private elevator to the bridal suite. He had a courier service deliver their bags to the hotel earlier that day and the concierge made sure everything was in order.

Cicely couldn't believe her eyes. She felt like a princess in a fairy tale. The suite was beautiful. Her things were organized, a bottle of champagne was being chilled, and there was fruit and cheese on a silver tray. A few minutes after they were there, the room phone rang. Clay was obviously expecting the call. He answered a few questions and hung up.

"Dinner will be here at six o'clock," he said.

Cicely smiled and said "okay." She was a little overwhelmed. Clay liked things done right so she shouldn't be surprised. If all this was set up in Charlotte, she couldn't wait to see what he had planned for Hawaii. The only details she knew was they were going to visit three islands during their ten day stay.

$\mathscr{S}$IXTY-SEVEN

Chloe and her dad drove to Atlanta, met the attorney at his office and Chloe turned herself in. Sandra had a case in court, and couldn't go with them. It was just as well, Roderick thought. She was still in denial about the reality of the situation. That reality being Chloe may be going to jail, and at the very least she would have a criminal record that would prevent her from getting into law school. She was already going to graduate a semester later, if at all. Spelman College had not decided if she could come back. They were waiting for the disposition of the matter.

Chloe didn't want Campbell or Natalia to go with them. She wanted to deal with this on her own. As far as Chloe was concerned she created the situation and had to deal with the consequences. Roderick was concerned that Chloe didn't show any emotion. He asked her attorney to petition the judge for a psychological evaluation. The attorney agreed.

When Sandra's court case was done for the day she went back to her office. There was a message from Roderick that Chloe made bail and he would call her later. After sitting and thinking for a long while, Sandra decided to call Kirby Casebier. She had to choose her words carefully if she could even get Kirby to talk to her. Sandra knew this was an act of desperation, but she had to try and save Chloe. All she wanted was Kirby and Enoch to understand that Chloe made a mistake. She never intended to hurt Nicholas or Blake. As a mother Sandra hoped she could get through to Kirby.

Enoch got a call from their attorney. Chloe turned herself in, but was out on bail. Interestingly the judge had ordered a psychological evaluation. "What if they find she really is suffering from some kind of trauma?" Enoch asked the attorney.

"Then that makes prosecuting her harder, but it shouldn't prohibit us from being able to keep her from petitioning for Nicholas. As a matter of fact that works to our advantage." Enoch was satisfied with what the attorney told him.

"Go on with your life, Enoch. It will be weeks before we get any movement on this," the attorney said.

"Got it," Enoch replied.

"One caution though; don't have any contact with Chloe Matthews or her family."

"Man, we live in a small community..."

"I know that, but we don't want another situation like you had at the restaurant," the lawyer interrupted Enoch.

"We go to the same church!" Enoch interrupted him.

"I can get a restraining order, to keep her from coming."

"Man, how do you keep somebody from coming to church?" Enoch chuckled.
"I can do it!" The lawyer laughed too.

Enoch sighed heavily. "Let me talk to Kirby about that."

Enoch actually felt sorry for Chloe; for everybody involved in the situation. "If Chloe had not antagonized Kirby at the restaurant none of this would be necessary. "The kid had an out but she didn't take it," Enoch was thinking as he drove. "Now her life is turned upside down." Enoch didn't agree

216

with prosecuting Chloe. He and Aunt Avis tried to talk Kirby out of it, but she was adamant to teach Chloe a lesson. He knew how he felt as a father when the boys were missing but he knew it was compounded for Kirby. In the depths of his heart he still hoped they could resolve all this without Chloe going to jail. Maybe she really was suffering from PTSD and she could get some help.

ϴIXTY-EIGHT

Kathy couldn't believe her ears. She and Campbell were talking and he was telling her about the kidnapping incident and the possibility of Chloe going to jail. "Ms. Robinson, it's a big mess. I can't help Chloe and everything is out of control." Campbell's voice was pleading.

"Oh my gosh, Campbell, I am so sorry, so very sorry you are having to deal with this. How are you coping? How are your classes?" Campbell chuckled at Kathy's question. She was and had always been all about education.

"I'm actually doing okay, all things considered." He knew what the next question would be so he pre-empted her. "I started on my law school applications, too, and scheduled my classes to study for the LSAT." Kathy was pleased with what he said, but she also knew how much he loved Chloe. She had to ask.

"How does any of this change depending on what happens with Chloe?"

Campbell didn't answer right away. Finally he said "I'm not sure. We were talking about coming to New York together." Kathy frowned at that comment. "Getting married and then coming back here. Her parents are depending on her to take over their firm."

From day one Kathy didn't like Campbell and Chloe together. She thought Chloe was too "fast" for Campbell.

She had a lot of influence over him. She was a good kid from a great family, but in Kathy's opinion she was just too much for Campbell. And exactly what Kathy had been afraid of had happened—not their having a baby—she never thought that—but that he would be "all in" and his life's trajectory would change because of his relationship with her. Kathy also knew it was her idea to approach Enoch and Kirby Casebier about adopting Chloe and Campbell's baby, and she felt somewhat responsible.

They talked a few more minutes and Kathy finally told Campbell, "I am going to call Kirby and see what I can do."

"Ms. Robinson, I hope you can convince her that Chloe didn't mean any harm."

"I don't know if I can convince her of that because I don't know if I believe it, but maybe I can get her to re-think prosecution."

Coupled with the Dr. Gasquet situation, the information Campbell gave Kathy added to her stress level. She wanted to go home. She wanted to see her parents and she wanted to see Sterling. She still wasn't sure that she wanted to be in a relationship with him. Her priority was still to earn a Ph.D., but she at least wanted to hear what he had to say. The night he told her he lied about dating someone and told her he loved her, they didn't finish their conversation. She was so upset about her situation at school that was what they ended up talking about.

It appeared that Dr. Gasquet wasn't going down without a fight. He hired an attorney who told Kathy's attorney and the Columbia University attorney that Kathy initiated a relationship with him and was a willing participant until she didn't get what she wanted. He way lying, and trying to buy time. What he didn't understand was who he was dealing with. Bishop Robinson told their attorney to get to the bottom of the situation and do it quickly. "My daughter has been distracted with this long enough." He wasn't a ruthless man but he was resourceful and he kept people in arm's reach who could be ruthless. "I want Gasquet fired and away from my daughter," Bishop Robinson said to the attorney.

When Kathy met with the attorney her father hired for her she was quite amused. He was not the guy she expected; obviously bright but not her father's "type".

"Ms. Robinson…"

"You can call me Kathy," she said.

"Thank you, Kathy. Did you ever sleep with Dr. Gasquet?"

"No! Absolutely not! Let's get this straight, I am a virgin and will be until I'm married. Dr. Gasquet sexually harassed me and I want him fired!"

That was the fire he was looking for. "Consider it handled," was all the attorney said in response to her statement. But he thought to himself, "a virgin."

Kathy showed him the email Dr. Gasquet sent inviting her to meet him at the conference.

"He's dumb and stupid," the attorney thought.

"Will you need to see me again in the next few days?" she asked.

"No, I think this can be handled without us meeting again."

"I am going home for a few days, but you can call me if you need to."

Kathy went back to her apartment, made a reservation for the next morning, and then started to get things organized with her study group. A couple of hours later she packed a bag and went to bed.

$\mathscr{S}$IXTY-NINE

The Casebier Collection Company office was busy. Kirby was grateful that their business continued to grow, but she had to convince Enoch they needed to hire one more person. She worked the hours that Nicholas and Blake were in school and Aunt Avis helped with the boys after school and on school breaks. But Kirby was determined to be their mother.

When the phone rang she didn't look at the caller id, she just answered.

"Kirby, this is Sandra Matthews." There was silence on the line for a few seconds.

"How may I assist you Mrs. Matthews?"

"Are you free to talk for a moment?"

A few more seconds of silence. "Let me go to another office, hold just a moment please." Kirby went to Enoch's office and closed the door. She took a deep breath and picked up the phone. "Yes Sandra."

"Kirby, I'll get right to the point," Sandra said.

"Please do."

"I hope you will take a moment and reconsider the charges you are bringing against Chloe."

"Why would I do that Sandra?" Kirby asked calmly.

Sandra chose her words carefully. "Chloe made a bad decision. She is not a criminal, she is not malicious, and she is not a bad person. Please allow her an opportunity to get some help and have a future."

"Did she tell you about our encounter at the restaurant?"

Sandra sighed. "Yes, she told me."

"Well, she had a chance to go on with her life until then."

"Another bad decision," Sandra said.

"How many bad decisions does she get to make before she has to deal with the results?"

Sandra didn't answer immediately. She didn't really have an answer.

"I know how you feel…"

Kirby's laughter interrupted Sandra. "No you don't. You don't know how it feels to have your children taken, you don't know where they are, how they are, when or if they're coming back."

"I was worried about your boys and Chloe."

"Sandra, you're not helping your case. Chloe is an adult, my boys are barely five years old. She was calling the shots, she made all the decisions; they were helpless in that situation."

As Kirby was talking the office door opened, and Enoch walked in. It didn't take him long to realize she was talking to Sandra. "Babe, our lawyer said we should not talk with them," he said. Enoch said it loud enough for Sandra to hear his voice. She didn't know exactly what he said but she wasn't getting anywhere with Kirby, and Enoch being there wasn't going to help.

"Sandra, is there anything else?" Kirby asked a little sarcastically.

"I want to help my daughter, I hope as a mother you can understand that," Sandra said.

"Oh absolutely, I understand perfectly, and like you I want to help my sons; help them stay away from your daughter."

Enoch asked Kirby one question about a client. She answered him and then he sat down in the chair in front of his desk. She reiterated the conversation with Sandra, and then Enoch told Kirby about the conversation with their attorney. "So are you asking if I want to drop the charges? No I don't!"

"I'm not asking that at all. I think we should see it through. I just don't want you to be surprised if it doesn't go the way we want it to." Before Kirby could respond Enoch made another comment. "Do you really want Chloe to go to jail? Does that serve any purpose?"

"I want Chloe to learn a lesson. I want her to have a real world experience. There is a reaction to every action and I just don't think Chloe has ever had to own her mess!"

"But why is that our responsibility?" Enoch asked.

" 'Cause she crossed me! The minute she drove off with my boys, making her pay became my responsibility!" Kirby was leaning across the desk pointing her finger at Enoch. He was surprised to see her act like that. "When do we go to court?" Kirby asked him, changing the tone of her voice.

"I don't know yet. They are going to do the psych evaluation first, maybe have a hearing on that. The lawyer said for us to go on with our lives, he'll call us."

Kirby smiled and said "okay!"

$\mathscr{S}$EVENTY

Grant lay the mail on the kitchen counter as he walked over to the stove. He peeped in the pot with the vegetables, then kissed Sunny on the cheek. She didn't respond. As they ate Grant wanted to talk about their counseling. Sunny didn't but she obliged him. "Do what you gotta do" she said to herself. As Grant talked, Sunny was thinking he recalled everything the counselor said and every response they had. She was amazed at how into this he was. He was really serious about the counseling.

She turned her attention back to him just as he asked her would she be okay not to have a wedding and eloping. She didn't know where that questions came from. The counselor hadn't asked that; at least not that she remembered. The question caught her off guard, but it also made her angry. She was tired of pretending so she answered him truthfully. "No Grant! No, I will not be okay with eloping. I want to have a wedding. I deserve to have a wedding." Her voice went up an octave and she was speaking loudly.

"And you are still making plans based on our original date, even though I asked you not to!" Sunny was stunned. She had covered her tracks so the only way he would know that was her mother telling him. She didn't recover quickly enough. "I take your silence as an acknowledgement that I'm right." Grant said seriously. Sunny rested her elbows on her thighs, with her hands clasped together and her index fingers to her lips. She was looking directly into Grant's eyes.

"The email receipt came for the payment on the honeymoon. Did you forget it was on my credit card?"

She had forgotten. Everything else was being handled from a joint account. How had she forgotten that? She still hadn't responded. Grant sat back but didn't take his eyes off her. She took a deep breath, got up and walked over to the counter where he had laid the mail. She flipped through it and saw a peach colored envelope addressed to her and Grant. She opened it. It was a letter from Cicely and Clay. Grant was watching her as she read. Her eyes were getting wider. She dropped the envelope. He picked it up and saw the return address. "Did you know about this?" She screamed.

"Know about what?

"Cicely and Clay are married!"

She threw the letter at him. He picked it up, read the short letter and looked up at Sunny with a smile on his face. "This dude has the nerve to say don't call him! My man!" Grant laughed.

"Do you think that's funny?" Sunny said squinting and frowning. Grant didn't immediately respond. "Why are they married and we're not?" Sunny was still screaming. "They broke up, she left town, she came back, they got back together, now they are married and in Hawaii! What the hell? I bet they didn't go through any freakin' counseling." Sunny's accent had kicked in and she was talking fast. She ranted, raved, cursed and cried. Grant just watched her for a few minutes. Then the truth came out in the midst of the rant. "And Cicely didn't have to tell her friends her wedding date changed because her fiancé doesn't trust her. There's no way she should be married before me!"

She finally realized Grant wasn't saying anything. He was leaning forward in his seat. His elbows rested right

226

above his knees. His chin rested on his fists. He was looking up at her. His face was expressionless. At that moment he wasn't sure what to do or say. His dream had turned into a nightmare. He had to face his reality. That reality being Sunny wanted a wedding. She wanted to impress her friends and she wanted that more than she wanted a marriage. He stood, cleared his throat, picked up the letter and walked to the door.

"Grant! Where are you going?" He looked over his shoulder as he walked away.

$\mathscr{S}$EVENTY-ONE

"I'm taking the day off and I think I'm keeping LaLa at home today, you know, a daddy daughter day."

"Oh, you decide to hang out on the day I can't take off with you!"

Raja shrugged his shoulders and laughed. They talked about some other things and then Jill asked about his mother. "So dear husband, what do you plan to do with your mother on this daddy daughter day?"

"I guess she can hang out with us but she will need to keep up."

Raja and Jill went to LaLa's room but she wasn't there. She was in the kitchen sitting on her grandmother's lap and having breakfast. She lost interest in the food when she saw her parents.

"You must finish your breakfast Leah." Mrs. Rajagopal said. LaLa ignored her and reached for her dad. "I wanted her to eat before you came in."

"It's okay Mother, I'm keeping her home today."

Raja and LaLa played for a while and he did get her to eat a little more. They went downstairs to see if his mother wanted to go to the park with them. She smiled. "I have plans. I am meeting a friend for lunch."

"Good for you. I'm glad you're getting out." Raja said.

"I have said no several times but she insisted this time." his mother said.
"Do you want me to drop you off somewhere?"

"Yes, thank you, that will be nice, then I won't have to leave so early."

Raja dropped his mother off at a small café and he and LaLa headed to the waterpark. On the way home, the hospital in Chapel Hill called. They wanted Raja to come up for an emergency surgery. "Not today" he groaned to himself. He had to think fast. He called his mother's cell phone but she didn't answer. He went back to the café but she wasn't there any longer. He knew if she was home she wouldn't answer their landline. He drove home. If she wasn't there he would take LaLa to Jill's mom. About five minutes after he got home, he heard a car - it was his mother. He quickly told her the situation and left. He would call Jill when he was on the road.

LaLa was asleep. Mrs. Rajagopal hoped she would awaken in time for them to go back out for a short errand. Jill wasn't happy with Raja's decision but she didn't tell him that. There wasn't much she could do. She was his mother.

After a snack and some clean clothes, Mrs. Rajagopal put LaLa in her stroller and left the house. It was a nice day, the weather was comfortable, and so she decided to walk. The library was only three blocks away, and LaLa liked seeing the ducks by the lake.

Jill's day was productive but very hectic, and now Raja was in Chapel Hill and probably wouldn't be back until tomorrow. She engaged her phone and called Raja's cousin Tara. They talked a few minutes and Jill was home. Tara always made Jill laugh. As she walked in she shook her head and smiled thinking about what Tara said. "Hello, anybody here? LaLa!" The house was quiet. Jill went downstairs to Mrs. Rajagopal's suite. Her mother-in-law had been living with them for months but she still felt uncomfortable around her and she still didn't trust her. The worst part, she couldn't think of what to call her. Usually she didn't say anything, just started a conversation, the few instances that they talked. When she reached the bottom step she felt something was wrong. "LaLa, Dadi!" she called. The silence was huge. Jill's heart dropped. "Oh my God!" She screamed. "She took LaLa. My baby is gone!" Jill was walking around in circles. She couldn't think. Finally she took out her phone and called Mrs. Rajagopal's mobile number. It went straight to voice mail. Jill started to cry and her hands were shaking. She didn't know whether to call Raja, call Tara back, or call the police. She decided to call the police. She got nowhere with them. The child was with her grandmother and they had been away for a few hours. Jill told the officer Mrs. Rajagopal had threatened to kidnap her. He asked all the obvious questions, but finally told Jill she should wait a few hours and call them back. She called Raja and got his voice mail. She left a frantic message for him to call her.

She called Tara. "What? Jill you can't be serious! Surely to God she didn't kidnap LaLa. There has to be an explanation." Tara asked sensible questions. "Are there clothes missing? Are there toys missing?" Jill had not looked around.

"No, the clothes and toys are here but if she wanted to get away quickly she didn't have time to get those things!"

"Jill! Do you hear yourself?"

230

"Her rabbit isn't here and her cup is gone!" Jill said.

"Of course it is. She doesn't go anywhere without that rabbit and if they went for a walk, Auntie probably took the cup! Please calm down!"

It had not occurred to Jill they could be out just for a walk. The phone beeped. It was Raja. She told Tara she would call her back. "What's wrong honey?" Jill told him she thought his mother had taken LaLa. "I'm sure you're wrong. Get in the car and ride toward the lake." Raja said calmly. She walked out the door with Raja still on the phone. She was almost running. She didn't get the car, she started walking. She didn't make it to the lake when she saw Mrs. Rajagopal pushing the stroller a block from the house. LaLa was fine, kicking her legs and obviously enjoying the ride.

"I see them," Jill said breathing hard.

"Sweetheart, please calm down, and you know what; you need to have a talk with my mother. I'll be back late tonight and if you two haven't talked, the three of us will."

Mrs. Rajagopal and LaLa approached Jill, not knowing anything was wrong. "Oh, hello Jillian."

"Hi", was all Jill said. She stooped to kiss LaLa and get a good look at her. Everything was fine. Jill took a deep breath, and took over pushing the stroller. "I looked for a note or something when I got home to see where you were."

"Oh my, I went to the library for some books, not knowing there was a puppet show. Of course I couldn't get Leah away from there until they finished. I intended to be back before you were home," Mrs. Rajagopal answered politely.

Jill took another deep breath. "I called your mobile phone and the call went to voice mail. You should keep it on."

"I am still not accustomed to carrying it. I think it is in my bedroom, I will try to remember."

They reached the house and LaLa held out her arms for her mother to pick her up. Jill lifted her out of the stroller and hugged her tightly, while Mrs. Rajagopal brought it up the steps. Jill realized in her haste she didn't lock the front door.

Jill took LaLa to her room, and Mrs. Rajagopal went downstairs. A few minutes later they were both in the kitchen. "I know she's hungry," Mrs. Rajagopal said. It's a good thing I prepared a meal before we left." Jill felt bad, but she tried to justify being angry in her own mind. But she had to fix this before Raja came home.

$\mathscr{S}$EVENTY-TWO

In all the years Belinda had known Grammy this was the first time she knew of that Grammy had slept late. Something had to be wrong. She didn't draw any attention to it while Ben and the girls were there, but as soon as they left she went to Grammy's room and knocked on the door. There was no answer. When there was no answer the second time, Belinda opened the door slowly. "Gram, Gram." She was in the bathroom. She pushed the door open slightly, she was leaning on the counter. "Gram, what is it?"

"Just a stomach virus, but I feel bad."

Belinda put her had on Grammy's arm, she was clammy and obviously had a fever. "Can you get some clothes on? I'm taking you to the doctor." Belinda knew she was sick when she didn't protest. They left the boys with Thelma. "If Ben comes home for some reason, just tell him Grammy and I are shopping."

By the time they arrived at the doctor, Grammy was really sick. Belinda had to get a wheelchair to get her in the office. "Mrs. Coffey, I think we have something going on here other than a virus. I want to admit you to the hospital," the doctor said.
Grammy interrupted him. "Hospital! I have too much to do…"

Belinda interrupted her. "Grammy, there is nothing more important than your health." Belinda turned her attention to the doctor who gave her some instructions.

"No sir, I am not going by ambulance. Belinda can take me in the car," Grammy said as she rubbed her head. Her eyes were closed.

The doctor agreed she could go by car but they had to go directly there. Once they were in the car Belinda called home to check on the boys and update Thelma. Everything was under control there. Thelma said she would call the school, and leave a message for the girls to walk home. Next Belinda called Ben. She knew he was in a meeting, but he would be angry if she didn't call. Her message simply said call her cell phone.

As the time passed Belinda was nervous. If something was really wrong with Grammy, if she really was sick, Ben would not do well. He was still puzzled why she gave him the hundred thousand dollars the year before with no explanation. He thought she was hiding something. Just as the thought cleared her head, he walked in. "Hey babe, any news?" he asked, hugging her.

"No, they're still running tests."

"You wouldn't hide anything from me would you?" Ben asked seriously.

"No I wouldn't. I promise. I don't know any more than I told you on the phone."

"Do you need to go home and feed the boys?"

"No there's milk there. I want to hear what the doctor has to say." Belinda sounded serious. "I called the nurse so Thelma has an additional set of hands." Ben laughed.

"You didn't want Hampton to hire the nurse but you sure are using her."

"Well, he insisted! I don't want him to waste his money! On another note, I think you should call Auntie" Belinda said to Ben.

"Don't we need to have something to tell her?"

"Maybe we should prepare her, just in case."

Ben sighed heavily, but he knew his wife was right. He called right then before he had a chance to talk himself out of it.

"How long has this episode been going on?" Aunt Avis asked.

"Belinda found her sick this morning. What do you mean 'this episode'?" Ben asked, looking at Belinda.

"Honey, she was sick about a month ago and she was sick when she was here the last time with the same symptoms. I told her the second time it wasn't a virus."

"Auntie, why didn't you tell me?" Ben asked.

"Sugar, I trusted my sister to tell you because she said she would."

Ben was shaking his head and rubbing his hands across his chin. Belinda took the phone from Ben. "Aunt Avis, does Grammy have any health history we may not know about?"

"No, she's healthy, never really been sick," Aunt Avis replied confidently.

"That's good, really good."

Auntie changed the subject to ask about the children. As they talked, the doctor came in.

"Mrs. Coffey will be back up soon, but here's where we are" the doctor said. "We ran a battery of tests, including checking her liver function, kidney function and we are doing a colonoscopy now and the CA125."

"What are you looking for, doctor?" Belinda said. The two of them proceeded to discuss the tests, but Ben was just standing there. Finally he interrupted them. "What kind of test is the CA125? What does that mean?"

Belinda swallowed hard before she answered him. "He's taking a precaution to see if there is any type of cancer." Nobody said anything for a few seconds.

Aunt Avis was still on the phone and listening to the conversation on the speaker. She spoke first. "By precautionary you mean to rule out cancer?"

"Yes ma'am." The doctor answered.

Ben didn't realize he was holding his breath until he exhaled.

$\mathscr{S}$EVENTY-THREE

Today was the first day in many days, actually weeks that Min had not communicated with the doctor. She attempted to reach him earlier in the day but he hadn't responded. She sat down with a magazine but couldn't concentrate. "Where is he?" she thought to herself. "Why hasn't he called me? He knows we talk every day."

The third day she hadn't heard from him, Min called the office, and left a message for him to call her. An hour or so later, she got a call from another physician's assistant asking how she could help. Min was caught a little off guard and she hesitated before she spoke. "Dr. Ryan has been helping me with my continual care after an exacerbation of my Multiple Sclerosis."

"Yes ma'am I have your records in front of me. Is there something new or different that has occurred?" the P.A. asked.

"No, I just needed to ask about some supplements he suggested I get." Min was not telling the truth.

"Mrs. Baye I don't see any notation of that in the file."

"Oh that's okay. I will just wait until he is back in the office."

"He's on vacation and won't be back for a couple more weeks. If you need anything please let me know."

When they hung up, Min experienced a gamut of emotions. She was embarrassed, angry, puzzled and jealous. "Why would he be away for so long without telling me and I wonder who he's with," Min thought. "I know that lady is wondering why I didn't tell her any more than I did." Minutes passed and Min said aloud, "I am very angry with him." She thought over and over what to do. Finally she got online, went to the website and booked the first available appointment.

Things were more strained now than they previously were between Jackson and Min since the night Anderson and Jacksa witnessed what they determined to be the aftermath of Jackson hitting Min. He knew that she knew he did not hit her but she had not told the truth. She let their daughter, her FBI agent boyfriend and most likely their son think he was crazy again.

The night of the incident when Jackson left the house, he drove to her house - the woman with whom he had the affair and ended up in this situation. He turned into the cul-de-sac, slowed down a few feet from her driveway, and then thought better of what he was going to do and kept driving. He drove back to Hattiesville to a Waffle House where he sat for two hours before going home.

As Jackson sat drinking a cup of coffee and waiting on his waffle, he realized what he almost did. "Why was that my reaction?" He thought to himself. "I was about to make a bad situation worse. Plus, what makes me think I could just show up there, uninvited and unannounced after all these months?" he chuckled to himself, shaking his head.

Anderson knew Jacksa was affected by her parents' situation. She had only briefly spoken to her dad, and her brother said he believed him. JJ said in spite of everything else, he didn't believe for one minute Jackson hit Min. Jacksa didn't know what to believe. Although Anderson had been instrumental in defusing the situation, in a calm moment he pointed out to Jacksa that Min didn't ever say her husband hit her. She didn't really say anything. Anderson wanted Jacksa to let her parents work out their situation. He wanted them to work on their relationship.

The ring was in the safe deposit box. He was trying to plan something special to ask her to marry him. His sisters told him that an engagement needed to be its own occasion, and he shouldn't propose on a holiday or for her birthday. "What if I ask her on my birthday?" he asked. His mother and aunt said yes, his sisters said no!

Honey didn't offer any advice about the timing of the proposal. She only said they shouldn't spend a lot of money on a wedding. In a private moment away from the rest of the family, Honey told Anderson to "stay out of Jacksa's family business. I know you love her, but blood is thicker than water. You don't want to say something that you have to defend later or worse, you regret."

He didn't tell Honey she was right. Jacksa said to him at one point, "let me handle this." Honey also told him that the dynamics between a husband and wife cannot be explained by other people. "Your granddaddy and I would have a disagreement and five minutes later we would be laughing about something. That's just how it is."

$\mathscr{S}$EVENTY-FOUR

Hawaii was amazing, and Cicely was having the time of her life. Clay left no stone unturned. Their days were filled with beautiful sites, great food and excursions. Their nights were quiet and intimate.

They flew into Honolulu, spent a couple of days there, then on to Oahu, and then were on their way to Maui where they would be for four days before heading home. Cicely had no idea how much money Clay spent, he only told her he added a year to his retirement date. She was absolutely impressed with how he pulled all this off in such a short window of time. "Your husband has skills, girl!" She loved the sound of him saying "husband."

On the flights they talked. She told him about running into Jeremy and Javier and about her conversation with Javier. "He encouraged me to forgive you. Things were really tough between him and Delia for a while, but they worked it out and they should be married by now."

"So I have Javier to thank for you coming back," Clay said sarcastically.

"No, I admit I gave a lot of thought to what he said, but I can back to Hattiesville because I needed to go back to work. I came back to you because I love you, I missed you and I wanted to be your wife."

When Grant was in his car he sat for a few minutes, and thought about the scene with Sunny. She was jealous because Clay and Cicely got married first and had a meltdown. She also lied to her mother about the counseling. "Sunny has no respect for me. I cannot marry a woman who will lie and disrespect me," Grant said out loud. Just as he started the car, his phone rang. It was his mother's number. "Hey Mama."

"It's me G! Did you get a letter from Clay?" It was Gretchen calling from their mother's phone. Grant laughed. "Yep, just read it a few minutes ago."

"I haven't been home, I read Mama and Daddy's! Can you believe they eloped?" Gretchen asked.

"Sure, I believe it. Works for me!" Grant answered.

"What do you mean it works for you? Sunny is planning a big wedding and you're okay with that. You're not eloping!"

"Maybe not, but I'll talk to you about that when you're not at Mama's house," Grant said to his sister sadly. "What did Pop and Ma say?" Grant asked, laughing.

"Pop laughed and of course Ma is crying."

"Crying for what?" Grant asked.

"She can't believe he didn't tell her, she wanted to be there." Gretchen was mocking her mother. "Aunt Millie and Uncle Clayton would be so proud 'cause Cicely is so sweet…blah, blah, blah!" Grant and Gretchen were laughing loudly.

He spoke with each of his parents for a few minutes. By the time he hung up he had completely forgotten about the situation with Sunny. He got a beer from the refrigerator, turned the television on Sports Center and sat on the sofa. He was surprised Sunny hadn't called. He laughed out loud

241

thinking about Clay. "He did the thing!" Grant laughed again. He groaned when he heard his phone. He expected it was Sunny, but it was Gretchen.

They began their conversation laughing again about Cicely and Clay. Gretchen told him that her letter included a copy of their itinerary and a check to get started on a reception. "I think we should call them!" Gretchen said. "You know Clay is expecting me to call. I never follow directions."

"Don't call GG, let them be! Just plan the reception, you can have your time with him when they get back."

"Well, I'll see! Now, tell me why you said you may be eloping." Gretchen said seriously.

Grant sighed loudly and didn't immediately respond. Finally he said, "I'm not thinking about eloping. I'm thinking about not getting married."

Gretchen swallowed hard. "Why G, what happened?" He took a deep breath and started at the beginning. Gretchen didn't say much, just listened intently. "She went crazy when she read the letter. It's like she's competing with her friends and now Cicely. If you had seen her you wouldn't believe how she was acting," Grant said shaking his head. "GG I am so disappointed."

"I can't even imagine how you feel, but what I know for sure, marriage is forever. As Bishop Robinson always says, 'she will be the same person on the other side of the altar as she is on this side'. Don't do it unless you are absolutely sure. I do think you two should continue your counseling," Gretchen said.

"Why, what's the point?" Grant asked.

"You want to know in your heart of hearts you did everything you could to make it work."

"Yeah, I get that."

"Be transparent, be honest, and at the end of the day if you and Sunny decided it's not the thing to do, your conscious will be clear," Gretchen said evenly. She was stifling her emotions. She was angry at Sunny and hurting for Grant. He had endured enough hurt, and she just didn't know how he would bounce back from another heartbreak. They talked a few minutes more and Grant assured her he was fine. "Okay, call me tomorrow, love you Grant."

"Love you sis."

About the time Grant dozed off, Sunny called. He didn't answer.

$\mathscr{S}$EVENTY-FIVE

When Kathy's flight landed, she had a text from the attorney to call him when she had a few minutes to talk. She would call him later. She texted her mother who was waiting in the cell phone lot. Her priority at the moment was going home to see her parents and Sterling.

Katherine was excited that her baby daughter, now her only daughter, her only child, was coming home. She knew it was just for a few days but she was glad just the same. She missed Leah terribly and Kathy being so far away in school made it worse. Katherine filled her days with her work at the church and her work with the Board of DavisTown College but she had a need, a desire to nurture. She wanted grandchildren and really hoped Sterling could convince Kathy to come home and finish school there so they could get married.

Sterling was meeting with a recruit and his parents when he felt his phone vibrate at his side. It was Kathy texting to let him know she was headed home. He wanted to pick her up but he couldn't afford to miss this appointment. He needed to sign this kid for next season.

Once Kathy and Katherine were home and Kathy was settled she called the attorney. "I have noteworthy news."

"'Noteworthy', that's a curious term," Kathy responded to him.

He chuckled. "Dr. Gasquet's attorney says that he will resign if we agree not to press charges."

Now Kathy laughed. "Are you kidding me, so he can go to another school and sexually harass someone else? No way! I want to press charges, I want him fired, not given a chance to resign, and I want him to face the judicial system!"

"Kathy, chances are he won't go to trial but the police record and bad press should keep him from getting another job in this country."

"What do you mean?" Kathy asked.

"That's the noteworthy part; Dr. Gasquet is not a citizen. He's here on a work visa, so we will ask that his privileges be revoked and he will have to go back to France."

"That works for me," Kathy said smiling. "I will tell my dad and see if he advises me to do anything else." Kathy thanked the attorney, glad to have this behind her for now. Her priority at the moment was talking to Sterling.

As soon as the recruit Sterling met with left, he headed to the Robinson's home. When he arrived Katherine greeted him at the door with a hug. She whispered in his ear, "Lee wants the four of us to go to dinner. You should tell him you made plans and I will back you up."

"Got it," Sterling said.

Like clockwork, Lee suggested dinner and Sterling said he made reservations for himself and Kathy.
"They need to talk," Katherine said, looking at Lee.

He didn't protest, but he wasn't exactly happy. Katherine thought to herself that he was clueless about what was going on.

A few minutes later, Sterling and Kathy were in his car. It was an awkward moment. "I don't have dinner reservations" Sterling finally said.

"Why did you…"
He interrupted her, "I want us to talk without an audience. Cards on the table Kathy. We need to make some decisions. When you leave here to go back to New York we will be a couple…or not."
Kathy relaxed a little. She thought he was going to say something about marriage.

As he turned into the parking lot of a barbeque restaurant, Kathy finally spoke. "We have a lot of territory to cover, we need to start at the beginning. I don't know that by the time I leave we can make that kind of decision."

"Kathy Robinson, we are going to settle some things if we have to say up all night."

Now that Kathy was home and had to face the music, she was scared. She missed him when she was away, but now she didn't want Sterling to press her about their relationship.

SEVENTY-SIX

When the doctor came in, Belinda was waiting by herself. Ben had gone to get his phone charger from the car.

"Belinda, Mrs. Coffey's test results are back. Let me put your mind at ease. The CA125 was negative for any type of cancer."

Belinda closed her eyes, blew out a long breathe and said "Thank you God."

The doctor continued. "Her liver and kidneys are fine too."

Belinda was starting to feel relived until he said "but".

"Her gallbladder is diseased. There are so many gall stones, there is no way to remove them all. It looks like somebody sprinkled salt over it."

Belinda had seen many diseased gallbladders in her career, but that was an unusual description. And it didn't sound good at all. "So the gallbladder will have to be removed," she said.

"Yes. I've scheduled the surgery for first thing in the morning."

"Okay. Is she awake, does she know?" Before the doctor could answer, Ben walked in. His eyes widened when he saw the doctor. "It's okay sweetie, I'll fill you in," Belinda said putting her arms around his waist.

The doctor continued. "No, she's in recovery from the tests. I gave her a mild sedative, she was nauseous. I will tell her when she awakens."

"Will you let me tell her?" Belinda asked, looking at Ben and smiling.

"I don't have a problem with that."

"Please have her brought up here when she is awake. I'll handle giving her the news."

Ben was quiet, looking from his wife to the doctor and back. As the doctor left the room Belinda told Ben everything he said. Ben looked relieved, but before he said anything Belinda looked at him seriously. "I have no reason to think anything will go wrong but there are risks with any surgery and anytime there is anesthesia involved."

"The good thing is she's otherwise healthy." Ben said, smiling.

"Use my phone to call Auntie." She gave him her phone and took his to plug it in. She needed a moment out of his sight. She was grateful not to have to tell him anything more serious.

Grammy's surgery went well, and she was discharged the next day. Belinda didn't say anything but she was a little bit overwhelmed and Grammy was going to need some help for a little bit, the girls had their schedules and then there was Bryce and Bradley who were growing so fast. She couldn't ask Auntie to come to Landridge because that would leave Kirby without any help, especially now that she didn't trust Natalia any longer. Thelma would help, they would just have to work it out. She had two surgeries scheduled for the week that would have to go to someone else. "My family first," she said aloud.

248

No sooner than the thought went through her head, her phone rang. It was Hampton. "Hello," she said in a friendly tone.

"Hey sweetheart, how are you?"

"I'm okay. How are you?"

"I'm good. Why just okay?" Hampton asked, sounding sincere. For whatever reason, Belinda shared with Hampton the things that were going on in her life. He listened attentively.

"Honey, do you want me to send the nurse back or help with Britt and Bree?"

Belinda laughed to herself, thinking about Brianna saying 'he acts like he knows us'. "I don't think the nurse is necessary, but some transportation help for them would be great!" She couldn't believe she was doing this, especially without talking to the girls.

"Have one of them text me their schedule for the next few days and I'll work it out," Hampton said.

"I will," she said. Then asked, "What's going on in your world?"

"I played in the police chief's golf tournament this morning."

"How did you do?" She asked, relaxing a bit.

"Did alright, my team came in second, behind a group of twenty-somethings, so I feel pretty good." They both laughed.

"Ben keeps saying he wants to play..."

"That's no problem, I can get him out there anytime, just let me know."

They talked about five minutes more and Belinda said she needed to go and call the girls. As they were saying their good-byes, Hampton said what he always said; "you need to call your sister."

SEVENTY-SEVEN

The conversation Raja forced Jill and his mother to have yielded major results. Jill and Mrs. Rajagopal were much more forthcoming than he expected. Mrs. Rajagopal admitted to Jill she didn't want Raja to marry her because she is an American. "He defied us and embarrassed his family," she said.

Jill confronted her about wanting to kidnap LaLa. "I knew if I took the baby he would come back to me." At the end of the day the air was clear. They did not promise to be friends, but they did promise to live cordially for Raja and LaLa's sake.

So far it was working. Jill was busy at work and Mrs. Rajagopal was cooking almost daily and caring for LaLa. She would walk or ride the bus the mile to pick her up from pre-school. Jill admitted to her mother it was working and "Dadi" was a lot of help.

Raja was pleased he didn't have to feel like he was walking on egg shells with Jill or his mother. Now he and Jill could get back to discussing having another baby.

SEVENTY-EIGHT

Min was anxious to see the doctor. She wanted an explanation for why he hadn't continued to correspond with her. Jackson offered to go to the doctor with her but she declined. Things were still tense between them, and for his best efforts, Min was not giving in, she just wasn't interested in reconciling with him.

The nurse escorted Min to an exam room and went through the routine procedure. The last thing, she sent Min to the lab to give some blood.

When she was done in the lab, an assistant walked her to the doctor's small office.

"Good morning Min, how are you today?

"Hello, I'm well, how are you?" she answered cheerfully.

As he sat behind his desk, her eyes landed on his hand. He was wearing a ring she hadn't noticed before now; a wedding band. Her heart jumped into her throat. She swallowed hard. He was looking at notes on the computer. "Everything looks good here, tell me what's going on." He looked away from the computer and directly at Min.

"I'm perfectly fine. I made the appointment because I couldn't get in touch with you. I called and emailed you and you didn't answer." He frowned. She continued. "We were communicating every day and then you just dropped off the earth!" There was a moment of silence. Min was waiting for him to respond as he was trying to decide what to say.

Dr. Ryan spoke. "Min, this appointment is inappropriate if you aren't sick."

Now she frowned. She couldn't believe he was being this way with her.

"First, I was out of the office and I see that you were told that."

She interrupted him. "Did you get my messages?"

"Yes, when I got back."

"They were giving me the run around."

"Min, nobody gave you the run around. The staff followed protocol. My personal time off is not for public knowledge."

"Public knowledge" she said shifting in her seat. "I'm not the public, we're friends."

"We are acquaintances, we haven't known each other long enough, nor do we know each other well enough to consider ourselves friends." The expression on her face told him she was surprised he said that.

"You were calling every day, checking on me and talking to me about my problems with Jackson."

"Part of the treatment is to make sure you are free of stress. I apologize if I crossed the line, but my intention was to help you through the tension so you can get better physically."

Min and Dr. Ryan debated the nature of their relationship and slowly the reality set in. "Think about this," he said to her. "Jackson had an affair. He got caught up in a situation that probably started just like with us, talking, communicating every day, then one thing leads to another and the rest is history. In your mind that's where we were headed." The tone of his voice was firm but not accusing.

"The difference is, you are not married and my marriage is in name only. Jackson was a married man when he got involved with another woman," Min said.

"I am married. We were celebrating our thirtieth anniversary while I was on vacation last week."

She was quiet but she knew he was right. She wanted, needed and enjoyed his attention, but didn't understand that she was really living in a fantasy. Dr. Ryan's comments stung. She didn't know what to say, she didn't have a comeback. He was married. Was he right? Just like Jackson, he wanted a woman who could respond to him physically. "I guess congratulations are in order then."

"Thank you Min."

"Under the circumstances I think you should transfer me to another doctor."

"I don't think that's necessary, I think you're ready to be discharged."

She smiled. "Yes I think so too."

Min left the doctor's office with a myriad of emotions but the bottom line was that she had a decision to make. What would she do about her marriage?

$\mathscr{S}$EVENTY-NINE

Days became weeks and one day when Enoch was not expecting it, the attorney called. He wanted to meet and discuss the disposition of the case with Chloe Matthews. "I need to prepare my wife, can you give me anything over the phone?" Enoch asked the attorney.

"I don't have the full disclosure, but according to what I do know, the psychiatrist says Chloe is suffering from PTSD."

Enoch didn't saying anything to Kirby until after they put the boys to bed. They were relaxed on the sofa, talking and enjoying each other's company. He eased into the conversation. "Are you freakin' kidding me? PTSD! That's a likely story, but I guess it makes a good defense!" Kirby said. She was quiet for a moment. Then she looked at Enoch sadly, "Do you think they are going to try to take Nicholas from us?" Tears rolled down her cheeks as she asked the question. Enoch pulled his wife into his arms and held her tight. She looked up at him and he kissed her forehead.

"Baby, Nicholas is our son. You are his mother. I promise you nobody, nobody is going to take him away from us, and you know I don't make promises I can't keep."

Roderick Matthews received the call from his attorney who had more information than Enoch's attorney had. "Chloe has been diagnosed with Post Traumatic Stress Disorder, the attorney told Roderick.

"That works to our advantage," Roderick replied.

"On one hand; in terms of her not getting jail time, but not to our advantage with Chloe getting custody of the child."

"I know Chloe told you to file for custody, and I know she thinks that's what she wants, but Sandra and I want her to go back to school, go to law school and not concern herself with raising a child right now. Nicholas is four years old and he probably won't adjust well in a new environment, away from the parents he knows and his brother."

"You just made the prosecution's case."

Roderick didn't respond "What you need to remember Rod, I represent Chloe. She's an adult and she can tell me what she wants. If she directs me to pursue custody I will. I have to."

"What you need to remember is, I'm paying you."

The attorney didn't respond.

Roderick called Campbell and asked him to come to his office. "We need to discuss some things," he told him. When Campbell arrived at the office, Roderick got right to the point. He told Campbell about his conversation with the attorney.

Campbell told Roderick he agreed that filing for custody "is not the right thing to do." Campbell went on to tell Roderick about some previous conversations he had with Chloe. He told him that Chloe was doing research on getting custody and he knew on several occasions she went to the school to watch Nicholas on the playground.

Roderick let out a big sigh. "Campbell, please don't tell anybody about these incidents. If they find out, the

256

prosecution can make a case for premediated kidnaping. That will land her in jail for sure."

After Campbell and Roderick talked he called home. "Hey doll, how are you? Is Chloe home?"

"Yes, she's here. Why?" Sandra asked, shrugging her shoulders.

"Campbell and I are on our way for dinner!" Roderick said and Sandra laughed.

She was amused that Roderick and Campbell were together. But she had the presence of mind to know Roderick had a plan.

"Okay, I will call Lola's and order the food, you pick it up."

"That's good. Order me pork chops and okra, Campbell wants barbeque chicken and collards and we want corn bread, no biscuits."

The four of them had dinner and then Roderick eased into the conversation about the information from the attorney. He was very firm with Chloe and Sandra. They had to understand their options were limited. If Chloe wanted to stay out of jail, if she wanted to go back to Spelman and on to law school, she needed to go with the diagnosis and not file for custody. Campbell was supportive, "Chloe I love you and I'm committed to us being together and having a family, and putting all this behind us."

Chloe was quiet, but fully engaged in what her dad and Campbell were saying. Sandra was not totally on board. She said she thought they should at least ask for visitation. Interestingly, it was Chloe who spoke up. "No Mama. That's not what I want to do. I've given the situation a lot of prayerful consideration, and I have made a few decisions. I am going to ask the Casebiers if we can meet. I want to apologize to them in person and tell them I am going on with my life and I won't bother them or Nicholas anymore. I need to especially apologize to Kirby. I was awful to her and if the situation was reversed I would have beat somebody's butt!" Chloe's voice cracked as she continued to talk. There were tears in her eyes. "Mama, Daddy, please forgive me, and thank you for having my back. I will never let you down again."

"We love you Chloe…" her mother started to talk, but Chloe interrupted her.

"Let me finish Ma." The tears came then. "Campbell, I ask for your forgiveness too." He started to say something but she held up her hand to stop him. She thanked him for loving her and supporting her through the ordeal and thanked him for being the voice of reason. "You consistently give me practical advice and don't act out of emotion, and if you still want me, I would be honored to be your wife and the mother of your children."

"Of course I still want you. I love you. You are more important to me than anybody else in my life." Before Campbell could continue, Chloe spoke again.

"Mama, Daddy, I know the plan was for me to take over the practice, but I've decided not to come back to Hattiesville to live. When I finish at Spelman and get in law school, I want to live somewhere else. The least I can do for Nicholas is let him grow up in this town in peace."

"Maybe we should investigate going to New York like Ms. Robinson mentioned to me," Campbell said.

"I think we should," Chloe said, smiling at him.

EIGHTY

"This is my letter of resignation."

"What the hell are you talking about Melissa? Why are you resigning?"

She dropped her head, took a deep breath and explained. "I have terminal cancer. I am going to endure the treatments to buy myself some time. I have some things I need to handle state side."

"You can transfer to New York or Los Angeles. Plus you need the money and the benefits."

Melissa sighed again. "I do need the insurance. Can I take a leave of absence?"

"Yeah, that's a viable option. I will make the arrangements. You will need to at least report to…which office do you want to go to?"

"New York, it's closer," she said.

"Okay, I'll make the arrangements right away."

Melissa and her editor talked a few more minutes. When she left his office she called her assistant. "Can I be ready to leave day after tomorrow?"

"Yes ma'am." her assistant said.

"And when can you ship my things?" Melissa asked.

"A week from today. Is that acceptable?"

"That's fine and I want you to come too, to help me get settled."

"I'm prepared to do that, and to stay as long as you want me to."

"Thank you."

EIGHTY-ONE

Kathy and Sterling caught up on the regular things; her classes, the football team, and then Sterling changed the subject. "Darling, I want you to move back to Hattiesville, transfer to an area school, let me court you so your daddy won't kill me, and then you marry me." He paused just for a couple of seconds. "Now I know things may not happen exactly like that, but you have to give me something."

She smiled, blushing a little. "Sterling, how do you know you want to marry me?"

"I knew you were my wife the first time I saw you. I just didn't like the way that felt. I side-stepped the reality of it," he said.

"We were apart for years so that's hard for me to believe."

"I know," he chuckled. "But, I didn't stop thinking about you and when we ran into each other at that conference it was easy for me to rekindle those old feelings. Can you honestly tell me you didn't think about me at all during the hiatus?"

Now she chuckled at this choice of words. "Honestly, no I can't tell you that," she said quietly.

They were quiet for a few minutes, and then Sterling asked again. "What will our status be when you leave to go back to New York?"
"Sterling, I don't know how to answer that."

"But you have to," he said in a firm voice. He put down his fork and looked directly into her eyes.

"I miss you when I'm away. I admit that. I want us to have a relationship. I admit that too, but I don't know what that looks like. I want to be Dr. Kathy Robinson, president of some college, not a soccer mom!"

"Ain't no child of mine playing soccer!" They both laughed. "Well, not the football team mom either. I'm just not that person."

"How do you know you're not that person?" he asked.

"I have no desire for it, and that's not the thing you want to find out after the fact."

The waiter came to see if they wanted dessert. It was a welcome break. "Yes I'll have the brownie thing with the vanilla ice cream and chocolate syrup. No whip cream please."

"I can't believe you are going to eat that after those ribs and fries!" Kathy said shaking her head.

"I will work it off tomorrow at practice. Now back to the subject at hand."

"Why did you come home, why did you call me? Cards on the table Ms. soon to be Doctor Kathy Robinson."

She took a deep breath. "I came home to say I want us to have a relationship, I guess a long distance relationship. Being at Columbia is working for me. Yes, it's far, but if we try we can make it work." She said it all in one breath.

"A long distance relationship will be tough, but I'm willing to give it a try."

Kathy relaxed a little.

"But answer me this," Sterling continued, "Do you expect us to date forever?"

She swallowed hard. "I know that's not realistic, but do we have to make those decisions today? Can we please just take one step at a time?" she asked.

"No! Unless I know we have a future as husband and wife, I don't want to do this. I am not going to spend three years waiting on you to get out of school, trying to negotiate a long distance relationship, not to mention trying to nurture said relationship, for you to tell me you don't want me. I love you girl, but its doo-doo or get off the pot!"

"I don't know if I can manage a career and a family and do it well."

Sterling didn't let her finish. "You can do whatever you want to do."

She dropped her eyes. Her mind raced. She knew he was serious, and her back was against the wall. This was her only chance with him. "I love you too, and I don't want to lose you," she said softly. "If you can support my decision to stay in New York for now, and let me graduate, we can get married and work out the rest."

"That's what I'm talking about!" Sterling said smiling. "Kathy, all I want in life is a family and football. We can do this."

EIGHTY-TWO

Brianna and Brittani were quite intrigued when they came out of school and Hampton was standing in the foyer in front of the office. A young lady was with him. They were talking and she was taking notes.

"Hi G-Pop!" Brittani said.

Hampton liked the sound of that.

"Hey girls," he responded, hugging them. He had actually figured out a way to tell them apart. "Girls, this is Felecia, and these are my beautiful granddaughters, Brittani and Brianna Coffey." Everybody said hello.
"Felecia is one of the interns in our office."

As they started toward the car, Brianna started asking questions. Felecia was engaging and Hampton appreciated that. She explained what her job was at the firm as an architectural design intern. "Felecia is going to help me get you two where you need to be, so your mom won't have so much to do."

"Okay," they said in unison.

As they were riding from school to ballet, they talked. "So G-Pop, can I be an intern at your firm one day?" Brittani was asking.

"Absolutely Britt, as a matter of fact, you can come over anytime and get to know what we do."

"Will Aunt April be all right with that?" Brianna asked. "I don't want her to be angry with my sister because you are doing something for her."

Hampton was stunned at how matter of fact Brianna was about everything. He liked her fire but he also knew it needed to be channeled in the right direction. Felecia was looking at him from the corner of her eye. "Your Aunt April will be fine, trust me on that. Bree, are you interested in coming too?"

"I may come with Brittani just for information but I am not interested in architecture. I am going to be an actress. I am going to New York to Broadway as soon as I get out of school!"

"She means college, G-Pop. Don't worry, Daddy said so," Brittani said.

Hampton laughed. "That's a good plan sweetheart. Let me know how I can help."

"Maybe we can go to New York to a play on school break - that would be helpful."

"Brianna! You know better!" Brittani said covering her face with both hands.

Hampton and Felecia laughed. "Its fine, it really is. You two can ask me for anything and if it's in my power you can have it." They were in the parking lot of the dance studio. "I will pick you up," Felecia said, looking into the back seat. She told them what type of car she would be driving. Hampton opened the car doors for them, walked them to the door of the studio, holding their hands. Walking back to the car, he pumped his fist. He knew the way to his daughter's heart was through his granddaughters.

The Coffey household was quiet, and that was an unusual occurrence. Grammy was resting, the boys were asleep, and Ben and the girls were at work and school. Thelma was off today. It had been on Belinda's mind all morning—calling April. She didn't want to talk to her sister but it was necessary and the only way to control the conversation was for Belinda to make the call. She couldn't ignore April at church and pretty soon they would need to meet for the final approval on the new house.

Belinda realized she didn't have April's number in her phone; she had to find the business card. She dialed without thinking so she wouldn't talk herself out of it. The phone rang several times and as Belinda was preparing to leave a message April answered.

April hesitated when she saw Belinda's name come up on the screen. Her initial thought was to let the call go to voice mail. She answered because, one, she was curious why Belinda was calling and two, she could hear her dad saying "you need to talk to your sister."

"Hi Belinda, is everything okay?"

"Hi April, yes everything is fine. Do you have a few minutes to talk?"

"Sure," April said as she closed the door to her office.

"I'm not sure what to say now that I have you on the line," Belinda said.

"I get it. Daddy has been telling me we need to talk," April said with a slight laugh.

"He said it to me a dozen times too. I guess you know about all the things he's doing for my children."

266

"I'm sure I don't know everything, but I know our intern is helping with their transportation. How is Mrs. Coffey, by the way?"

Belinda answered April and told her more about the current state of her life than she intended to or that she would have expected to.

"What can I do to help?" April asked.

Belinda was caught off guard. "Thanks April, I will let you know."

They talked about the house for a few minutes, and then about the retreat Belinda was planning for the women at church. "Belinda, I'm really glad you called. Let's get together soon," April said sincerely.

"Yes, let's do that."

After they hung up. Belinda was glad she called too. She thought maybe they could be friendly after all.

April held the phone for a few seconds after she and Belinda hung up. Gradually tears welled up in her eyes. She lay the phone down and covered her face with both hands. She cried softly for a few minutes. Belinda had forgiven her and she was glad. She didn't think she would like having a sister but maybe it would be okay. "I almost ruined her life." April thought to herself. "Thank God for His grace."

ℰIGHTY-THREE

"Hello," Honey said, answering the landline when the number showed up on the television. She expected it was Anderson calling from work. It was a Charlotte area code, even though she didn't recognize the number.

"Hi Honey, it's Jacksa."

"Hi there, is everything okay?"

"Yes ma'am, everything is fine."

Honey asked about Min, and about King.

"I am planning a birthday party for Anderson, and I need your help."

"Sure, what do you need?" Honey asked, thinking about the engagement ring discussion.

"My first thought was to have a surprise party but his work schedule is so crazy that may not work."

"You try to surprise that boy and you get surprised," Honey said. They both laughed. After a few minutes they decided to have the party at the clubhouse in Jacksa's subdivision. Honey offered to coordinate the food with Anderson's mom but Jacksa declined.

"I'll have it catered. I don't want you all to have to do all that work." Jacksa said. "But you can make the cake!"

Honey laughed and agreed, and said she would have Anderson's sisters send Jacksa the names of a couple of friends she probably didn't know. Jacksa was excited. The plan was coming together nicely. Now she just needed to tell him what she was planning.

As soon as Jacksa and Honey hung up, Honey called Anderson. "Had you made other plans?" Honey asked Anderson.

"No, I've been so busy I hadn't given my birthday much thought, plus the girls said not to get engaged on my birthday."

"And how many times have either of them been engaged?" Honey laughed.

"Good point!" Anderson laughed too. "Good lookin' out, I gotta go, I'll call you later."

Anderson thought while he drove. By the time he reached his destination he decided. He was going to ask Jacksa to marry him at his birthday party. He needed to take the ring to the jeweler and have the diamonds reset.

Anderson worked late, and didn't get to see Jacksa that evening. They did talk and she told him about the party. He protested as she expected him to, eventually conceded and made sure she was inviting her parents, her brother and a couple of her friends.

Since taking the job with the FBI, Anderson's schedule was so irregular he stepped down as chief of the security team at Hattiesville Community Church. He still received all communications and still advised the team and Bishop Robinson on various things, but he wasn't a part of the day-to-day operation. As he checked his email, he saw a change in the Bishop's schedule. "Good, he will be in the office tomorrow, I will go by and see him," Anderson thought to himself. He wanted to tell Bishop Robinson of his intention to marry Jacksa. Suddenly, he had a bad feeling in his gut; the thought came to him, she could say no.

EIGHTY-FOUR

Min was on an emotional roller coaster by the time she got home. She was embarrassed, angry—at him and at herself—and she was hurt. Much to her surprise Jackson was home when she arrived. He was in the recliner watching a golf match on television. He hadn't cooked, like he was in a habit of doing—in his attempt to win her back. When she came in he looked up, said hello and turned his attention back to the match. He didn't ask where she'd been or how she got home.

Min went into the bedroom, changed clothes and sat for a moment. She had to make a decision and quickly. Did she want to resume her relationship, her marriage, or did she want to continue to live with her husband as roommates? The reality of what Dr. Ryan told her set in on the ride home. He was probably right, Jackson's affair most likely started as a conversation. He was wrong for letting it go that far, but she couldn't truthfully say she would have made a better decision if the door had opened with the doctor. "The truth of the matter is, neither of them are attracted to a woman who cannot respond physically," she thought to herself. Sadness washed over her.

Jackson walked down the hall to the room he was sleeping in. He didn't even look her way. She heard his keys as he walked back by. Then she heard the door alarm beep and the door close. At that moment she knew Jackson had given up on their marriage. "I guess he's headed to see her," she thought.

A half hour later he came back. Min was glad. Even considering what she knew and what transpired over the last few months. She couldn't bear the thought that he had completely given up on them. He brought back wings and beer; "bachelor food," she thought. She was standing in the hall where she could see him but he couldn't see her. She took a deep breath and walked in. "How long has King been outside?" she asked casually.

"A while, probably time to bring him in."

She opened the door to the deck. King ran in and went straight to his water. Jackson grabbed a bag of barbeque chips and headed back to his recliner. "Everything on that plate is brown," Min said with a chuckle. "Where's the green?"

"Got celery right here," he said without looking at her.

"Do you want a salad?" she asked, trying to engage him.

"No thanks," he said.

She continued to make small talk. He continued to give her one word answers. He was totally involved in the golf match. Min left the room, leaving her salad half made. She went to her room and cried. Her life was falling apart.

A short while later, she heard the door open. She thought Jackson was leaving until she heard King bark, and Anderson's voice. After all this time, King still barked at him. Jackson said "the dog knows he doesn't need to be here." Anderson said King could smell his gun, and the barking was a warning to him that King knows what to do if he thinks Min is threatened. Min looked in the mirror to make sure she didn't look like she was crying. "Mom, where are you?"

Jacksa was coming down the hall. "Coming, be right there." They hugged and headed back to the den where then men were having a decent conversation about golf. Min went back to her salad and Jacksa was cleaning up her dad's chicken bones and beer bottles. Min noticed he already drank three. Jackson and Jacksa didn't make eye contact but he thanked her.

"Ma, your daughter is planning a birthday party for me." Anderson said to break the tension. "I hope both of you will plan to come."

"That sounds like fun, Anderson. Thanks for the invitation." Min said enthusiastically. All eyes were on Jackson, but he didn't say anything. "Tell me the date and time so I can put it on my calendar," Min said. Jacksa gave her the details, and told them Anderson's family was coming. "Oh, please tell Honey to let me know what she needs me to do."

Anderson laughed. "You probably don't want to get in that. My family is over the top when it comes to special occasions." Anderson, Min and Jacksa laughed. Jackson still didn't say anything. Jacksa told her mother she would tell her more about it when Anderson wasn't around. Anderson was thinking he had to get Jackson to say he was coming. He knew Jacksa was angry with her dad but years from now they would both regret his not being there when Anderson asked her to marry him.

A commercial came on and Jackson got up to get another beer. "Can I get you something?" Min asked him.

"A beer." She gave it to him. "Thanks," he said and went back to the recliner.

"Pop, I need you and JJ to be at the party too, can't let the women take over. They already out number us!" Anderson said laughing.

Jackson chuckled. "We should be able to work that out."

Just then one of the golfers missed a putt and his opponent won. Jackson and Anderson cheered, and for a few minutes they talked about the match.

"I need to tell you all something," Min said.

Jacksa and Anderson turned their attention to her. Jackson was flipping through the channels.

"The night you two came in and thought Jackson hit me, he did not."

Jackson stopped flipping channels but did not look at Min. "It happened just like he said. I lost my balance and he caught me."

"Mom, why did you let us think he hurt you?" Jacksa asked, looking at her dad, who hadn't said anything. "I was angry with him and that was my opportunity to hurt him."

"Mother, that's not good, Anderson was going to arrest him!"

Anderson had a very serious look on his face. "Mama Min, like I said the night of the incident, domestic violence is serious, not something to play with because you want to get back at somebody."

Jackson was sitting on the edge of the recliner seat, and his body was turned to face the other three people in the room. On one hand he felt relieved, on the other hand he was ticked off. His mind was racing.

"I know, you're right, and I sincerely apologize," Min said with tears in her eyes.

Jacksa looked at her father. Jackson took a deep breath and then stood slowly. "Now what, Detective Thorn?" Jackson asked. "I told you the truth, but you threatened to arrest me,

274

and Jacksa, you know me better than that but you believed I was capable of hitting my wife."

"Jackson, I hope you will forgive me." Min said.

Anderson was not moved by the emotion. "Pop, I deal with the information I have at the time. I'm glad we didn't get to the next step, but if I observe that situation again, I can't say I will react differently."

Jackson wanted to hit him in his chest. He turned up the bottle, finished the beer and walked out onto the deck, leaving the three of them standing there. King followed him out.

EIGHTY-FIVE

"Mother, Raja and I really need some time to ourselves."

"Well take a few days off," Ellen told Jill.

"I want to but I'm afraid to leave LaLa with Dadi."

"I thought that was going okay now."

"It is, but I'm nervous about leaving them overnight, and for more than one day."

Ellen and Jill talked and Ellen advised Jill to discuss her concerns with Raja. Jill knew her mother was right, but she called Tara first.

"I thought my mother would offer to keep her but she and Daddy are going on another cruise." Jill told Tara.

"Girl, your parents are retired. That's what retired people do," Tara said laughing. "And I'm sorry to say I can't help you. I can't get away anytime soon."

"So I'm stuck with Trey or Dadi; what a choice!" They both laughed.

Raja assured Jill that LaLa and his mother would be fine. He said he would ask Trey to check in with them to make sure they had what they needed. Jill took a deep breath and agreed. At dinner that night they told Mrs. Rajagopal they wanted to go away for a long weekend and asked if she would mind babysitting. "Of course I will attend to Leah that goes without saying" she responded. As they were discussing the plan, Jill's phone rang. "It's Grant," she told Raja as she walked out of the room.

The first few minutes of their conversation revolved around LaLa. Then Grant told Jill that Clay and Cicely were married and told her how Sunny reacted. "She flipped! She was screaming at me because they eloped," Grant told Jill. He went on to tell Jill about Sunny lying to him about the counseling and changing the wedding plans. Jill didn't say much, she mostly listened. She wanted to tell Grant to run, and that she knew there was something about Sunny she didn't like. But, she didn't want to be prejudiced because Leah was her best friend. She also knew Grant well enough to know he called her because she was Leah's best friend.

"G, don't do it if you have any reservations. Marriage is forever. There's enough general uncertainty, don't set yourself up for failure."

"I know you're right. I just can't believe it's happening again," Grant said sadly.

"What's happening again?"

"That I'm not getting married," he said.

"Don't do that Grant. These are two totally different sets of circumstances. If you really love Sunny, the two of you may be able to still work this out. You just need to get to the bottom, to the root of why Sunny changed."

Grant sighed heavily. "You're right, but how is that going to happen if we can't complete the counseling?"

"You know I'm not an ultimatum person," Jill said, "but I think that's where you are. She has to be totally engaged in the process, or you two are finished. It's just that simple."

They didn't talk much longer. Jill was very proud of herself for being fair to Sunny. As far as she was concerned really, Sunny could disappear. She didn't want Grant to marry her anyway.

By the time Jill rejoined her family in the kitchen, Raja and Mrs. Rajagopal had worked out the details of their being away. She was downstairs in her suite and Raja and LaLa were playing on the floor. They left the dirty dishes for Jill. "That's your punishment for leaving the dinner table," Raja said laughing. Jill told him about her conversation with Grant and she told him how she really felt. "You gave him good advice, and I'm proud of you for putting your personal feeling aside, but at the end of the day, he has a decision to make."

EIGHTY-SIX

Grant lay across the bed, thinking about Sunny and thinking about his conversation with Jill. He recognized Jill could have said a lot more than she did. He appreciated her being fair. He decided to take her advice. He would contact the marriage counselor, and make appointments for himself and Sunny. He wanted to complete the counseling sessions regardless, but Sunny's choices were, finish the sessions or call off the engagement, plain and simple. He would make that crystal clear to her.

The next day Grant made the arrangements, called Sunny and told her what he did, advised her of her options and told his family he was going back to Washington. He got on the road feeling good that progress was being made. He loved Sunny and wanted to marry her but not with this level of uncertainty.

Sunny was surprised but glad to hear from Grant. They only talked briefly while he was in Hattiesville. Her mother warned her that she needed to do what Grant asked or she would lose him forever. Sunny was quite taken aback at Grant's attitude. He was very demanding, not his usual soft-hearted, loving self. This would be her last chance to save her relationship and like it or not, she was going back to counseling.

What Sunny didn't tell Grant on the phone was, she did cancel all the plans, and she told her friends they were postponing the wedding. She lied about the reason though. Sunny let her friends believe she put off the wedding because it came out in the pre-marital counseling that Grant was still dealing with the tragedy of Leah's death. She told them she and the counselor agreed that he needed to work through all those emotions first. That also explained his going home to Hattiesville without her. She saved face with her "girls"; they were sympathetic with her situation. Now she had to fix things with Grant.

Sunny was really busy at work and didn't notice she hadn't heard from Grant all day. They were going to see the counselor after work. She didn't know if they were riding together or meeting there. Sunny reached for the phone to call Grant, but quickly decided against it. She sighed loudly and went back to work. She felt like crying.

She arrived at the counselor's office first. Her mind was made up to be agreeable to everything, be apologetic and give in. She didn't want to compromise on having a wedding, but if that was the last straw she would. She could tell her friends the wedding was too much for Grant, and they decided to have a quiet small ceremony and a reception. Sunny took a deep breath. Everything was settled in her mind.

When Grant walked in and they made eye contact his heart melted. He realized then how much he missed her. They shared a long hug, and Sunny relaxed a bit. The counselor called them in before they said much to each other.

The session started with a review of what they previously covered. Two minutes in her presence and Sunny remembered why she disliked the counselor. Grant told the counselor about the scene when they received the letter from Clay and Cicely. Sunny squirmed in her seat as she heard Grant describe how she acted. "I just needed a break, so I took some time off and went home." Grant said.

"Now that I'm up to speed, Sunny let's start with you. How was your break from Grant?" The counselor asked.

"I missed him terribly." Sunny started by saying. "I was really sad that he left without our resolving the issue. I just don't think he understands how I feel." Grant didn't say anything.

"How do you feel?" The counselor asked putting emphasis on the word 'feel'.

"I feel misunderstood, unsupported, like he's jerking me around."

"Go on," the counselor said.

"Grant acts like because of Leah he gets to make all the decisions."

"There it is," Grant thought to himself.

"What does that have to do with you feeling 'unsupported'?"

"It's not Leah per se, it's the fact that Grant is making decisions for us based on his experience with her."

"What are you talking about Sunny?" Grant snapped.

"Give me an example please Sunny," the counselor said nicely.

Sunny sighed loudly, crossed her legs and her arms. "Because he had counseling with Leah, he thinks we need to do this," she said waving her hand around the office. "Because they planned a big wedding and it didn't happen, he doesn't want to have a big wedding with me, regardless of what I want."

"Grant, what do you have to say?" the counselor asked.

Sunny looked directly at him, she wasn't smiling. Grant wasn't smiling either. "She's right, I don't want a big wedding, but Sunny wants a wedding more than she wants to be married, and that's evidenced by the fact that she didn't think counseling was necessary and she didn't cancel the plans she made when I asked her to and then lied about it."

The conversation went downhill from there. There was a heated debate but the tide was turned when the counselor asked Grant if his relationship with Sunny was a "rebound" relationship.
"No, why would you ask that?" Grant answered frowning.

Sunny was stunned that the counselor asked that question. It never crossed her mind that she was his rebound from Leah.

"If I was going to have a rebound relationship I wouldn't wait three years," Grant said.

"Grant, that's probably true in theory, but think about how the basic premise of your relationship with Sunny is the exact opposite from you and Leah. Starting with the fact that you did not have sex with Leah before you were married...supposed to get married," the counselor said.

Before Grant could respond, Sunny sprang to her feet. "You and Leah never had sex? We had sex on our third date! So were you thinking about her when you were with me?" Sunny screamed at him.

Grant looked up at her but didn't say anything.

"Answer me damnit!" Sunny shouted again.

"Sunny, please sit down," Grant said quietly.

She didn't move. "Were you thinking about Leah when you were with me?" Sunny asked again. She didn't scream but her voice was forceful.

Grant took a deep breath and blew it out slowly. He looked at the counselor with pleading in his eyes. She met his gaze but gave him nothing. "I love you Sunny," he started by saying.

"What does love have to do with anything?" Sunny said, her voice still louder than it needed to be.

"No I didn't have sex with Leah. It was important to her, to both of us, to wait until we were married."

"But waiting wasn't important for you and Sunny?" the counselor asked.

Grant sighed. "No, to be perfectly honest it wasn't." Sunny drew in her breath and held it. She finally sat down on the edge of the sofa. Grant kept talking. "In the months after Leah passed I regretted not ever being intimate with her, not ever feeling her love or showing her how much I loved her in a physical way." Grant was looking straight ahead, staring as he talked like nobody was in the room but him. "I told myself I wouldn't ever let that happen again. My attitude was why wait, life is too short."

"So you did base the decisions you made about us on your relationship with Leah?" Sunny asked.

"Not really on Leah, but on past experience," he answered.

"And what about the fact that Sunny's looks are the opposite of Leah?" the counselor asked.

"I don't think that matters, that's just how they looked."

"So you weren't looking for different?"

"Not in terms of looks, no. Leah was beautiful in her own way and Sunny is beautiful in her own way," Grant said. Sunny relaxed a little.

The counselor was attempting to prove to Grant that Sunny was a rebound for him. She wanted him to admit it just to clear the air between them. She thought it was important for them to get married with a full understanding of each other. She asked Sunny questions about her past relationships. Grant knew she was previously engaged and that they broke up because he was a gambler, and stole some money from Sunny.

"Sunny, where were you in the planning stages of the wedding?" The counselor asked.

"Why does that matter?" Sunny snapped at her.

"I'm making a point Sunny, that's all."

Sunny rolled her eyes but she did answer. "We were about a month from the wedding. The invitations had been out about two weeks."

"Were you embarrassed when you had to call off the wedding?"

Sunny looked at the counselor and then at Grant. Neither one said anything or took their eyes off her.

"Of course I was embarrassed! Wouldn't you be?"

"What did your friends say?" the counselor asked.

That was when it happened. Sunny started screaming at the counselor, accent and all. Grant just watched. He was glad she saw it for herself.

"One said I should've known, and my mother even said his character was questionable."

"And you did not want to be embarrassed again, so you made plans without consulting me and didn't think counseling was necessary," Grant said.

"Shut up Grant. Just shut the hell up. You care more about a dead girl than you do me!"

EIGHTY-SEVEN

It was a cool, rainy Tuesday morning. Kirby and Enoch dropped the boys at school and then drove to Charlotte to the courthouse. They would finally know today if Chloe would be punished for kidnapping Blake and Nicholas. Their attorney cautioned them against expecting the judge to severely punish Chloe, and reminded them the PTSD defense was still on the table.

Natalia was sitting right outside the courtroom when Kirby and Enoch arrived. Jacksa Baye was with her at Sandra and Roderick Matthew's request. When Natalia looked up and saw Kirby and Enoch she stood to say something to them. Jacksa tried to stop her. "Mrs. Casebier, Mr. Casebier, can I talk to you please?"

"Natalia, I don't think that's appropriate," Enoch said. Kirby didn't say anything. She didn't even stop walking.

The Casebiers' attorney presented the facts; Chloe Matthews stole Natalia Durant's car and kidnapped Nicholas and Blake Casebier, and took them to Georgia. "Although Nicholas is her biological son he doesn't know her or anything about her, she gave up all legal rights to him at his birth." The attorney went on to talk about her using her friendship with Natalia to get access to Nicholas.

"Chloe Matthews is an intelligent, privileged young lady who has an easy life. She is remorseful about giving up her son, so she decided to get him back. Kidnapping him was the only way to make that happen." He painted a rather ugly picture of Chloe. His closing remark was, "Chloe Matthews should be punished for what she did and understand the consequences will be severe if she tries it again."

Chloe's face was expressionless. Sandra wiped a steady stream of tears and Roderick looked really sad. Chloe's attorney said that she was confused, acted on the spur of the moment and without a plan. "There was no way her actions were premeditated. She did not prepare anything - no clothes, or food for herself or the boys." He talked about Chloe being an A student and planning to attend law school. He briefly mentioned that she and Campbell planned to get married. He didn't say much about her friendship with Natalia.

Things proceeded pretty much the way the Casebiers expected and they knew it was about time for Chloe's attorney to introduce the PTSD defense. "Your Honor, the defense asks that Chloe Matthews be exonerated due to a diagnosis of Post-Traumatic Stress Disorder. She was examined by a psychiatrist, and continues in therapy with a doctor who specializes in PTSD and is the top psychologist in this region." He presented a written statement from the doctor stating her agreement that "Chloe suffers from PTSD, and the kidnapping incident is an example of the disorder and a cry for help."

The presentation of evidence went back and forth for over an hour before the judge said she would render her verdict after recess. Enoch and Kirby went to lunch. Their attorney told them he would meet them back at the courthouse. The Matthews and their attorney went to a conference room and had lunch brought in. They wanted to talk about their options. "I feel optimistic" the attorney said, "that the PTSD defense will work in our favor. That should get us probation at most."

"But probation will still give Chloe a criminal record and keep her out of law school," Sandra said.

At that moment Chloe slammed her fist on the table. "Is that all you care about?" she screamed at her mother. Everyone in the room was startled. She had been perfectly quiet until that moment. "My life is in shambles, I may be going to jail, my son doesn't know me and all you can think about is whether I can get in law school!"

Chloe left the table and walked to the window. She started to cry. Campbell went to her and put his arms around her. After a couple of minutes her mother came over to where Chloe and Campbell were standing. "Campbell, may I speak with Chloe alone please?" Sandra asked. He walked away without saying anything. "Sweetheart, I am really sorry. Please don't think I'm being insensitive. I know in time we will put all of this behind us and I just want you to be able to move forward with your plans." Chloe didn't say anything. She was looking out of the window at a bird. Sandra kept talking. "I am well aware of the reality of all this. I only want to keep you encouraged." Chloe kept her eyes on the bird who was drinking from a puddle.

Enoch and Kirby talked about other things at lunch, rather than what was going on in the courtroom. They checked work messages and email. When they were back at the courthouse and met their attorney he didn't tell them anything they didn't expect to hear. "I fully expect the judge to accept the PTSD defense. Now what she does with it I can't call," he told them.

Jacksa and Natalia sat in the technology lobby. Natalia wasn't hungry. They did get some work done, and it seemed the time went by quickly. When they went back upstairs they saw Kirby and Enoch going into the courtroom. Natalia didn't try to approach them this time.

Chloe, Campbell and her parents walked in about one minute before the judge. It was obvious Sandra and Chloe had been crying. Natalia made eye contact with Chloe and winked at her. Chloe smiled slightly.

"All rise," the bailiff said as the judge entered the room. Kirby reached for Enoch's hand, and Sandra reached for Roderick's hand. Chloe's heart was beating rapidly, as was Campbell's.

"In reviewing all aspects of this case, several things are clear to me. First, the system should not have allowed this young couple to choose an open adoption without more appropriate counseling. The open adoption process also failed the adoptive parents, or else they wouldn't be subjected to this. It is also very clear to me that Nicholas Casebier is fortunate to have birth parents who realized they couldn't care for him and knew that adoption was best for him, and he's fortunate to have adoptive parents who obviously love him and are taking very good care of him." Enoch squeezed Kirby's hand. "The facts in this case are irrefutable. Miss Matthews did kidnap Blake and Nicholas Casebier." The judge paused. "But I don't believe she committed the act with any malice or forethought. I do believe she acted on impulse, and I don't believe the boys were ever in danger." Sandra squeezed Roderick's hand and felt a glimmer of hope. The judge continued. "However, a serious crime was committed." She paused again.

"Miss Matthews, please stand." Chloe and her attorney stood. She had to hold onto the table to steady herself. The judge started by scolding Chloe. She stopped short of calling her a spoiled brat, but told her she needed to make better decisions. "I know you want to go to law school, and I hope this episode in your life taught you some valuable lessons." The judge paused for a moment, took a deep breath, looked at Chloe's parents, at Campbell and then at Chloe. She was not smiling.

EIGHTY-EIGHT

A few days passed before Min and Jackson had the talk they needed to have. The night Min told Anderson and Jacksa the truth about the incident with Jackson, he was as angry as he was relieved. Jacksa tried talking to him that night, but he wouldn't talk to her. Finally on Sunday, JJ called, and through the course of the conversation with him, Jackson decided to talk to Min. If for no other reason, he knew things needed to be smoothed over before Anderson's birthday party. Jackson didn't want Anderson's family to pick up on the tension. He still thought Anderson was arrogant and he still didn't want him around Jacksa, but it appeared he was outnumbered and outgunned on that.

Jackson called Min after lunch on Monday to ask if they could have dinner. It took him all morning to decide how to ask her. He was disgusted that they had grown so far apart that after thirty plus years of marriage, he didn't know how to ask his wife to dinner.

Min was genuinely glad to hear from Jackson but she didn't want to go out. She told him she would cook and they could have dinner at home. The fact was they hadn't eaten a meal together in weeks. "We can have a better conversation here," she said.

"I agree," was his response.

Min worked all afternoon to prepare Jackson's favorites. She worked slowly because she had to. She stayed busy to avoid thinking about why she was cooking - to make up with her husband.

When Jackson came in he had flowers he picked up at the grocery store. Min appreciated the gesture, and Jackson appreciated her cooking for him. The tension was still there when they sat down to eat. Jackson started the conversation by complimenting her on the meal. He was determined not to apologize again. He had done that over and over to no avail. "We need to clear the air," Jackson said. "A lot has happened in the last year, and we both made mistakes. We need to move past all that, and get back on track." Min started to say something but he interrupted her. "Min, there's no point in rehashing all that happened. We need to decide to move forward or end things for good." He hadn't planned to say "end things", and, based on the expression on Min's face, she didn't expect that either.

Min swallowed hard. She did not expect Jackson to be so blunt, and she never considered ending their marriage. For a split second she was angry. This all started with his affair. Like he said, they both made bad decisions, but she hadn't been unfaithful - not really. "Jack, are you willing to go to counseling?"

"Counseling?" he repeated, frowning.

"I think we need some help."

His first thought made his heart race. His "friend", the woman who was at the center of the issues he was having in his marriage was a counselor. Marriage counseling was not her specialty but because Min knew her and she did work with married couples...he was afraid she would want them to see her. "Let me think about it," he said, quickly moving past the topic. "I do think we need a change of scenery", he continued. "After the big birthday party, I think we need to get away for a few days."

"Okay, where should we go?"

"You know I like the beach in the fall," he said.

"Okay, I'll make the arrangements. Do you want to fish or play golf?"

They talked about the trip while they finished eating. "Do you care for coffee?" he asked as he took their plates off the table.

"Yes, thank you," she answered.

They had successfully glossed over their problems, and they both knew it. Jackson knew he needed to do something, though, that would diffuse the whole counseling thing. He couldn't take a chance that Min would pursue a session with his friend, and he couldn't take a chance on letting the friend know anything about his marriage. Because he had ignored her frequent attempts to re-connect with him, he didn't know what frame of mind she was in. He was getting his life back in order without her and it needed to stay that way.

EIGHTY-EIGHT

A week after the blow up in the counselor's office, Grant received a package in the mail he had to sign for. It was from Sunny. He opened it slowly. There was a note on top, and under the note the box from the jeweler. Her engagement ring was inside.

The counseling session ended with Sunny screaming at him and walking out. He stayed a few minutes and talked with the counselor. She advised him to give it three days and then call Sunny. On the fourth day, Grant went to her office to invite her to lunch. She declined, and asked him to leave. He knew at that moment she was done with him and the relationship. The truth; he was okay with that. Grant knew he loved Sunny but truthfully not the way he loved Leah. He never thought of Sunny as a rebound but according to the counselor she was. He was heartbroken, but more because of the failed relationship than because he and Sunny were not getting married.

He looked at the ring, closed the box and took it to his safe. He put the box in the safe, closed the door and walked away. He didn't want to think about it. Nobody knew what was going on. Clay was just back from his honeymoon and he didn't tell Gretchen because he expected her to overreact and he didn't want to deal with it. It was time to face the music. He decided to make it a three way call, tell Gretchen and Clay at the same time and be done with it.

Sunny's mother convinced her to give the ring back and come home for a visit. She told her it was better to know now than for Grant to figure out after they were married that he still loved Leah. Sunny tried to think of something to tell her friends. Her mother told her to tell them the truth. "Why lie when the truth will do?" her mother said. Sunny told her friends that Grant was not over Leah and she called off the wedding. Surprisingly they were very understanding, and very supportive.

Sunny bought a first class airline ticket to Eleuthera with the credit card Grant gave her for the wedding expenses, and then closed the account. From one day to the next she wavered between anger and hurt. The counselor called and offered to meet with her, but Sunny refused.

The first couple of days Sunny spent on the beach. She realized how much she missed the sun and the beautiful blue water. Finally, her mother made her talk. She cried and cried, but came clean to her mom about everything. Interestingly, Grant called Sunny's mother while she was there. "I know you talked to Sunny, but I want to talk to you myself. I regret things didn't work out with Sunny. I'm sure her version of the story blames me, and her perception that I'm still in love with my deceased fiancé; and some of that may be true, but Sunny lied to me repeatedly. She was more interested in the wedding than the marriage," he said.

"Grant, I know my daughter. I know she wasn't without her share of the blame but three's a crowd. You had not closed the door on your relationship with Leah before you were involved with Sunny."

"Mrs. Dorsett, if that's true, that was not my intention. In my head and my heart I worked through Leah's death. I've had time to think about what the counselor said, and Sunny was not my rebound," Grant told her.

"Let's not rehash this please. I've been with Sunny for a week…"

"Are you in town Mrs. Dorsett?" Grant interrupted her.

"No, she is here is Eleuthera with me."

"Is she going to stay?" Grant asked.

"I don't know yet. She's thinking about it," Mrs. Dorsett said.

Grant sighed loudly. They talked only a few more minutes. She wished Grant well, as if they would never speak again.

What Mrs. Dorsett told Grant was not the absolute truth. She asked Sunny to stay but after a few days Sunny said no. She didn't want to leave her job, and her life in D.C. She would stay another week and then go back.

NINETY

Melissa was in New York and settled in her new place. Her assistant did a good job in a space smaller than they were accustomed to. Today was a good day and she knew she needed to call her attorney. "Melissa, Mr. Josephs did not sign for the letter. The post office returned it to our office", the attorney's assistant told her. Melissa sighed and shook her head. She didn't know what else to do. He wouldn't take her calls either. "Oh well, for the next two weeks I can't do anything."

NINETY-ONE

The judge didn't say anything for what seemed like a full minute. Chloe's heart was pounding as were her parent's hearts and Natalia's. Finally she spoke.

"Chloe Nichole Matthews. I find you not guilty of the felony kidnapping of Nicholas and Blake Casebier by reason of mental disease, specifically Post Traumatic Stress Disorder." Chloe dropped her head and tears fell on the table she was still holding on to. The judge looked at the court reporter. "This portion is off the record." The reporter nodded and stopped typing. "Miss Matthews, you are absolutely guilty of making bad decisions, but because that's not against the law I can't do anything about it. I also cannot sentence you to seek counseling but I strongly suggest you continue; young lady, you need help." Sandra and Roderick were holding hands and she squeezed his hand when the judge made that comment. She didn't like it at all. "We are back on the record." The reporter resumed typing. "Under the circumstances I am issuing a restraining order against you. You are prohibited from coming in contact with Blake or Nicholas. And finally, you are responsible for covering the Casebiers' attorney's fees."

"Your Honor," Chloe's attorney was speaking, "the Matthews and the Casebiers are members of the same church. It will be hard to abide by the restraining order in that instance."

"She's a smart girl, she'll figure it out. Court is adjourned," the judge said matter-of-factly and hit the gavel on her desk.

Sandra and Chloe's attorney were taken aback by the judge's attitude, but Roderick reminded them both that was irrelevant. "The important thing is Chloe is not going to jail and she is not convicted of a felony." Chloe and Campbell hugged for a long moment, both so glad that was over. Natalia was very relieved too. She felt guilty and felt the whole ordeal was her fault, despite all of them assuring her it wasn't.

Enoch and Kirby left the courtroom immediately. They were not surprised at the verdict, but Kirby was glad about the things the judge said to Chloe and pleasantly surprised the judge ordered Chloe - her parents actually - to take care of their attorney's fees.

They didn't talk much until they stopped for dinner. They called Aunt Avis to make sure she was home and settled with the boys and she suggested they have dinner out, she had everything under control at home. "We can close this chapter," Enoch said to Kirby, squeezing her hands. They sat across from each other waiting to order. "Now that this is behind us you know what I want to talk about?" Enoch said, smiling and raising his brows. Kirby looked puzzled. "You really don't know huh?" he asked.

"No I don't."

"I think we should have another baby."

"Enoch! Are you for real?"

"Yes," he answered and shrugged. "We always said we would have a big family."

Kirby was quiet for a moment. "Yes we did, but I don't know if I can go through the emotion again of not getting pregnant and deciding to do the in-vitro."

"Let's pray about it, but I don't think we will have to go through all that again."

"Wow", she said just above a whisper.

NINETY-TWO

Clay and Cicely were getting settled into married life. They were preparing to move into the new house but first was their reception. Gretchen planned it and perfected every detail. Grant was coming home alone and that was the only blemish on the celebration.

The day after Clay and Grant talked, Cicely called Sunny. She did congratulate Cicely but also told her how angry she was when she received the letter. "I hate that you feel that way, Sunny. But you and Grant may eventually work things out just like we did. I forgave Clay because I love him, and I want to be with him. Life is too short to be bitter." Sunny rolled her eyes as she listened to Cicely.

Cicely told her about Hawaii. Sunny was really quiet. Then Cicely mentioned the reception. Sunny sighed loudly. "Sunny, I hope you will come to the reception and celebrate with Clay and me," Cicely said.

"I don't know about that," Sunny replied. "I don't want to see Grant and I really don't want to see his family."

"Sunny, nobody is angry with you."

"I know. I just think it will be awkward, and I don't feel like dealing with it," Sunny said.

"I get it, but please at least think about it."

Sunny rolled her eyes again. "Okay, I will think about it," Sunny said but didn't mean it.

Sunny couldn't sleep. She kept thinking about Grant. She turned over and looked at the clock. It was 2:17 am. Sunny started to cry. After a few minutes, she was very angry at Grant for hurting her and angry with herself for still crying about it. She sat up, wiped her face with her hands, reached for the phone and called Grant.

The phone startled him. He didn't look at the screen he just answered. "Grant Sturdivant, I hate you!" Sunny shouted into the phone as soon as he answered.

"What?" He took the phone away from his ear to look at the screen. "Sunny what are you screaming about?" She started to cry again. Grant sat and listened to her cry for a minute or two. When she settled down, he took a deep breath, trying to decide what to say. "Sunny, I'm sorry you hate me." That sounded so horrible to hear because she really didn't hate him; in fact just the opposite, she loved him. Grant continued, "I don't hate you, I love you Sunny, but love isn't enough."

They talked for about thirty minutes rehashing their last encounter with the counselor. When Grant yawned, Sunny looked at the clock. She knew they both had to get up in a few hours. "I'll let you go Grant, we aren't accomplishing anything through this conversation." They hung up. Sunny cried herself to sleep. Grant tossed and turned for a while.

"Sunny, it's me."

"What is it Grant?"

"I'm at the door." He still had his key but he didn't want to scare her. She opened the door. Neither of them said anything, they went straight to bed.

NINETY-THREE

Belinda and April were meeting for lunch. April wanted to take Belinda to a new restaurant close to the hospital. She designed it and wanted her big sister to see the finished product. Their relationship was still a work in progress but thanks to Hampton's insistence and April seeing the twins pretty regularly they were working on it. G-Pop had the twins in the office a couple of times a week. Brittani really did seem interested in the business, and she had an eye for detail. As far as Brianna was concerned it was just something to do.

April picked up Belinda in front of the hospital. When she arrived, Belinda was at the curb talking to a very handsome man. He opened the car door for Belinda. "April, this is Dr. Lane Silver." He spoke to April and smiled. He and Belinda said a few more words about a patient, then he looked at April. "It's nice to meet you, April."

"Thanks, nice meeting you too."

"Why do I feel like I'm being set up?" April asked Belinda, not smiling.

"Because you are," Belinda responded very matter-of-factly. She went on to list Dr. Silver's qualities and ended with "and he is not hard on the eyes either!" They both laughed.

"Then why is he single?"

"I don't know all the details but as I understand it, he had a bad break up in Houston and moved here to distance himself from the situation."

"Oh I see. Umph. I guess he's angry and bitter. I pass!" April said.

"No, it's not like that at all," Belinda responded to her.

"Does he know he's being set up?"

"Yes, it was his idea!"

The conversation soon shifted from Dr. Silver to Thanksgiving dinner. "I compromised with Grammy and the girls. We're going to Hattiesville for Thanksgiving and having Christmas dinner at G-Pop's house." April didn't respond.

Belinda told her how much she liked the restaurant. "April, you are really good at what you do," Belinda said, looking around.

"You know I think Brittani may be headed in this direction too, especially if 'G-Pop' has anything to do with it," April said, moving her fingers in the quote sign and laughing.

Belinda didn't respond for a few seconds. Then she said seriously, "I don't want Brittani to expect too much. I appreciate what you and..." Belinda hesitated. She still didn't know what to call Hampton.

"...G-Pop are doing, but I don't want her in any way to interfere with what you have planned for your company." April knew Belinda was referencing the comments she made to her previously about the business.

"We have plenty of time to work that out. She has to finish college and that's years down the road. I just want to encourage her gifts, and Bree too. Daddy told Felecia to set up a desk for Brittani and he said he is going to get Brianna an acting coach."

Belinda looked at April like she was speaking a foreign language. April laughed and shrugged. "He's really serious," April said.

"Does he realize they're in middle school?" Belinda said.

April told Belinda how Hampton pushed her growing up. "If he had raised you, you wouldn't be a top surgical nurse, you would be a top surgeon."

NINETY-FOUR

"I won't travel back with the team, I will catch the train after the game."

"That sounds good, Sterling. I hate I can't come down for the game," Kathy said.

"No problem. I just want to see you," Sterling said. Kathy smiled.

Sterling was spending as much time with Kathy as he could and spending a considerable amount of money in the process. But he wanted Kathy and he was willing to do what he had to do. On his last visit they finally consummated the relationship. He knew she was finally convinced that he loved her, otherwise she would not have had sex with him and if his plan worked they would be getting married for Christmas. He was also glad she would be home for Thanksgiving. He even promised her mother the football team would help with the church's Thanksgiving dinner.

Katherine Robinson met with her staff including the volunteer coordinators who would help with the annual Thanksgiving event. Each year Hattiesville Community Church provided meals for homeless families and residents in the area shelters. Through the course of the day hundreds of people would be fed. The project was bittersweet for Katherine. While she loved serving the community, she prayed for the day there would be no need. One of the volunteers reminded her that the scripture said "the poor would always be among us."

Katherine was also delighted that Kathy would be home and Sterling would be there too. She was glad they worked things out, but she knew her daughter, and until and unless they were married she didn't know what to expect.

Landridge Community Church was also providing meals for the women and children shelter residents and some homeless people. Belinda was re-creating what she helped Katherine do for the years she was in Hattiesville. Hampton and April volunteered to get the business community to underwrite the cost and a couple of other churches used their buses to provide transportation to and from the shelters. Their dinner was scheduled for the Sunday before Thanksgiving so the Coffey's could go to Hattiesville for Thanksgiving.

Everybody had an assignment. Grammy and Thelma were taking care of Bryce and Bradley. Brittani and Brianna were hostesses for the children from the shelters. Ben made sure they understood the magnitude of the experience. Lili Marcos helped Belinda get things organized and did a good job engaging the Hispanic community. Juan handled all the logistics and Carlotta and Jorge were to help Brittani and Brianna.

This was very different for Hampton. He attended church and financially supported it in a big way but it was unusual for him to take an active role. Brittani and Brianna assumed he was going to help and when they mentioned it, he couldn't say no.

When his phone rang his hands were full and he couldn't reach it. Several minutes later when he had a chance to look at it he was glad he didn't answer. It was Melissa…again. He didn't know why she kept calling. He had ignored her calls and messages for weeks. "I better get somebody on this, figure out what she's up to," he thought to himself.

Carlos Reyes, the private Investigator Hampton kept on retainer, listened intently as he got his assignment. He made a few notes, never writing names. After they hung up, Hampton exhaled loudly. He knew he would have some answers soon.

The next order of business was to check with Felecia to see if the travel arrangements were complete for the trip to New York for him, Brianna and Brittani. They knew they were going but didn't know the details. Felecia was going also. Hampton had some friends in New York that he wanted to see while they were there, so she would accompany the girls to a couple of events. April cautioned Felecia not to get side tracked and become the sitter. But Felecia was fine with these extra assignments. Being an interior design major, she was getting ideas she could use in her portfolio, so it was a win-win.

NINETY-FIVE

Jacksa was nervous. She triple checked her lists for Anderson's party. She wanted everything to be perfect, especially because his family and friends would be there. She wanted to impress them, and she wanted Anderson to be happy. Honey, Anderson's grandmother, was bringing his favorite cake - chocolate pound cake with chocolate frosting. Lola's Restaurant was catering the food; all of his favorites including ribs and gumbo.

Anderson was nervous, too. He went over and over in his mind what he wanted to say. He knew in his heart he would know when the moment was right. Only Honey knew what he was going to do. All she said was "follow your heart."

Min was looking forward to the party and to visiting with Anderson's family. Jackson was mediocre. He just wanted it to be over. He was glad JJ was home. That was the highlight of the event for him. Jackson told JJ that he and Min were working through their challenges.

When Jacksa and Anderson arrived at the party, the music was pumping and Anderson danced into the room. He was surprised to see some of his friends and cousins and was glad they were invited. Jacksa didn't miss anything. After an hour of dancing and eating some of everything he saw, Anderson was ready to cut his birthday cake. He looked across the room for Jacksa who was laughing with a friend. She looked so beautiful. He wanted to make her smile forever. He walked across the room and asked the DJ if he would play "Made to Love You" by Gerald LeVert, and when it ended he was going to say a few things. With that done, he took a deep breath and walked over to Jacksa and led her to the dance floor. They danced and he sang in her ear. When the song ended the DJ didn't start another one. Anderson was holding Jacksa's hand. He thanked everyone for coming to celebrate his birthday. "Most of all, I want to say thank you to the most amazing woman in the world. Jacksa Baye, you are the best. When I found you, I won!" She was looking at him smiling. Everybody laughed. "Jacksa, I'm not a perfect man, but I have a perfect love for you." He got down on his knee. The room was perfectly quiet. "If you are patient with me, I promise I will be the best husband, father, and grandfather I can possibly be." She trembled like it was cold; she was looking directly into his eyes. When she saw the tears in his eyes, the ones in her eyes spilled over the lids. "Will you do me the honor of being my wife? Will you marry me?" She swallowed hard. "Yes," she said.

He took the ring from his pocket and slipped it on her finger. Then he picked her up and spun her around. She was screaming, everybody in the room was cheering and he was laughing. Her arms were around his neck and she got a good look at the ring. It was absolutely gorgeous.

Jackson couldn't believe his eyes. Detective Thorn had just proposed to his daughter, and she said yes. How was this going to play out? As soon as the thought went through his mind, Jackson felt guilty. This was not about him, or his mess, this was about Jacksa, and as much as he didn't want Anderson around he wanted his daughter to be happy. Eventually Jackson made his way to Anderson and shook his hand but didn't say anything except congratulations. He and Jacksa hugged for a long moment. Neither said anything.

After they were congratulated by every person there, Anderson pulled Jacksa aside to tell her about the ring, and to show her a picture of the original ring. Jacksa went to

Honey to thank her. "You're welcome baby," Honey said, and then whispered in her ear, "I have my husband's band too, if you want it. I didn't tell Anderson." Jacksa gasped. "No don't tell him and yes I want it. Thank you!"

NINETY-SIX

A couple of days passed before Campbell and Chloe had time to debrief. Her parents, actually her mother, kept her close. Kathy Robinson heard from her mother and Campbell how things went in court, and Kathy had a long, strong conversation with Campbell. She encouraged him to cut his ties with Chloe. "I can't just abandon her Ms. Robinson."

"Campbell, I'm not suggesting you abandon her, I'm suggesting you change the nature of your relationship."

"Ms. Robinson I love Chloe, and my intention is to make a life with her. My future is with her."

Kathy sighed heavily. "Campbell, do you realize you haven't gotten to know any other young ladies? You and Chloe have been together five years and you are only twenty-two years old!" He was relentless in protecting Chloe. The more Kathy talked the more he tried to convince her Chloe was not bad for him.

Eventually Kathy gave up. She was going in circles with him. Finally she mentioned law school in New York. "We applied to Hofstra and NYU…"

"Campbell, when you say 'we' do you mean Chloe too?"

"Yes, ma'am. After what happened with her kidnapping Nicholas and all that, we decided a change of scenery is what we need. I am applying for scholarships and Chloe's parents are good with paying her tuition." Kathy rolled her eyes.

"And Mrs. Matthews said she will take care of our living expenses." Kathy was speechless.

Chloe felt better than she had in weeks. The counseling was actually helping, and she was notified by Spelman College that they would let her come back to school. She would graduate in the summer. That meant if she was accepted into law school she wouldn't have a break, but she was okay with that.

She and Campbell had a plan. He was a good man, even her mother admitted that. Her parents always thought he was a nice guy but was from the proverbial wrong side of the tracks. The only part of the plan that wasn't worked out - what they would do after law school. The Matthews Law Firm was her inheritance, and Campbell could for certain work there, but Chloe wasn't sure she wanted to come back to Hattiesville. She was making peace with allowing Nicholas to grow up there without any interference from her. Campbell said that wasn't a decision they had to make yet. They hadn't told her parents they may not come back. Again Campbell said that wasn't something they had to share right now.

Chloe was ready to go back to school. She wanted to be back in Atlanta, back on campus, back in her classes, with her friends and away from her parents. She would miss Campbell but she needed some air. "This town is just too small," she told one of her friends. "I went to the salon and I know they were talking about me."

Because of the judge's order Chloe couldn't go to church and she didn't dare go back to the school to see Nicholas. The Casebiers were not allowing Natalia to sit with the boys anymore and the church child care director moved her to another age group so she wouldn't see Blake and Nicholas. Chloe felt really bad. Her decision affected so many people. But she refused to stay stuck in the past. The only way she could move forward was to stop looking in the rear view mirror.

NINETY-SEVEN

Carlos Reyes found out from the magazine's Milan office that Melissa was now working in New York. The New York office was tight lipped but he eventually learned that she was on medical leave. It took some doing, more than he expected or liked, but he finally found out the diagnosis and the prognosis. "Yes, Señor Josephs that is the situation here."

Hampton thanked Reyes for the information, but he wasn't sure how to respond. Melissa is dying and now she wanted to make peace with April. "The only peace April needs from her mother is a piece of that estate," he thought. "A part of what she traded her daughter's peace for."

In the big scheme of things he was grateful she didn't go directly to April. But that also puzzled him. April wasn't that hard to find, especially now that Melissa was back in the states. Hampton chuckled out loud. As usual Melissa was not facing her responsibility, he thought. It was easy to call him, give him information and walk away. She did it well, and Hampton preferred it that way.

Interestingly, a couple of hours later, Hampton's phone buzzed and he could see it was a picture on the screen. He laughed thinking it was Brittani or Brianna. They sent him pictures regularly; selfies, pictures of the boys, and pictures of their school and extra-curricular activities. When he looked more closely he saw that the message was from Carlos Reyes. He opened it quickly. There were six pictures all of Melissa. She was very thin, wearing sunglasses and a stylish hat. One of the close up pictures was taken in the doctor's office. He could see how weak her eyes looked.

He looked at the pictures over and over. The beautiful Melissa Angelique Montgomery; smart, rich, terribly ambitious, and immensely successful. "I bet she would trade all that now," he said out loud. "Having a child to raise didn't fit into her life plan," he thought. "What was the life plan now?"

As the day went on, Hampton decided he wanted to know what the letter said. He called his attorney. He explained the situation. "Hampton, I will call up there right now and call you back," the attorney said. "Thanks, man."

Twenty minutes later, Hampton's attorney called back. "They are going to overnight the letter to me. It will be here tomorrow by noon. I'll be in court but my assistant will call you when it gets here, and you can pick it up." Hampton was quiet for a minute, "Hamp, are you there?"

"Yeah, I'm here." He was quiet again for moment. Finally he spoke. "Why don't you read it and tell me if there are any legal ramifications. If not, I don't care what it says."

"If you're sure, then that's what we'll do," the attorney said.

"Yeah, I'm sure."

NINETY-EIGHT

Grant didn't think, he just drove over to Sunny's house. Despite it all, the lies, the deceit, and the revelation from the counselor he had to face his truth. That truth being he wanted Sunny.

She awakened first the next morning. He felt her move from under his arm. "Where are you going?" Grant asked. She went in the bathroom without answering. He was on the phone when she came out. "You need to call in sick," Grant told her when he hung up.

"Why, so we can have more angry sex?" she said sarcastically.

"Do what I asked you to do please," Grant said ignoring her attitude.

She was surprised at the tone of his voice. She reached for her phone, sent two text messages, and then lay it on the night stand. She put her hands on her hips. "Now what?" He pulled her back in bed.

When Sunny and Grant got up, he made coffee and she cooked breakfast. They didn't talk much until they finished eating. "What do you want Grant? Why are you here?" Sunny asked breaking the silence.

"I want us to work this out," he said quietly. The expression on his face and the tone of his voice tugged at her heart strings.

"Why, Grant? Don't say you love me because we both know that's not enough. If anything came out of the counseling you insisted we have, we know you're not ready to be in a relationship with me."

"And you're not ready to marry me," Grant said to her.

"So I ask you again, why are you here?" Sunny said looking directly into his eyes.

"Can we start over? Can we start with what we know, date again and see where it goes?" Grant asked Sunny sincerely.

They talked for a couple of hours. Neither of them raised their voice. They went to the gym together. Sunny talked Grant into going to a yoga class with her and he talked her into cycling. They picked up a pizza on the way from the gym. They were both pretty quiet - each considering their own thoughts. Later in the evening Sunny looked out the window. "It's snowing!" she said.

"No joke?" Grant asked her.

"No joke, and it's coming down pretty hard."

He went over to the window where she was standing. He leaned his body against hers and rested his chin on her shoulder. He wrapped his arms around her waist.

NINETY-NINE

Campbell received an acceptance letter from Hofstra Law School but Chloe hadn't heard from any school. He was waiting to hear from NYU but he was getting a little anxious. He didn't want to lose his spot at Hofstra. He was also concerned about Chloe's applications. What were they going to do if neither school accepted her? He didn't want to leave her but how could he turn down this chance? Chloe seemed to think she hadn't heard anything because she applied relatively late and wasn't actually graduating until summer.

"If I don't get accepted, I'll stay in Atlanta and maybe apply to law school at Emory," Chloe told Campbell with no emotion.

"What about our plans? What about us?" Campbell asked her.

"We'll have to be 'us' long distance," she said.

Campbell was tired; emotionally tired. He had been on a roller coaster with Chloe for almost five years. "Maybe Ms. Robinson is right," he thought. "Maybe I do need to change my situation with Chloe."

A few days passed and Campbell received more good news; he was getting a full scholarship. This was the greatest news ever. Law school and no student loans was beyond his comprehension. Even health care coverage was included. He was absolutely ecstatic but he was hesitant to share the news with Chloe. She still had not received anything. He decided to keep the news to himself for the time being.

Chloe called Campbell as soon as she read the email. She received a "provisional" acceptance to Hofstra based on her graduating in the summer. "Let's go to New York for Christmas to look for a place," Chloe said. Her bubbly demeanor was back.

"Maybe you and your mom can go," he said. I need to work every shift I can over the holidays."

"Okay, that's fine. We'll tell them at Christmas dinner what we're going to do!"

"I have some news too!" Campbell said. He told her about his scholarship. Chloe screamed like a little girl. "That is so good! I am so proud of you! I will take you out tonight to celebrate!"

*O*NE HUNDRED

Min and Jacksa spent two entire days shopping for a wedding gown. Jacksa was determined to find a dress in a store and not have to order one. She and Anderson decided to get married on New Year's Day. Jackson just didn't understand the rush, but when he asked Min if Jacksa was pregnant she told him off and said he better not ask Jacksa that. JJ assured him she wasn't pregnant.

They opted for a small wedding; about one hundred guests, and a cake and punch reception. They would have a sit down family dinner after the rehearsal. The wedding party was all family. Anderson asked JJ to be his best man and Jacksa asked Anderson's younger sister to be her maid of honor.

Min and Jackson's next door neighbor suggested a boutique in Raleigh to look for a dress. They drove there the second day and found the perfect dress. Because of Jacksa's skin tone the white dress looked better on her than the off-white or candlelight colors. She even tried a pale pink dress but they decided the white one was perfect. They left it for the minor alterations. The couturier promised to ship it to her the following week.

Jackson took Min back to the first store she and Jacksa visited to purchase Min's dress and shoes. He found a dinner jacket and slacks there too. All of a sudden the shopping didn't seem so crazy to him after all. Everything was coming together. Jacksa was so excited. In the span of a few days they ordered flowers, and three kinds of cake, punch and a champagne punch. Anderson's mother and sisters addressed the invitations and mailed them. Anderson's assignment was to get his tuxedo and coordinate things at church with Bishop Robinson.

"Hey babe," Anderson said when Jacksa answered her desk phone.

"Hey!" She responded with excitement. "Why did you call this phone?"

"I'm in the office. Headed to a meeting."

"Oh, okay." She knew the rules about the phones in the FBI office.

He told her he talked to Bishop Robinson's assistant and they were good with the counseling schedule. "We see Mrs. Robinson for the first session, each have an individual session and then the final session together with the bishop," Anderson told Jacksa. It was a short turn around, they knew, and they were happy Bishop Robinson was available on New Year's Day.

"That's fine. We will just have to make it work," Jacksa replied. Anderson gave her the details; she wrote them on a note pad and would transfer them to her phone when they hung up. They talked another minute and Anderson had to go.

"What the hell, boss?" Anderson leaned forward in the chair. "I'm getting married January first. You have to get me reassigned! I will talk to the chief myself if I need to." Anderson and his supervisor went back and forth. Anderson was adamant about not taking this assignment unless the schedule could be adjusted.

"A.T., the crime won't stop 'cause you gettin' married. Damn man!"

"And I'm not disappointing the woman of my dreams, her Mama and my Mama 'cause fools want to traffic cocaine!"

Five more minutes of the same, and the supervisor gave in and said he would talk to the chief.

Jacksa and Min went through the checklist with Anderson's mother and sister. Things had fallen into place nicely. It was going so smoothly Jacksa was nervous.

After the first counseling with Mrs. Robinson, Anderson and Jacksa rode home discussing the session topics she brought up. "This counseling is pretty intense," Anderson remarked, sort of thinking out loud. "Are you having second thoughts?" Jacksa asked.

"No!" He reached over and held her hand. "That's the point of counseling, to make you think," he said. "When will we have time to do our homework?" Jacksa asked.

"Let's do it tomorrow since I go back the next day. How did I get to go first, anyway?" They both laughed.

"Because you asked me to marry you."

"Touché," he said, and laughed.

Bishop Robinson knew a lot about Anderson and his background, but in the counseling session they talked about how growing up without his dad affected him. Anderson was six years old when his father died. They talked about him growing up on the Catawba Indian Reservation and how the men on the reservation rallied around him and how their influence will affect him as a married man. The last question Bishop Robinson asked Anderson gave him pause. "How is your relationship with Jacksa's parents?"

Anderson told him how much he loved Min, how well they got along, and how she and his family have a good relationship. He talked about JJ and their relationship. He didn't mention Jackson. But he should have known the bishop wasn't going to let him get away with that.

"You didn't mention her father," Bishop Robinson said. Anderson had to think quickly. Jackson and Min were not members of Hattiesville Community Church. But they visited from time to time. Jacksa joined and was baptized after Anderson started courting her and that prompted Min to come more regularly, but not Jackson.

He couldn't, or at least he didn't want to tell Bishop Robinson what he knew about Jackson Baye. Anderson chuckled. "I would say, Bishop, that my relationship with Mr. Baye is difficult at best. I don't think it's any different than any other father would be about his only daughter. He's just more vocal about it. He says he doesn't want a man who carries a gun for a living to marry his daughter. But he also conceded it's not his decision." Anderson said.

"Do you think that's the real reason?"

Anderson shrugged. "That's what he said to me, Jacksa and even the guys at the barber shop."

The bishop chuckled, before he leaned toward Anderson and looked at him seriously. "That may be what he's saying and that may be your story, but I know in my spirit that's not it." He waited for Anderson to respond. Anderson shifted in his seat. He couldn't break Jacksa's confidence, not even to Bishop Robinson.

"Sir, Jacksa shared something with me about her father in confidence. He knows I know, so that's part of his problem with me."

"I respect you, son, for being a man of your word. But I have to ask. Is, was, or did he hurt Jacksa?"

"No sir. If that was the case I would have handled that myself."

The bishop just nodded.

Jacksa and Mrs. Robinson had a good talk. They talked about sex and having children, they discussed interracial relationships. Mrs. Robinson asked Jacksa why they were rushing to get married. "Mrs. Robinson, I'm not pregnant if that's what you're asking!" Jacksa laughed. "Anderson and I haven't had sex." They ended their session talking about the demands of Anderson's job.

Following the second combined counseling session, The Robinsons were satisfied that Anderson and Jacksa were ready to get married, but they had them agree to two additional sessions after they got married, so they would have the prescribed six sessions.

Anderson was still waiting for the final decision from his supervisor. He couldn't imagine telling Jacksa they would need to postpone their wedding date. There had to be a compromise. He couldn't go another day without telling Jacksa something. She had no idea there even a challenge.

"What's up boss?" Anderson said, walking into his supervisor's office and taking a seat. They talked about a couple of case matters and then the supervisor addressed what he knew Anderson really wanted to know.

"A.T., the chief only offered one option. You take the case in Memphis instead, you come back on December 31st, get married, have a week off, but go back. The caveat; you have to leave tomorrow."

*O*NE HUNDRED-ONE

Things in the Rajagopal household were on track. Raja and Jill had their long weekend, and implemented a regular date night. Having a live-in babysitter turned out to be a good thing. Mrs. Rajagopal really took responsibility to care for LaLa, and Raja made sure that she discussed things with them before making decisions. There was peace in their lives and all parties were appreciative.

Christmas was a little over a week away and Jill was overwhelmed. Raja's family was coming from London. Tara's parents, her brother Yash and his wife would arrive on Christmas Eve. Tara and Robert were coming the day before. Mrs. Rajagopal talked the family into coming. She and Raja talked about it; he talked to Jill whose only stipulation was they stay in a hotel, and Mrs. Rajagopal made the initial call. Tara and Robert were staying with Raja and Jill, allegedly to help Jill around the house, but truthfully they were there for Tara to police all the activities, and everybody's actions.

The first time they were all together was for an early dinner on Christmas Day. Jill invited her parents, her brother Trey and his girlfriend. LaLa was overwhelmed because there were so many people, and she stuck pretty close to Trey and her dad.

Yash and Tara were genuinely glad to see each other. They hadn't seen each other since his wedding four years before. They talked periodically but he had taken their parents side against Tara for marrying Robert and against

Raja for marrying Jill. Tara and Jill thought his wife was nice enough but she was really quiet.

Tara and her parents were cordial, and they were kind to Robert. That was all she really cared about. Yash did tell her Mrs. Rajagopal scolded his parents and he knew that changed their attitude.

Dinner was a buffet of traditional American and traditional Indian dishes. Jill and Tara said privately that Yash's wife wasn't Miss Personality but she was an excellent cook. When they complimented her she told them she came from a big family that owned a restaurant, and she had cooked since she was a teen. They teased Yash, saying that's why he was gaining weight.

After coffee and dessert, Ellen and Dr. Strauss excused themselves. They were leaving for New York the next morning to meet some friends for a few days. Before they left there were hugs and handshakes. Ellen and Mrs. Rajagopal shared a long hug. Jill walked her parents to the door. "This was really nice sweetie," her mother said. "I think you all have turned the corner."

"I think you're right, Mom," Jill said.

The men gathered in front of the television to watch the basketball game - even Tara and Yash's father, who knew very little about the game. Usually Tara, Jill and Trey's girlfriend would watch the game with the guys, but they decided to sit in the dining room with the other ladies. Yash's wife and Tara's mom told Mrs. Rajagopal about her friends in London. They had asked about her. "Tell them I am well, but I have responsibility to my family in the United States. I won't be coming back to London." She told them about LaLa and their time together. They talked a little about Mr. Rajagopal.

At the end of the evening when all the guests were gone, Jill and Raja reviewed the events of the past two days. Their conclusion; Christmas dinner was a success.

ONE HUNDRED-TWO

Kathy and Sterling's Thanksgiving weekend was somewhat of a whirlwind. There was so much going on they had little one-on-one time. Though Sterling didn't like her being so far away it was working because he could control the situation - his relationship with her.

She was a highly intelligent woman but a bit naïve. When they had sex the first time it "just happened." When she asked if he had a condom he told her no. "I didn't come up here with this in mind, but I just love you so much," he had said. "It's your first time, you can't get pregnant." She believed him. They lay in bed the next morning and talked about the experience. Mostly about how she was feeling and what she experienced physically and emotionally. He was very gentle with her and talked her through it all; even when she said she felt guilty losing her virginity outside of marriage.

"I do love you, Sterling, but I made up my mind a long time ago to be a virgin until I was married. I broke my promise to God, to my parents and to myself."

"Babe, please, you're making me feel terrible."

"I don't mean to," she said, and snuggled closer.

"I love you Kathy, you know that, and in my heart we are married. You are the woman I am going to spend the rest of my life with," he said to her.

She believed him.

On his next visit he brought a box of condoms to leave at her apartment. He left the box as a decoy. The ones he would really use were in his bag tucked away. He didn't want her to see that he had tampered with them. He had fixed them to guarantee the condom would break.

ONE HUNDRED-THREE

Clay came home every day expecting something new. There were drapes, rugs, lamps. Day by day, Cicely was making a home of their new house. She was doing it alone since Sunny wasn't around to help.

Cicely's work schedule was four days on and three days off, but the days she worked were long days, and from time to time the shifts changed, and she worked nights. She was currently on nights and she was glad. Clay was gone in the morning before she got home. She didn't want him to know how sick she was. The diagnosis; Hyperemesis Gruvidarum. In non-medical terms, morning sickness. Except in her case it was anytime of the day sickness. She was doing her best to hide the pregnancy from him.

Clay and Enoch took Enoch's truck to a Christmas tree lot in Mooresville to buy a tree for each of their homes, and one for Gretchen and Paul and Grace. They laughed as they reminisced about going to the tree lot with their fathers and Clay's Uncle Paul. Their families had bought trees from this family for as long as either of them could remember. Clay skipped a few years because he was single and didn't want to bother with all that.

The two of them spent the better part of Saturday setting up the trees. Gretchen and Grace would take great care in decorating their trees. Enoch and Kirby knew their three would have lots of decorations hand-made by two five-year-olds. Clay was excited about him and Cicely decorating their first Christmas tree together. They would get it done the next day after church. Cicely chose silver and white ornaments, white lights and a beautiful angel dressed in white to go on top. They were spending so much money on the house they said they wouldn't exchange gifts. At some point they both admitted they wouldn't stick to it so they decided on a reasonable spending cap.

"I want us to start a tradition," Cicely said to Clay one day when they were just talking.

"Okay, what is it?" he asked, smiling at her.

"Each year let's buy each other an ornament."

"I like it," he said, "but not just any ornament, one that represents something special about our relationship or our life together."

"Exactly!" she said, excited that Clay was on board.

He started looking the next day. He looked online, he talked to some of his female co-workers. One of them gave him an amazing idea. He took a picture of the front of their home and sent it to an artist who reproduced the picture as an etching onto a wooden block and etched their last name and the year.

He was nervous though. The artist told him he was cutting it close to have the finished product before Christmas. Fortunately the package arrived the day before Christmas Eve.

ONE HUNDRED-FOUR

It was after work hours when Hampton's attorney called him. "I read the letter, went through the other papers..."

"Other papers?" Hampton asked, frowning.

"Yep, there are some other pretty important documents."

"Is there anything I need to do legally?"

"Not so much you. This is more for April," the attorney said.

"She doesn't know anything about any of this," Hampton replied, leaning back in the chair and closing his eyes.

"She's going to need to know Hamp; and you need to be the one to tell her."

Sighing loudly, Hampton agreed. "I'll come to your office tomorrow and take a look at everything first."

"I'll have somebody call to confirm the time, but plan for early afternoon," the attorney said.

They hung up, and Hampton was trying to decide what to do. His phone buzzed; another picture. This time it was from Brianna. It was a picture of a model Brittani created for a school project. She was posing beside it. It was a model of an amphitheater. Brianna's text message said she would perform on that stage one day. Hampton smiled, then said "Belinda" into his blue tooth.

"Hey sweetie;" he said when she answered. "Can I drop by for a few minutes? I want to talk with you about something." Something in his voice made her uneasy.

"Sure," she said. "That was Hampton, he asked to come over," Belinda was saying to Ben.

"Okay, what's up with him?"

"Don't know but he sounds funny."

"He's fine" Brittani said, coming into the kitchen where Ben was feeding Bryce and Belinda was feeding Bradley. "We sent him a picture of my model, so he probably wants to see it in person!"

When he arrived, Hampton spent the first part of his visit with the girls. He gave Brittani some pointers and when he was sure that Brianna was satisfied he went into the den to talk to Ben and Belinda. He told them about Melissa, and that he would see the information she was trying to send him the next day. "I don't know what to do." Hampton was looking at Ben but really talking to Belinda. Ben spoke first.

"What you don't want to do is to have regrets; yours or April's."

"Ben's right. She needs, at least deserves, to know and then deal with the facts and make her own decisions," Belinda said.

"Melissa never wanted April. She hasn't seen her in twenty years. I have covered for her, never told April the whole story - the real story."

"Pop..." Belinda paused, "...you did the right thing for her, and now the right thing is to let her decide." They were all quiet for a moment.

"Don't do anything until you see what's in the packet," Ben said.

"That's a good point. You may be overreacting," Belinda said in agreement.

They discussed the situation in detail. Hampton was glad to have them to talk to. Belinda saw a side of him she hadn't seen, didn't think existed, a softer side. "Are you here because you want me to tell her?" Belinda asked.

"No, you're not getting into that," Ben said.

"No sugar, that's not why I'm here, but please be open to talking to her if she wants to," Hampton said.

"Sure, I can do that," she replied.

"April is going to be fine. She is strong and level-headed. She will probably surprise us," Ben said seriously.

Ben was still cautious about Belinda and April's relationship, and he definitely didn't want Belinda getting involved with this situation between April and her mother. They talked about how April made a point of being sisterly. "Sweetie, my mom used to say to Kirby and me there are some people you feed with a long handled spoon. That's the way I am with April," Belinda said to Ben.

"I hear you babe, but it seems the spoon handle is getting shorter."
"Don't worry, I have a long memory," she said.

Hampton didn't have to wait long to see the attorney, and they got right down to business. Hampton took a deep breath and opened the packet. There was an envelope addressed to Hampton, one addressed to April and a document with at least a dozen pages inside a blue cover. It was a certified copy of Melissa's will. Hampton lay it on the table, took the letter opener from the pencil holder in the center of the table, and easily opened the letter addressed to him.

"Hello Hamp,

It's been way too long. You never liked it when I didn't get right to the point, so here it is. I have terminal cancer. I am in treatment to only prolong the inevitable. I am going to die—soon. So I am getting my affairs in order. Including making peace with you and April.

No, I haven't done the right thing by our daughter. And you know why; I had her for you. I did my best for as long as I could. You might as well forgive me 'cause God has forgiven me and I've forgiven myself. Fortunately, she is the best of me. The things you loved most about me is who she is. I know that her success, who she is in business and as a person is because of you. I didn't have the capacity to do all that Hampton. Thank you for being such a good father to her.

My career was my priority, my passion or as you once said; 'my drug of choice.' I excelled in the world of fashion. I did well and made a lot of money but that couldn't save my life.

I'm sure April will tell you if she hasn't already, I am leaving the bulk of my estate to her. I am taking care of my assistant, giving some money to a couple of charities, my alma mater, and of course my mother's old church! The administrative fees are taken care of.

In closing, yes, Hampton I loved you, but not enough to be a wife and mother. I didn't want family outings and Christmas dinner and PTA meetings. I wanted glitz and glamour. You are a remarkable man, a great human being and from what I remember a sensational lover, but I wasn't the woman for you. And I hope you have the two things you always wanted; a loving wife, and I hope that soon April will give you the grandchildren you want and deserve.

Be well,

Melissa

Hampton sat quietly for a moment, re-reading parts of Melissa's letter to him. He appreciated her transparency but she didn't say anything he didn't know. He had made peace with her in his heart and mind long ago. He wanted to read what she wrote to April but decided he wouldn't. He wanted to see the Will, though.

The attorney opened the packet and handed it to him. Hampton looked and started to say something, but the attorney spoke instead. "We can re-seal it."

The first paragraph was legal jargon stating it was Melissa's Last Will and Testament, and that she was in sound mind and not coerced into making these statements. The second paragraph identified her assistant as the Executor of the Estate, and gave her the Power of Attorney and more legal jargon related to the Executor's duties.

The third paragraph told the story. It stated April Angelique Josephs, the only child of Melissa Angelique Montgomery and Hampton Josephs, will receive in cash three million dollars, a house previously owned by her maternal grandparents, valued at ninety thousand dollars, jewelry, paintings and sculptures valued at one point six million dollars and a list of other things such as a mink coat, camera, designer luggage, and a collection of limited edition leather purses, valued at half a million dollars.

"Damn!" Hampton said shaking his head. "I had no idea Melissa had accumulated this kind of wealth." He took a deep breath, didn't say anything for a moment but gave the attorney the will back.

"How do you want to proceed?" the attorney asked.

Hampton blew out a long breath. "Let me sleep on it. I will call you tomorrow."

ONE HUNDRED-FIVE

"April?" She turned around expecting to see the man her dad sent her to have lunch with. Instead, standing there was Lane Silver, the doctor Belinda introduced her to.

"Lane, hi, how are you?"

"I'm good, how are you?"

"Fine," she answered.

"What are you doing here?" Lane asked, smiling.

This was the first time he got a good look at her. She was checking him out too. She rolled her eyes as she answered. "My wonderful father who is also my business partner, wants me to meet with a business associate of his because he over scheduled himself." She rolled her eyes again.

Lane laughed. "Why don't you want to meet with the guy?"

"Because he's a jerk."

Lane was laughing again. "I'm off today so I can hang around if you have a little time to talk when your meeting is done."

April smiled. "Sure, that sounds good."

April's meeting lasted about forty-five minutes. She didn't know Lane was watching her. He took a seat at the bar where he could see her. He paid close attention to her body language. She was very serious and though he couldn't hear what she was saying to "the jerk" it was obvious she had command of the meeting. All Lane knew about April was she and Belinda were sisters and she was the most sought after architect in town. He wasn't sure he wanted to know her better but he was sure he needed to get back "out there" as his mother told him.

When her guest left, April took out her phone, and started typing. After a couple of minutes Lane walked over to her table. She looked up, "Have a seat!" she said. Lane sat and she kept typing. She smiled as she did.

When April put the phone down, Lane asked "So is the jerk going to do business with you?"

"He already is, I just needed to update some things about the project. Ugggh!"

Lane laughed loudly. April stifled her laugh but smiled and blinked her eyes over and over.

"Ms. Josephs may I get you something else?" the waiter asked.

"Lane?"

"I'll have another one of these," he said lifting his glass to the waiter, and ordered an appetizer. Lane and April talked for almost an hour.

"Lane, this was really fun! Thanks for waiting. I have to get back to work..." April was saying when he interrupted her.

"April, I'm really glad we ran into each other. When can I see you again?"

April looked at him closely. "Maybe we can get together over the weekend," she said, and they exchanged numbers.

He came to her side of the table, helped her out of her chair. They chatted while the valet brought her car. "I'll call you later," he said to her with a wink.

On the drive back to the office, April thought about what she and Lane talked about. She engaged her phone. "Hi April," Belinda said when she answered.

"Hi, can you talk for a few minutes?"

"Yes, what's wrong?" Belinda asked, afraid April was going to say something about her mother.

"Nothing's wrong. Have you talked to Daddy?"

Belinda hesitated. "Not today. He came by here last night to see the kids."

April laughed. "Yeah, I heard about the amphitheater!"

Belinda wanted her to get to the point.

"Did he tell you about…"

Belinda held her breath.

"…these family pictures he wants for Christmas?"

Belinda exhaled. "He didn't tell me, Brittani told me. I forgot to mention it last night."

"Well, as I understand it, he had Felecia hire a photographer."

"Based on what Brittani said, a professional needs to handle it, there are so many of us." They both laughed.

"Okay I need to change the channel," April said. "I ran into Lane at lunch today." April told Belinda about her impromptu lunch date.

342

ONE HUNDRED-SIX

The day after Lane and April ran into each other in the restaurant, he called to see if she was available for lunch. "April, hello it's Lane. Give me a call please. Are you available for lunch?" When he hung up he wondered if she didn't answer because it was him calling. He had back to back patients and was really hungry. He checked his phone and there was no message from April so he went to the cafeteria. At the end of the day as he was preparing to leave the office, April called. She agreed to meet him for dinner. Lane arrived before April, went to the bar and had one drink. He finished it before she arrived. He was standing right inside the door when she walked in. She looked amazing. Her hair was different, she had on jeans, a bright, colorful sweater, a purple jacket and boots. The previous times he'd seen her she was dressed in business attire. "Wow, you look incredible!" he said as he hugged her slightly. "Thank you!" She smiled.

When the server came they ordered an appetizer and a drink. He let her order first, and ordered a drink because she did.

"You must have gotten off early today, no business suit."

She laughed, "Yeah, I worked about half the day."

"What do you do other than work?" he asked.

"I'm active in church, in a book club, play golf, and since the kids have come into our lives, I support their extra-curricular activities."

"Kids? What kids?"

"Belinda's kids. You don't know that story?"

"Story! No I don't." Lane said frowning.

April took a deep breath, smiled and started talking. The server set their drinks in front of them but didn't linger. A couple of minutes later someone else brought the appetizer. Lane listened intently. This was the most incredible thing he had heard in a long time. He sipped his drink and had a few bites of the appetizer. She stopped talking when the server came to take the order. She resumed her story. "Our relationship is a work in progress but I think she's forgiven me," April said quietly.

He was shaking his head. "Whew! April, that's crazy. What about your mother?" he asked.

"That's a story for another day," she said. He didn't press her.

"What about you, Dr. Silver? What do you do outside of work?"

"I play golf too, I love movies, and I read. I haven't gone to church since I've been here."

"May I extend an invitation for you to visit Landridge Community Church?" she said excitedly.

"Thank you, I will take you up on that," he said.

"I can't believe Belinda hasn't invited you."

"She has several times, I just haven't come."

At the end of the evening he asked to see her again and she agreed. When the valet brought her car, Lane took her hand, walked her to the driver's side and kissed her forehead. He walked to his car thinking about her. He decided to call his mother and tell her he had a date.

ONE HUNDRED-SEVEN

After a few days, Sunny and Grant settled back into their original routine minus the sex. But, her mother wasn't happy about it. He didn't tell his parents, Gretchen or Clay. He also didn't tell Sunny they didn't know. And interestingly Sunny and Cicely had not talked either. Sunny had not told her friends she and Grant were back together. Her mother asked her if that meant she wasn't sure. "It means I don't want to have to explain again if things don't work out."

Grant was excited about going home. He wanted to see Gretchen and his parents and he wanted to celebrate with Clay and Cicely. He still loved that they eloped! He packed the car, stopped by the office to check on a couple things and then got on the road.

It was Saturday morning so there wasn't much traffic after he got out of D.C. A quick stop at Gretchen's house to shower and change clothes, then on to the church. The reception should be starting. Everybody was surprised when Grant and Sunny walked into the fellowship hall.

When Grant asked Sunny to go home with him she didn't know it would take the attention off Clay and Cicely and put it on them. That wasn't what she wanted. And that was when she figured out Grant's family didn't know they were back together. She was really hurt, really angry, but she wouldn't address it until they got back home.

At the end of the evening after Cicely and Clay left, Grant was waiting for Gretchen to give the cleanup crew some instructions. She had been busy and they hadn't really talked. Sunny was waiting and Gretchen knew they were going to her house. They would talk at home.

Grant heard Gretchen moving around downstairs. He eased out of bed. He didn't want to wake Sunny. He needed a few minutes alone with his sister. "Hey you."

"Good morning."

Those were the only civil words between them for several minutes. "That crazy girl gave you pure hell and you escort her back in here like nothing happened! You are crazy." Gretchen was screaming at Grant.

"Get over it G.G., she's here to stay. And she's coming to Christmas dinner!"

ONE HUNDRED-EIGHT

Roderick and Sandra were lying in bed just talking; something they hadn't done in so long. "We weathered the storm, Rod," Sandra said quietly.

"Yeah, we did. I still think Chloe's up to something, though," Roderick said.

"Of course she is, that's her! Probably some bombshell at Christmas!" Sandra laughed. "Speaking of Christmas, what are we doing?"

They talked about Roderick's sister Natalie coming from D.C. They talked about taking some time off together. "We need a vacation," Roderick said and kissed her.

Roderick and Natalie prepped dinner on Christmas Eve. They prepared ribs, steaks, coconut shrimp and lots of sides. Sandra's contribution was sweet potato pies. They talked and laughed and it felt good. As Sandra watched Roderick and Natalie, the thought occurred to her they didn't realize how out of control their lives had been over the last year, and how much stress they were dealing with. She literally exhaled. As much as she loved Chloe, she knew they needed to do some things differently. But was it too late?

Natalia was invited to dinner and she arrived early to help Chloe and Sandra with whatever they needed. Chloe and her cousins set the table and laughed about not sitting at the kids' table. The doorbell rang. It was Campbell. He went into the kitchen, spoke to Roderick, Sandra and Natalie, and then joined Chloe in the dining room. He was a little nervous about the announcement that he and Chloe were making at dinner but it had to be done.

The group ate, laughed, debated and enjoyed each other and the food. When one of her cousins started to clear the table, Chloe asked her to wait a few minutes. "Campbell and I have something to tell everybody! She started by saying she and Campbell were headed to New York City. "We are both accepted into law school there!" She continued by explaining that her acceptance was conditional. Campbell told them about his scholarship.

"Congratulations son, that's great," Roderick said. Other than that nobody commented.

"Thank you sir," Campbell said.

Chloe went on to discuss the details of their plans. Sandra finally gathered her thoughts. "Chloe, this sounds like a very good, however ambitious, plan. Why New York darling?"

"Ma, Campbell wanted to go to New York and after everything that happened I decided a change would be good for me too."

"I think you're right," her Aunt Natalie said.

Sandra looked at Natalie with a scowl. Natalie looked directly at Sandra but continued to talk to Chloe. Sandra loved her sister-in-law but she always took Chloe's side. It had been that way all of Chloe's life. "New York will offer both of you so many opportunities," Natalie said.

"I know, that's why we're so excited!" Chloe said with a big smile.

Natalia knew about Chloe and Campbell's plans; she sat and watched the interaction between Chloe and her parents, and she felt the tension. "Sis, that's exciting! We can have Christmas dinner in the city next year!"

Natalia and Chloe started talking about Natalia coming to visit and all the things they would do. Sandra interrupted them.

"Chloe, what about North Carolina Central Law School? What about you being here to take over our firm? Have you forgotten about all that?"

Chloe glanced at Campbell. "No ma'am," Campbell said.

"Chloe and I talked about all that before we made the decision to move to New York. N.C. Central is off the table, but we didn't make a decision about coming back to take over your firm. We won't have to make that decision for at least three years."

Sandra was amused that Campbell was doing the talking. That was a switch. Chloe wasn't in the habit of allowing anybody to speak for her.

"You two seem to have this all thought out." Roderick said somewhat sarcastically.

"Daddy, we have talked about this a dozen times. I can't live in this town; not now. I'm tired of people looking at me crazy, whispering, talking about me," Chloe said looking directly at her dad.

"Sir, we made the decision to get away so our son can live in this town in peace. He deserves that. It's not his fault the adults in this situation don't always make good decisions."

"Mama, I hope your offer to pay my tuition and living expenses still stands."

"Chloe, that offer was for Durham, North Carolina not New York City! The cost of living is much more and the tuition is higher."

Chloe cut her off before she finished. "Ma, I thought you would be proud of me for getting accepted, and for making a mature decision. Instead you're talking about money! Do we need to negotiate? Okay, you give me what you had planned to give me in Durham and Campbell and I will make up the difference."

What they all noticed was Chloe didn't whine or pout like she usually did when she wanted something from her parents.

"I'm sure Rod and Sandra will work something out with you," her Aunt Natalie said looking at Roderick. Sandra wanted Natalie to mind her business. She knew Rod would give in now. His sister had a lot of influence on him. He was no match for his sister and his daughter.

"I don't know Chloe. Your dad and I will have to talk about all this," Sandra said.

Chloe didn't like what her mother said. But she was determined not to be stressed about it. If she had to do it on her own, she would. She and Campbell. Chloe looked at her aunt. "Can Natalia and I go back with you and then you go to New York with us to help me look for a place?"

"Absolutely, I would love to!"

"Me too!" Her cousin said.

Natalia was ecstatic. "Oh my goodness! I have never been to New York City!" She kept talking. They all laughed. Natalia's accent kicked in and they weren't sure what she was saying.

The day after Christmas Roderick and Sandra left Hattiesville to drive to Charleston. On the drive down they talked about Campbell, Chloe and New York City. They agreed there wasn't much they could do to stop her, and obviously the threat of not giving her money didn't work. "I told you she was up to something," Roderick said.

"But that's more than I expected," Sandra said.

"I guess NCCU is off the table as Campbell said," Roderick told Sandra.

"I guess that was our dream."

Neither of them said anything for a few minutes. Finally Sandra mentioned the amenities at the hotel.

On the ride back to Hattiesville, Roderick and Sandra decided they would offer Chloe a contract. In exchange for them funding her education and living expenses she would have to work for them for three years, commencing no more than two years after graduation.

"That will give her time to study for the bar exam, take the exam and pass," Sandra said.

"What about Campbell?" Roderick asked.

"I guess we will make him the same offer, provided they're still together. We will just put a clause in the contract that states that." They talked about it a little longer and were satisfied with their decision.

ONE HUNDRED-NINE

Ben and Hampton met on Monday to review the punch list for the church. Ben couldn't believe it was almost done. The move-in date was the end of January. This was their last meeting before Christmas.

Hampton told April he would handle the walk through. The truth; he wanted to talk to Ben alone. They had a good list in about an hour. "I'm sure we will need to do this again before we give you the occupancy certificate," Hampton said.

"I just can't believe it happened. It's actually a church! Man! I can't wait for Belinda and Grammy to see it. And Bishop Robinson will be here next week. Can we get back in?"

"Oh yeah. No problem, just let me know when," Hampton said matter-of-factly. Ben was standing there with both hands on top of his head. "You have time for lunch?" Hampton asked him.

"Sure!"

After a few minutes of talking about the church and Ben and Belinda's new house, Hampton told Ben about Melissa's will. "I don't know what to do," Hampton said seriously. "Man, I'm absolutely stunned at the amount of money, plus that she's giving it to April. Don't get me wrong. It's the least she can do. The very least. April deserves it. She hasn't done anything else for her. As far as I know they haven't had any contact since Melissa left, over twenty years ago." Ben was listening intently. He leaned back in his chair, away from the table, and closed his eyes for a few seconds. When he leaned up, he looked directly into Hampton's eyes.

"You need to tell April. Some things just don't need to be a surprise. Then you need to trust her to make the right decisions and support whatever that decision is," Ben said very evenly. As far as he was concerned his role here was pastor and counselor, not son-in-law or brother-in-law. He could tell Hampton was thinking through what he said.

"I have protected April with everything in me her whole life..." Hampton was saying when Ben interrupted him.

"But you think you can't protect her from this."

"Right!"

"But by your telling her and not letting her get a letter in the mail or some arbitrary phone call from a stranger saying your mother died and left you three million dollars, you are protecting her. And based on what you're telling me, you should handle this sooner rather than later."

ONE HUNDRED-TEN

Jacksa thought she was dreaming. She couldn't process what Anderson was telling her. This made no sense. She couldn't fathom he had to leave the next day, wouldn't be home for Christmas and would get back less than twenty-four hours before the wedding.

Anderson could tell by the expression on her face Jacksa was devastated. He knew she didn't understand but that was the nature of the job. He couldn't give her the details of the case. If he could the seriousness of it may be more understandable to her.

Jacksa thought of the conversation she had with Mrs. Robinson. "You have to be willing to sacrifice sometimes to have the kind of lifestyle you want," Mrs. Robinson had said to her. "Ambitious men like Anderson need support and that may look like you being along when you don't want to be…" The thought stopped there. Jacksa knew she had to make the right comment. She didn't want to deflate Anderson.

"Sweetheart, you have to work. The timing just stinks."

"Yeah, but I can quit and when we get back from our honeymoon, I can go back to the police department."

"Anderson…"

"Baby, I don't want anything to stand in the way of you becoming my wife!"

She blushed a little. "Quitting is not the answer. We will make it work. Let's see what we need to adjust for you to leave in the morning." Jacksa sounded more positive than she felt.

ONE HUNDRED-ELEVEN

When Hampton pulled into the garage that evening, April's car was already there. He hoped she wasn't going out. He wanted to talk while he had the nerve. He called her.

"Hey Da, what's up?"

"Hey sunshine. You in for the evening?"

"I was going to Zumba, you need me?"

"Yep, how about coming down for a few minutes," he said.

She knew something was up; he only called her sunshine when it was serious.

A few minutes later she came in wearing workout gear and carrying her gym bag. Hampton was in the den, jazz music was playing in the background. This was serious, otherwise it would be R & B. April sat on the sofa, Hampton was in the recliner.

"The last time we met like this, you told me you have another daughter. Please don't tell me I have a brother now," April said seriously.

Hampton looked at her just as seriously. "No sugar - no brother, no more siblings. I have some news though."

The packet from the attorney was lying on the coffee table. "For a couple of months, I've been getting letters from an attorney representing your mother. I ignored them for a while."

"Why?" April asked.

"I, we hadn't heard from her in ages. I just couldn't imagine what she wanted. I had it checked out and what I found out is in that packet."

He nodded toward the coffee table. April looked at the envelope but didn't reach for it. She shifted from sitting on one leg to putting both feet on the floor. "Talk to me Daddy."

"Melissa has terminal cancer. She says she is in treatment only to give herself time to tie up some loose ends."

"What does that have to do with me? I haven't seen her in twenty-one years. I'm sorry..." her voice cracked...she cleared her throat..."I hate she has cancer." There were tears in her eyes.

"It's okay for you to feel bad. She is your mother."

"I think a better way to describe her is my egg donor," she shrugged. "I made peace with her a long time ago, Daddy. What does any of this have to do with that packet?" she asked with an annoyed tone of voice. Now she nodded toward it.

"You need to read what's in there." Hampton said getting the envelope to give to her.

"Did you read it?" April asked her dad, but not reaching for the envelope.

"I read a letter she wrote me and I looked at the Will."

"The Will! Now I'm really amused. Why would I be interested in her Will?"

"Baby, she left the bulk of her estate to you!"

"To me! Why? She doesn't even know me! Just tell me what it says." She rolled her eyes.

Hampton sighed. This conversation was not going as he expected. She had been angry with him for not telling her about her grandmother passing, so he thought she would be glad he let her review The Will herself. He opened the envelope, took out the document, intending to read it to her. She looked so annoyed he decided to just tell her and get this over with. He told her about the mink coat, the purses, and the camera first. She said nothing. Her face was expressionless. He went on to mention the paintings and sculptures, still no expression until he stated the value. "Really," she said. "One point six million dollars. That stuff should be easy to sell, so the kid's college just got funded." Hampton looked up. She was not being sarcastic, she was serious.

"Your grandmother's house…"

She interrupted him, "I will find a homeless family to give that to. Is that it?" She stood to get her gym bag.

"No, that's not it."

April crossed her arms and stared at Hampton. "Melissa is leaving you three million dollars in cash."

"Are you freakin' kidding me?" April screamed. "Three million dollars, does she think she can buy me? I haven't heard from her in twenty plus years and she thinks three million dollars will make it okay!" She was yelling and Hampton didn't say anything. He wasn't trying to defend Melissa because he agreed with April. It was too little too late. "Well, the mortgage on the church just got reduced! Is there ANYTHING else?"

"No sweetie."

"Thank you!" April said. She threw her gym bag on her shoulder and walked out. She drove about half a mile before the flood gates opened. She was crying so hard she couldn't see to drive. She turned into a parking lot and cried for several minutes. When she finally calmed down she wasn't sure why she was crying. Was the emotion out of anger, or because she cared about her mother? "Am I mad because she opened a door that's been closed forever or because I don't want her to die?" She sat and thought for five minutes or so then wiped her face, blew her nose and drove to the gym.

April missed the Zumba class so she went to a spin class and then decided to swim a couple of laps. When she finished and was headed to the locker room she ran into Lane and a couple of his friends.

"You are beautiful even soaking wet!" he said. She blushed. He introduced her to his friends, and then they chatted for just a minute. He told her they had played basketball and he was on his way home, he had an early surgery. "Why don't you come over to my place tomorrow night? I will cook you dinner," he said.

"Oh, you cook?"

"Yep, and I'm good at it!"

They made plans and she walked into the locker room. It was cold outside and she didn't usually swim in the winter but she needed the stress reliever. She dried her hair as best she could, holding her head under the hand dryer. She didn't have a hat so she wrapped a towel around her head. When she got to the door she ran to her car. She hoped neither Lane nor his friends saw her.

April got home to see the den lights still on in her dad's part of the house. He would hear the garage door open but she hoped he wouldn't want to talk again. She made it into the house without any contact with her dad. She showered, popped some popcorn and sat in bed. Pretty sure she had made a decision, she reached for the telephone.

"Hey, how are you?"

"Good, and you?" Belinda said puzzled that April was calling this late and for the second time that day.

"Can you have lunch tomorrow?"

"No can't have lunch but I can have breakfast," Belinda said cheerfully.

"That's too early to drink but, okay!" April said and laughed.

"Are you okay? Is it Lane?"

"Oh, no he's good. As a matter of fact I ran into him at the gym tonight. How about he invited me to dinner at his place tomorrow night and he's cooking!

"Alright now!" Belinda said with a laugh.

"Why do you need a drink?" Belinda asked seriously.

"I'll tell you all about it in the morning." They made breakfast plans and hung up.

Belinda told Ben about her conversation with April. He was quiet for a moment. Then he told her about meeting with Hampton.

"Oh Jesus. I'm glad you told me. At least I can think of what to say, and be prayed up when I meet her." They both laughed. Belinda's phone rang again. It was Hampton. She showed Ben the screen before she answered.

Hampton asked about the children then told Belinda about the encounter with April. Her thought as she listened to him talk was why they were involving her. She looked at

Ben and shrugged. "It's ministry darling" was Ben's reply as he left the room.

"Well…she called me a few minutes ago. We're meeting in the morning."

"Good…"

"I don't really know why she's confiding in me though," Belinda said interrupting Hampton. "Six months ago she hated my guts, now she wants to be friends; I don't get it." There, she said it. He was quiet for a moment.

"Belinda, April is your sister. Now I know all of this happened suddenly and the circumstances were crazy and you two did get off to a horrible start. But, you need to forgive me and forgive her. This isn't anything I haven't said to you or to her. You had a tough start to life and I didn't do anything to make it better. I know you think April lived a charmed life and maybe she did, but her mother left her! The lady who raised you wasn't your biological mother but she obviously loved you and did well by you, and you had Kirby." As Hampton was talking, Belinda had a couple of emotions and thoughts. She felt like a little girl being chastised by her dad, and she thought he was expecting too much from her. The new family dynamic was taking some getting used to. "While I still have breath in my body we are going to get this right, Belinda." Neither of them said anything for a moment.

Finally Belinda spoke. "I am doing the best I can under the circumstances," she said.

"I know you are and I appreciate that," he replied.

"I will do what I can to help April, I know this has to be hard on her," Belinda assured him, thinking about Ben saying it was ministry.

Ben was back in the room, and caught the tail end of Belinda's conversation with Hampton. "You can get a good night's sleep!" she said, smiling at him.

"Why?" he asked, smiling back.

"April told Hampton she's going to use the three million dollars to pay down the mortgage on the church!"

"Hallelujah!" They both laughed.

At breakfast, April told Belinda about Melissa, her diagnosis and The Will. Belinda listened, didn't interrupt her and genuinely felt bad for April. "So don't worry, your children's education is covered and the mortgage on the church will be reduced," April said very seriously.

"April, that's terribly generous of you, but why don't you put the money away for your own children's education?"

"Because Brittani and Brianna will be in college before any children I have get out of elementary school. I have plenty of time to prepare for them. I want it out of my hands and doing something good as quickly as possible. I don't know the woman and I can't be bought!"

"Is that what you really think?"

"Yes, she gave some money to charity, her college; why not give it all to them? I don't need it!"

"You do realize she could make a full recovery?" "Good, then I won't have to deal with it at all," April said with attitude. "Plus she had the nerve to write me a letter. April took the sealed envelope from her purse, and handed it to Belinda.

"Why haven't you opened this?" Belinda asked handing it back to April who shrugged but didn't take the letter.

"You read it and tell me anything that you think is important; anything I don't already know." Belinda was staring at April. "Belinda, just read it or throw it away. I don't care but I don't want it."

Belinda took the knife from beside her plate and carefully opened the envelope. The letterhead had a New York City address and telephone number. April ate her food while Belinda read. The first two paragraphs reinforced in simple terms the contents of the Will. Starting with the third paragraph the letter became personal.

"April, I hope you can find it in your heart to forgive me. It is pointless to spend time now listing my many sins against you. Just suffice it to say I didn't have the emotional capacity to be your mother. The daughter your father wanted, I couldn't raise. He had a picture of what his family should look like and it was different from my picture. But that was good for you.

I kept up with your progress; despite Hampton's efforts to block me."

Belinda continued to read. April continued to eat. The letter talked a little about what Melissa had done over the years and mentioned several things about April like when she graduated from high school, made the college volleyball team and graduated from college. The mention of the volleyball team got April's attention. She wondered how Melissa knew about that, and she wondered how Melissa knew she was on the mayor's planning council.

"I did it all wrong April. You don't know me, and you didn't know my mother and she was angry with me about that for many years. I regret we didn't resolve it before she

passed. The bottom line is, I'm not a good mother. Please don't take this personally."

"How am I supposed to take it?" She laughed again.

"I hope when you have children you will be a good mother. Do that for me please and, I hope you marry a man like your dad. You deserve the life I didn't bother to have. Looking back there is nothing more important than the love of family, especially a husband and daughter who love you.

Now three million dollars is a lot of money. Invest it wisely, let Hampton help you, he has a talent for that kind of thing. You may have different taste in art, but I know you understand the value of those pieces.

In closing, please don't waste a lot of time hating me. Life is too short. I do love you, whether you believe it or not."

Melissa

Belinda looked up at April who had called the waiter over for another cup of coffee. "Did you hear a word I said?"

"Yep. I heard everything you said. What you don't understand is, I don't care! I don't give a damn about any of that! My mind has not changed because her conscious is bothering her."

Belinda shrugged. She didn't care either because she really didn't want to be involved anyway. She folded the letter put it back in the envelope took a sip of water and asked April about the new house.

ONE HUNDRED-TWELVE

Late in the day Lane called April to ask if they could have dinner a little later. His schedule had gotten re-arranged, and he needed ample time to "dazzle you with my culinary skills."

April was a little nervous when she arrived at Lane's house, but she had texted Belinda to tell her she was there. "Have fun" was Belinda's reply. It was dark so she couldn't see much of the house but the landscape lighting was nice. The house was dark also which puzzled her but she rang the bell, waited a minute and then rang it again. Another minute and no answer so she called him.

The phone startled Lane. "Oh shit!" He thought. "Hey April." He invited her in and she followed him into the great room. "I had a tough day, I am so sorry I'm not ready, but I promised you dinner."

"We can do this another time."

"No please don't go. Just give me a minute to re-group." She followed him to the kitchen.

April was impressed with Lane's kitchen. She liked the stainless steel appliances, the ceramic tile and marble counter tops and the island stove top with the grill. "This is really nice. How long have you lived here?" she asked quietly.

"Thanks, I've been here nine months. Please have a seat." She sat on a bar stool at the opposite end of the island from where he was standing. "May I fix you a cup of tea?" He took a wooden box from a cabinet and opened it. There were several kinds of tea bags. She took the box from him and looked through it. There was a thick silence in the room. He opened the refrigerator took out a bottle of water and a bowl of shrimp he had in marinate. He took a big gulp of the water. In a few minutes he had a Wok on the stove and was mixing vegetables and shrimp and boiling rice. It smelled delicious. This wasn't his original plan for dinner, but it would have to do. She sipped her tea; they made small talk about the house. He put a little oil in another skillet, let it get hot and poured the rice in for a few minutes. He served two plates, gave her chop sticks and a glass of water and sat across from her.

"This is delicious, Lane," April said, taking another bite.

"Thank you ma'am," he said with a big smile. "I promise to cook you a real dinner next time. I had bigger plans for your tonight, but I…"
"Went to sleep," she finished the sentence and they both laughed.

After a few minutes more of casual conversation, Lane asked April about her mother. "You told me that was a conversation for another time. This is another time," he said.

"You first," April said. "Tell me how you ended up in Landridge, Georgia from Houston, Texas.

"I ended up in Landridge because I wanted to live outside Atlanta. I came to Atlanta because I needed a change of scenery and I got the job here. If I'm going to tell you this story we need to be drinking something stronger than this water!" He went to the refrigerator and looked in. "I have wine, red or white."

"White please," she answered.

They moved to the great room and sat on the sofa. He used a remote to turn on some music very softly and another one to light the logs in the fireplace. "I was married for almost three years. My ex was a local news reporter when we got married. Shortly after, she was promoted to anchor. About the same time, I introduced the subject of having children. She asked me to give her a year in the new job. I was good with that until a year later she asked for another year. At the end of that year she said okay, but what I didn't know, she was on birth control pills."

"How did you find out?"

"I was concerned why she wasn't getting pregnant. When I asked her to go to the doctor, she came clean. I was pissed that she lied, but the real blow came when she told me she didn't want children." April shifted her body in the seat. "She said her career was more important than having a family. Saying I was shocked is an understatement." April swallowed hard, and there were tears in her eyes. Lane was still talking but April was half listening. The story he was telling her was the same story her dad told her about her mother. Before she knew it, she was crying. Lane frowned. A couple of minutes passed before she could tell him why she was crying.

Lane went to the kitchen to get April a napkin to wipe her face. He sat closer to her when he came back. "Why are you crying?" He asked her very carefully. She wiped her face, took a sip of wine and cleared her throat.

"I'm sorry." She sighed heavily. "That is the same thing my mother told my father after I was born, and then she left." She started to cry again. Lane put his arms around her and let her cry. When she was quiet, still holding her he asked, "Do you want to talk about it?"

She told him about the weeklong vacation she took with her father and her mother being gone when she got back. Then she told him about the letter, about Melissa having terminal cancer and about the Will. She didn't tell him what was in the Will. "Be grateful your ex-wife didn't have a baby and then decide she didn't want to be a mother."

"I am now, but I didn't understand it then," he said. They continued to talk. April wasn't accustomed to being this transparent and especially not with a man she didn't know any better than she knew Lane. But he was equally forthcoming. They talked about their childhoods; his growing up in rural Texas and her growing up in urban Georgia.

In the midst of the conversation Lane convinced April that she needed to confront her mother. "Clear your head and then tell her what's on your heart. You don't want to live with any regrets," he said.

"I guess I could write her a letter in response to her letter to me," April said more as a question than a statement.

"You could, but you're more courageous than that. Don't hide behind a note, I think you should call her!" When he said courageous, something stirred in her. Lane was right, she was bold and sure of herself. This was no different than any other challenge she had to face. "I will call her tomorrow!"

"That's my girl."

Lane's phone rang and they both looked at the time. "Dr. Silver," he said, answering and walking over to a desk a few feet away, in a small alcove off the room where they sat. It was obviously a call about a patient. He was making notes as he talked. The call was brief. When he walked back to where he left April sitting, she was on the edge of the sofa, getting her keys from her purse. He looked at her and frowned. "Where are you going?"

She smiled. "Home. It's after midnight."

"Please don't go. I'm enjoying your company."

She was enjoying his company too, but she wasn't sure what to do. "I have a good selection of DVDs. Let's watch a movie, your choice." They both laughed. She made a selection, he popped popcorn and they settled back on the sofa to watch the movie. When he awakened she was in his arms, sound asleep. He eased from behind her, went upstairs, found a Houston Rockets t-shirt and a toothbrush. He put the toothbrush in the bathroom and lay the shirt at the foot of the bed. When he went back downstairs he had a second thought about getting her up. She was sleeping so peacefully. He texted Belinda to tell her April was there and staying the night. He told Belinda April was pretty upset, but okay now. Belinda responded, "Thanks for letting me know. Talk tomorrow." He chuckled to himself then leaned down and picked her up.

"Put me down!" He carried her to the bottom step and set her down. "What are you doing?" she asked.

"I have things set up for you in the guest room upstairs," Lane said. April started to protest but he interrupted her. "It's cold, it's late, and you had a couple of drinks. You need to stay put tonight," he said. She started to say something else. He cut her off again. "I texted Belinda, and told her you are staying here tonight."

"Is that right?" She rolled her eyes. But she was tired, more emotionally drained than physically tired. "Good night Dr. Silver."

"Good night Ms. Josephs," he said with a smile. He stood at the bottom of the stairs until she closed the bedroom door.

At the top of the stairs was a den area with a huge television and book shelves. That's all she could see without turning on a light. There were three bedrooms, and two full bathrooms. She was familiar with this floor plan. There was a master bedroom upstairs and downstairs. The other bedrooms shared a bathroom.

The room was professionally decorated as she suspected the rest of the house was. She had seen these fabrics and color schemes at trade shows. She laughed at the t-shirt but quickly got ready for bed. She fell asleep thinking about what she would say to her mother.

ONE HUNDRED-THIRTEEN

Jacksa was cleaning up a few last minute things on her desk, to be off work until after her honeymoon. The phone rang on her desk. "Ms. Baye, there is someone in the reception area to see you." Natalia said.

"Thank you, I'll be right there." Jacksa was puzzled about who was out there. She smiled. It was probably nobody, just Natalia and another one of her surprises.

Jacksa walked down the hall and could see two gentleman standing there. "Ms. Baye, I'm Agent White," the man said showing her his ID. "May we talk somewhere privately?" Natalia got up from the desk and walked away.

"How may I help you Agent White?" Jacksa asked.

"You are listed as next of kin and emergency contact for Agent Anderson Thorn."

"Yes, he's my fiancé, she responded very matter-of-factly, and folded her arms.

"Ms. Baye, we are here to inform you that Agent Thorn was working an undercover assignment…"

"Yes, I know, get to the point!" Jacksa screamed.

"We have reason to believe Agent Thorn's identity has been compromised, and we haven't been in touch with him for forty-eight hours."

"Exactly what does that mean?" Jacksa screamed at him again. Natalia and Roderick were standing in the hall where they could see Jacksa but she couldn't see them.

"Ma'am, Agent Thorn is officially missing and we presume…"

Jacksa fainted.

ONE HUNDRED-FOURTEEN

The whole family assembled at the studio for pictures. Felecia was there to make sure it went well. There was a grand piano, and a huge Christmas tree just as Hampton requested. He wanted it to resemble the family room at his house. Everyone was dressed in black and white including Bradley and Bryce. Brianna and Brittani were wearing fuchsia sweaters for a pop of color. The photographer started with the boys, added the girls and added people until the whole group was in the picture. Then she moved the adults around and took people away until all the combinations were done. The final picture was Hampton, April and Belinda.

The session went off without a hitch. Hampton couldn't have been happier, and Felecia knew her Christmas bonus had just increased. As they were leaving the studio, Brianna told Felecia she would see her in New York City.

April was ready to go. She had an important call to make. Lane gave her a pep talk before she left his house that morning.

As soon as she got home, she took out the letter with the phone number, and dialed before she could think about it. She cleared her throat. The phone rang several times. Finally there was an answer. "April Josephs attempting to reach Melissa Montgomery please," she said in a very businesses-like tone of voice. After a brief silence the person answering said "just a moment please." April took a deep breath.

"Hi April, how are you?" Melissa said. Her voice was hoarse. "I can't say that I'm surprised you called."

"Well, I was surprised to hear from you after all these years." April said. "In all the research you did about me did you conclude that I could be bought? And did you decide that three million dollars in cash, an old house, some art work and a mink coat was the purchase price?" April laughed. "What were you trying to do; buy me or buy your way into Heaven? News flash, neither is for sale!"

"Trying to buy you was certainly not my intention." Melissa said. "I want to settle my affairs. Who else could I leave it to?"

"Whoever you spent the last twenty plus years with." The tone of April's voice was chilling.

"I spent all that time working, building a name for myself in the fashion industry. I'm not proud of what I did or didn't do, but I can't do anything about that now," Melissa said. "April I know I wasn't a good mother."

"No because you never wanted me. But thanks for donating the egg. It was a good one. I am highly intelligent. I have flawless skin, beautiful hair, great teeth, a shapely figure, great legs and a great sense of fashion. My friends say I'm one of those people who look good in anything! Like you told my dad, I am the best parts of you. Thanks for not passing on your stank attitude, your ability to throw people away and your inability to love. And let's be clear, I don't need your damn money. I have plenty of my own. I have a mink coat and a house. What I needed from you was for you to be my mother." April was screaming. "When my period started I had to tell my daddy, not my mama. When I was in fifth grade and that boy pulled up my dress 'cause he wanted to see my panties, I ran home and told the housekeeper 'cause my Mama wasn't there. When nine eleven happened and my friends were killed, my daddy's girlfriend stayed up with me all night! You're not in the prom pictures or the graduation pictures! And you know what? Just like I never mattered to you, you don't matter to me!" April could hear Melissa crying. "Know what else, tears don't move me!" Melissa didn't respond so April hung up. She called Lane.

"Hey girl!" Lane answered cheerfully.

"Hi, how are you?"

"I'm good and you?"

"Great!" she said. "You want to come over for a while?"

"I would love to," Lane said smiling.

ONE HUNDRED-FIFTEEN

The day following Kathy and Sterling's first intimate weekend together she was in a daze. She loved Sterling and she trusted him but she was condemning herself for giving in to temptation. She knew he loved her, and she believed him when he said they were married in his heart. But the truth was she didn't love him as much as he loved her.

After a couple of days Kathy finally decided to call her cousin Michelle. She had to tell somebody. "Finally! You did it!" Michelle said excitedly.

"Michelle, I'm not married."

"Damn, Kathy, you're thirty years old and still a virgin. Were still a virgin!" Michelle laughed.

Kathy was quiet. "You are really upset about this aren't you?"

"Yes, I am."

"Because you had sex with a man you love, who loves you, that you intend to marry, does not make you promiscuous or a bad girl. It simply means you physically expressed your feelings to him."

"But 'Chelle, I am supposed to be stronger than that."

"We all are Kathy, but everybody falls short. You act like you had a one night stand. I get why you feel guilty, but don't beat yourself up." They talked a while and by the time the conversation was over, Kathy was laughing at Michelle because of all the questions she asked.

"Hey Mrs. Robinson, how are you?" Sterling was calling Katherine. He needed to plant a seed. "This is a pleasant surprise, how are you Sterling?" she answered with a smile.

"Doing well. Team keeping me pretty busy but I have managed to get up to New York to see Kathy!" Katherine took a seat on the sofa in her office. She needed to hear this clearly.

"Oh really!"

"Yes ma'am and I'm going back next week just for a couple days. I'm giving the guys two days off from practice for exams. But the reason for my call, I need to see you and Bishop Robinson. I want to ask him for permission to propose to Kathy."

Katherine was quiet for a few seconds. "Oh Sterling, that's wonderful," she said. Her voice just above a whisper. "I am happy to hear you say that. I know you and Kathy had some challenges. I'm glad you found your way back to each other," Katherine said sincerely.

Sterling told her he wanted to come by the next evening to talk to the bishop and asked her not to tell him why. "Let me double check his schedule and confirm with you. Do you mind coming to his office if that works better?" she asked.

"I don't mind at all. I do have one more question." Sterling said. "What size ring does Kathy wear?"

ONE HUNDRED-SIXTEEN

Melissa had a massive round of chemotherapy, and a week later a massive radiation treatment. She was buying as much time as she could. Her hair was gone; all of it, including her eyebrows and eye lashes. She was surprised the first time she went through all this to lose her pubic hair, but losing the facial hair was worse. "I can't go to Landridge like this." Melissa said looking in the mirror.

"We will get a make-up artist to give you some eyelashes and draw you some eyebrows before you go," her assistant said. It was like she was reading Melissa's mind.

ONE HUNDRED-SEVENTEEN

Cicely made a "to do" list about two weeks before Christmas, and her latest review showed substantial progress. She and Clay were having her brothers and Clay's family, including Grant and Sunny, for Christmas dinner. Only Clay, Cicely and Gretchen knew Sunny was coming.

Originally Cicely was going to cook, then plan B was to ask Gretchen to help her. The end result was that she ordered her part of the food from Lola's Restaurant. She told Clay and her brothers her schedule just didn't allow her to cook like she wanted to. The truth was despite taking two pre-natal vitamins every day, her energy level was low.

Christmas Eve Cicely got off work at seven in the morning, and she would be off five days. Clay told her he had evening plans for them. He made shrimp cocktails, steak and salad. Cicely was nervous that he would want to have a glass of wine with dinner. She would need a reasonable explanation to say no.

Clay was curious what Cicely's ornament gift would be. He expected it would have some significance to their first Christmas as husband and wife. They talked a lot about creating their own traditions. Cicely was raised with her two brothers by their father when their mother left. He was a good man who was physically available and provided for them but he was emotionally unavailable. She longed for a different life with Clay.

After dinner, before Clay could mention having a drink, Cicely asked him to make a fire so they could open their gifts. "Ornaments first or last?" she asked.

"Last," he said. They opened the regular stuff and then Clay gave Cicely the ornament he had made for her. She loved it!

"Clay, it's amazing," she said, not taking her eyes off of it. After a few minutes Cicely gave Clay the red box with the ornament she had made for him. He opened it quickly, then stared at it. He looked back at the ornament and then back at her. It was several minutes before he said anything.

Christmas morning was a blur for Clay. All the family arrived within ten minutes of each other. After everybody's initial shock of seeing Sunny, things settled down. Gretchen, Cicely and Grace organized everything while the guys watched basketball. Sunny helped but she was pretty quiet. She was as uneasy about being there as they were having her there.

They ate, laughed and talked. Cicely and Clay didn't have a plan so he just said "I need to share some news with everybody." He said it very seriously, without smiling. Their guests were quiet. "Since this is our first Christmas together, CeCe and I started a tradition of exchanging an ornament." He showed all of them the one he had created for her. "I'm impressed," his cousin Gretchen said. Didn't know you had it in you bro!"

"GG, its Christmas. I'm calling a truce for the holidays." They all laughed.

"Well that will be boring," she responded.

"I will read the inscription on the heart-shaped ornament my beautiful wife gave me." He cleared his throat, took a deep breath and read; "Merry Christmas, we're having a baby!"

EPILOGUE

Christmas dinner at the Joseph's home was going just the way Hampton dreamed it would. Everyone was there; Belinda, Ben, Bryce, Bradley, Brittani and Brianna and Grammy. Kirby, Enoch, Nicholas, Blake and Auntie drove down from Hattiesville early in the day. April invited Lane.

There was more than enough food, and Hampton spent way too much money on the kids. The house was in total disarray and he couldn't have been happier.

They barely heard the doorbell ring. They were standing around the piano singing Christmas carols. "I'll get it," April said, laughing about how they sounded as she walked to the door. April opened the door and thought she was looking in a mirror.

Other books by this Author

The Wedding Party

Absent…One From Another

Cheryl McCullough Writes

P.O. Box 410971

Charlotte, North Carolina 28241

www.cherylmcculloughwrites.com

cheryl@cherylmcculloughwrites.com

Follow me on Twitter @cmwrites1

Like me on Facebook Cheryl McCullough Writes